KV-683-685

GWASANAETH LLYFRGELL WRECSAM
WREXHAM LIBRARY SERVICE

Tynnwyd   4/25   Withdrawn
o stoc   from stock

SPECIAL MESSAGE TO READERS

This book is published under the auspices of

THE ULVERSCROFT FOUNDATION

(registered charity No. 264873 UK)

Established in 1972 to provide funds for research, diagnosis and treatment of eye diseases. Examples of contributions made are: —

A Children's Assessment Unit at Moorfield's Hospital, London.

•

Twin operating theatres at the Western Ophthalmic Hospital, London.

•

A Chair of Ophthalmology at the Royal Australian College of Ophthalmologists.

•

The Ulverscroft Children's Eye Unit at the Great Ormond Street Hospital For Sick Children, London.

You can help further the work of the Foundation by making a donation or leaving a legacy. Every contribution, no matter how small, is received with gratitude. Please write for details to:

THE ULVERSCROFT FOUNDATION, The Green, Bradgate Road, Anstey, Leicester LE7 7FU, England. Telephone: (0116) 236 4325

In Australia write to: THE ULVERSCROFT FOUNDATION, c/o The Royal Australian and New Zealand College of Ophthalmologists, 94-98 Chalmers Street, Surry Hills, N.S.W. 2010, Australia

Kate Allan lives in St Albans, Hertford-shire. Her passions for history, adventure and romance inspire her writing.

PERFIDY AND PERFECTION

In the English village of Middleton, at the time of Jane Austen, the rector's daughter, Sophy Grantchester, keeps a shameful secret: she's a novelist. Seeking inspiration for her next book, she finds it in the form of her rakish cousin, Lord Hart. She writes him into her story, and — unwittingly — into her heart. To his surprise he falls for his poor and proper cousin — but she cannot be a wife. For surely no man would tolerate her novel writing . . . However, determined to win her, Lord Hart resorts to devious means. But Sophy could have told him that trickery is no recipe for success in love.

Books by Kate Allan
Published by The House of Ulverscroft:

FATEFUL DECEPTION

KATE ALLAN

PERFIDY AND PERFECTION

Complete and Unabridged

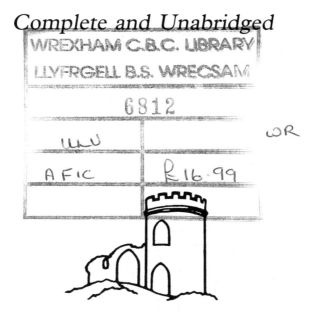

WREXHAM C.B.C. LIBRARY

LLYFRGELL B.S. WRECSAM

6812

uuu   WR

AFIC   £16.99

ULVERSCROFT
Leicester

First published in Great Britain in 2006 by
Robert Hale Limited
London

First Large Print Edition
published 2007
by arrangement with
Robert Hale Limited
London

The moral right of the author has been asserted

Copyright © 2006 by Kate Allan

All rights reserved

British Library CIP Data

Allan, Kate
    Perfidy and perfection.—Large print ed.—
Ulverscroft large print series: romance
    1. Women novelists, English—19th century—Fiction
    2. Children of clergy—Fiction
    3. Love stories
    4. Large type books
    I. Title
    823.9′2 [F]

    ISBN 978–1–84617–589–3

Published by
F. A. Thorpe (Publishing)
Anstey, Leicestershire

Set by Words & Graphics Ltd.
Anstey, Leicestershire
Printed and bound in Great Britain by
T. J. International Ltd., Padstow, Cornwall

This book is printed on acid-free paper

1

It is a truth universally acknowledged that a young lady of no fortune must be in want of one. Sophia Grantchester was one such young lady. She sought to end the painful worries about how all the tradesmen would be paid, not by finding a husband — but rather by being a lady novelist — like Mrs Radcliffe or Miss Edgeworth.

A shameful secret, of course, known to no one but herself. This was why, standing on the dark oak floorboards of Mr Pointer's general shop, her first instinct was to turn, and run.

Sophy chided herself and forced her feet to remain exactly where they were. Yet she could not stop the thoughts running through her mind: what if someone borrowed the volumes, and somehow found out that Miss Sophia Grantchester, daughter of the Reverend Grantchester, rector of Middleton parish in Wiltshire, was a *novelist?* Sophy gasped, then blinked. There they were, on the shelf in front of her. Both volumes. The gilded titles on their calf-leather spines glaring at her: *Caprice and Conventionality Vol. I* and

Caprice and Conventionality Vol. II. There was no one else in the shop apart from herself and Mr Pointer. She reached out towards the first volume. She trembled as her fingers gripped the spine of the book.

She had had the good sense to be published under a nom de plume, but what if people reading the book could tell that she was the author? Had she used a name or a turn of phrase that would give her secret away? Never would she have imagined that her book would be among the pitiful selection of books delivered by the circulating library to Mr Pointer's shop.

She must borrow them immediately and return them too late for anyone else to have a chance to do so. Or something. She picked up the second volume of *Caprice and Conventionality* and four other books selected without regard, and gave the pile to Mr Pointer, who sat behind his desk rubbing his spectacles with a fawn-coloured cloth.

Sophy turned back to the dusty two-foot-long shelf of circulating library books while Mr Pointer tied up her books in string for her. She willed her heart to stop thudding so rapidly. The bookshelf was in front of the shop's small-paned, bowed window with an unobstructed view of Stickleton post office across the street.

The vantage point was ideal. However, it didn't mean her plan was foolproof. Sophy swallowed. She simply had to get to the post office today. She needed her money.

The green door of the post office swung open and Mr Hannay, the postmaster, stepped out on to the street, his hands in his pockets and his collar pulled up high around his neck. He proceeded up the road in the direction of the Red Lion. Thank heavens Mr Hannay was a man of regular habits and enjoyed, without fail, his midday tipple. He was also a man of peculiar habits, and his post-office clerks never stayed beyond a few weeks in his employ.

His new clerk had been in Stickleton less than a week. Sophy could now go into the post office without being recognized.

'Here you are, Miss Grantchester.' Mr Pointer patted the pile of tied-up books and looked at her through his spectacles without focusing.

'Thank you.' Sophy smiled, snatched up her books, and hastened out and across the street to the post office.

★ ★ ★

'What a splendidly pretty bluestocking,' Viscount Merryford drawled. 'And you

3

always say that Wiltshire is so lacking in gentlemanly diversions, Harty!'

Benedict St Michael, Lord Hart, let his attention flicker away from his pair of greys, pulling his curricle at a slow trot, to his friend who sat beside him. Merryford adjusted his quizzing glass as he leaned forward and Ben followed his gaze. Was he looking at the girl hurrying down Stickleton High Street some way ahead of them? She wore a dull-coloured cloak, an equally dull-coloured dress underneath and a straw poke bonnet, trimmed with bright red felt. A pile of books tied with thick string dangled from one arm and she had a basket on her elbow.

Ben coughed. 'The girl with the books? That is only Miss Grantchester, my cousin.'

'Your cousin?' Merryford's eyes opened wide. He scrambled to retrieve his quizzing glass from his lap. 'Such fine ankles!'

Ben felt his brow creasing into a frown as an inexplicable surge of vexation directed against his old friend made his shoulders go stiff. 'Miss Grantchester is my cousin, indeed. And barely out of the schoolroom.'

'She looked womanly enough to me,' Merryford said, leaning back and placing his hands behind his head. 'Curves in all the right places. And hair the colour of spun gold!'

4

Ben stared as his cousin climbed the post-office steps in great haste and disappeared inside. How the devil could Merryford tell? Her grey woollen cloak had been buttoned up to the neck, and her hair seemed wholly hidden under her poke bonnet.

'Pothole!' Merryford exclaimed.

Ben snapped his attention back and steered them round it.

'And is she spoken for?' Merryford asked, rubbing his chin.

'What the devil do you mean by that?'

'*Carpe diem*, old friend.' Merryford nodded and winked. 'Take the opportunity.'

'I think you've got the wrong idea,' Ben said. For some reason his voice sounded agitated. He swallowed and made an effort to sound urbane as usual. 'Miss Grantchester is my cousin, but a very distant cousin; a poor relation if you like. She is not going to be expected to make an advantageous match.' Ben stopped there. He was sounding like his dear mama. And now he thought about it, why shouldn't she do something for Miss Grantchester to improve her prospects? He'd ask her about that for she had never mentioned such a thing.

'So she's not spoken for?' Merryford pressed.

'No, but she's as poor as a church mouse.

Remember, you need to marry money if you are going to stop the rot of that crumbling pile of yours in Devon.'

'Very true.' Merryford's mouth quirked into a lazy smile and Ben felt his neck prickle uncomfortably under his cravat. 'Well, in that case I can take her off your hands in a different fashion. Set her up in a nice little house somewhere. Chelsea, perhaps — '

'Oh no, you don't,' Ben said, and steered them through the doors and into the enclosed yard of the Rose and Crown public house.

★ ★ ★

Having made it into the post office without being seen, Sophy wasted no time in lifting the cloth of her basket and drawing out a letter, which she put down on the dark polished wood of the counter. A very stern letter to Lord Hart, her feckless cousin, reminding him most respectfully that it had been four weeks since his manager had visited and seen the appalling state of Middleton church roof, and promised that repairs would be arranged as a matter of urgency. Four weeks and still there was no sign of anyone coming to do anything!

'And is there any post come for a Mr John Chester?' she asked the clerk in a matter-of-fact way.

'Let me see.' The clerk, a lanky youth with a very pale complexion, squinted at a pile of letters stacked in one of the wooden pigeonholes behind him. Sophy held her breath and wished he would hurry up. If someone who knew her walked into the post office now . . .

'Yes, yes, there is,' the clerk said at last. He pulled out the letters one by one and handed them to her. There were three altogether. Sophy ignored the sinking feeling in her chest as she noticed that they were all addressed by different hands, and quickly tucked them under the cloth in her basket. Money was usually cut in half and sent in two separate letters but she needed both halves before she could then stick them together to make a five pound note.

'And I have one to post,' Sophy said, pushing her letter to Lord Hart forward across the counter. She drew open the strings of her reticule. 'How much do I owe you?'

The door of the post office crashed open. Mr Camberley, her father's curate, not a man known for rushing into post offices, shouted, 'Miss Grantchester! Miss Grantchester!' His chest rose and fell as he struggled for breath. 'I've been looking for you everywhere.'

'Mr Camberley! What is the matter?' Sophy

7

held her basket behind her back although she'd tucked the letters under her cloth. It was all right, he couldn't see.

'Mr Drayman has had an argument with someone about his hens. I don't know the whole of it but he is storming about looking as black as thunder and he says he is going to head back to Middleton right away! If we don't catch him, we'll miss our lift.' Mr Camberley's brow creased. He pulled some small coins from his pocket and splayed them down on the post-office counter.

Oh dear, Sophy thought. Mr Drayman was known for having a violent temper and if they missed him it would be a very long walk back to Middleton.

The clerk picked out the coins he wanted and pushed the remainder back towards Mr Camberley, who tucked them in his pocket and patted it. 'Take my arm,' Mr Camberley commanded. 'Quick, Miss Grantchester!'

Such an industrious, shy man ordinarily! Sophy did exactly as Mr Camberley asked. He led her out of the post office.

* * *

'I rather fancy a short promenade before we have our luncheon,' Merryford said with a yawn as he stepped down from the curricle.

'Work up an appetite, eh?'

Ben tossed the ribbons into the hands of the waiting ostler and drew in a long breath. He could not deny that Merryford's sudden interest in his cousin had disturbed him. He didn't even think of her as a young lady. She was simply a girl, and his cousin, and poor . . . and unchaperoned.

Merryford was already striding ahead, across the cobbles towards the street. And whistling a jaunty tune which grated. Ben hastened his step.

'Splendid,' Merryford muttered and turned right towards the post office. And then in a low voice, 'Ah, here she is now!'

Ben felt his fingers itch to be allowed to curl up into a fist. He pulled instead at his lapels as Miss Grantchester came down the post-office steps and on to the street in front of them. She did have rather fine ankles, Ben decided. Curious how he'd not noticed before.

Miss Grantchester was on the arm of a gentleman. From his clothes, a poor one.

'Don't be a bore, Harty,' Merryford said with a smile that did not move when he spoke. 'At least allow me the pleasure of an introduction?'

'She is my *cousin*, Merryford. Don't you forget — ' Ben's breath caught. She had seen them. Her dark lashes flickered. Her eyes widened as she looked up. She needed to be better dressed. The same reds that she had used to trim her bonnet would suit her far more than the grey she wore. And a fine gown would satisfy his curiosity as to what her neck looked like.

The line of her mouth hardened. She looked away. Confounded chit! Merryford might as well execute his designs on her.

What was he thinking? If anyone . . .

'Don't you forget, she's *my* cousin. *Mine*,' Ben said to Merryford under his breath as they came to a halt.

★ ★ ★

Two pairs of rather dashing black boots caught her eye, and Sophy looked up to see two fashionably dressed blades, both in immaculate black jackets, their chins held up by stiff, white cravats. One she did not recognize had greying brown hair and was staring at her rudely through his quizzing glass. However, that was nothing to the vexation she felt towards the other — her wayward, rakish cousin, Lord Hart.

Bother!

She reminded herself that every cloud has a silver lining and pushed a false smile into her

10

cheeks. She could take Lord Hart to task much more effectively in person than via letter.

'Good afternoon, Miss Grantchester.' Lord Hart lifted his black hat. The breeze tousled his hair. The winter sunshine highlighted chestnut flecks.

'Good afternoon, Lord Hart,' Sophy replied. Unfortunately, all that glitters is not gold. Lord Hart was handsome, certainly. He had a regularity of features that was arresting, yet nothing too sharp or angular. But he was feckless, and a rake. She kept her fingers on Mr Camberley's arm.

'May I introduce Mr Camberley,' she said. 'Mr Camberley, this is Lord Hart.' She could have informed Lord Hart that Mr Camberley was her father's curate. She would not. He could find out once he took an interest in the affairs of Middleton parish, for which he was supposed to be responsible.

'Mr Camberley.' Lord Hart tipped his hat again. His companion coughed. Lord Hart swallowed and frowned. The frown quickly disappeared. He said, 'May I introduce to you Viscount Merryford?'

'Your servant.' The viscount bowed.

Sophy ignored him. She had no interest in acquaintances of her wayward cousin. She held her chin high. 'It is unfortunate I did not see you a few moments earlier, Lord Hart. Before I had been to the post office. Will you wait here a moment, please?'

She was back from the post office in a moment, the three gentlemen still standing where she had left them. Not making conversation. Mr Camberley looked as though he'd rather be somewhere else. The two bucks were concentrating on looking fashionably bored. They were out of place in such ordinary surroundings. There were several shops in Stickleton, but little to tempt coins from a fine gentleman's purse. A breeze ruffled her cloak. The air tasted very cold. Cold enough maybe for snow. She remembered why she was vexed with her cousin.

She gave Mr Camberley back his coins and handed Lord Hart his letter. 'I had gone to the trouble and the expense of writing you a letter, my lord, on the subject of the repairs of the church roof.'

He took it without a word, glanced at the address, and tucked it in an upper pocket. Was he even going to bother to read it? He said, 'Is it fixed now?'

'Fixed?' Sophy felt a swell of anger rise in her chest. 'And who is supposed to have fixed it, my lord? The fairies?'

'Ah, I understood from my man that this

was all in hand. I shall look into the matter.'

'You may rest assured, Miss Grantchester,' the viscount said, 'that Lord Hart is a man who honours his word.'

Lord Hart sent his friend a look that should have turned him to stone and Sophy found herself piqued with curiosity. They must have quarrelled. Some sporting wager, no doubt.

'Well, good day to you, gentlemen.' Sophy nodded. 'I fear we really are in the most frightful hurry — '

'Good day, Lord Hart, Viscount Merryford,' Mr Camberley echoed and pulled them into a fast walk. 'Hurry, Miss Grantchester — we are in danger of missing Mr Drayman!'

'Wait!'

Sophy stopped. Mr Camberley stopped.

'Miss Grantchester,' came the voice of her cousin. 'I must enquire after your father.'

She turned around. Lord Hart's expression looked genuine. Could he really be concerned? He said, 'Is his health improved?'

'Yes, thank you,' she replied. 'He is able to carry out most of his duties.'

Mr Camberley coughed very loudly. 'Miss Grantchester — '

'Mr Camberley,' Lord Hart said with a charming smile and a flourish of his hand. He stepped forward so that he stood right in front of them. 'Meeting my dear cousin so unexpectedly today has been most fortunate for I have some matters of family business to discuss. If you would — '

'Really, Lord Hart?' Sophy interrupted. 'We are in a terrible hurry. As for — '

'Obedience is a virtue, Cousin. And most becoming in a maid.' He raised a single eyebrow.

Sophy breathed in very deeply through her nose. She could not trust herself if she allowed her mouth to open.

Mr Camberley pulled his sleeve across his damp brow.

'I shall see *my cousin*, Miss Grantchester, home,' said Lord Hart.

'How kind, Lord Hart!' Mr Camberley untangled his arm from beneath her fingers in a haste of which she would never have wagered him capable. 'I had better run and catch Mr Drayman. Good day, Miss Grantchester. Gentlemen.'

Sophy watched Mr Camberley's brown-coated figure speed off in dismay. She could run after him or . . . If Lord Hart was proposing to take her home in his curricle, she couldn't deny the prospect was exciting. A tiny tingle went down her spine. She had never been in such a dashing vehicle before.

'Merryford, get yourself a mount from the

14

Rose and Crown. I need to take *my cousin* home.'

'Delighted, Harty,' Viscount Merryford drawled. He flashed a smile. An unpleasant rash of gooseflesh ran up Sophy's neck. She was glad to see him disappear up the street ahead.

'You don't mind me taking you home, do you, Miss Grantchester?' her cousin said, pulling at his cravat. He might be a rake, with a rather high opinion of himself, but he did have gentlemanly manners, Sophy considered. She did not have the acquaintance of many gentlemen of such standing. Mr Camberley was a gentleman, but poor. The shopkeepers such as half-blind Mr Pointer and drunken Mr Hannay were better off financially, but not gentlemen.

'I am quite looking forward to it.' Sophy gave Lord Hart her sweetest smile. Mr Drayman's heavy cart clattered past at a dangerous pace. Mr Drayman looked thunderous. Mr Camberley briefly raised a hand, from where it clutched the side, and waved. 'Which is fortunate,' she added, 'as it would be a little late now for any alternative arrangements.'

She skipped forward before Lord Hart did something gentlemanly such as offer her his arm.

She heard the click of his boots as he strode after her but she didn't stop until she was in the yard of the Rose and Crown. There was only one vehicle black and dashing enough to be her cousin's.

'I have never been anywhere in such a handsome chariot,' she said.

'Really? I suppose not.' He raised his eyebrows, drew her eye and Sophy found herself staring into the dark-brown depths. She looked at the ground.

What was so compelling about one man's eyes anyhow? She hadn't seen Lord Hart for a while; over a year, she rather thought. He was the model for the hero in the story she was writing, she told herself, thus she was naturally curious to check that he was exactly as she remembered.

'Let me take these,' Lord Hart said and reached forward.

His face came very close to hers as she handed him her pile of books and basket. Something tickled her nose. A gentleman's scent? He tucked them safely in the curricle. He was not exactly as she remembered. He was far more compelling. Or had she been reading too many Gothic romances, which had sharpened her appetite for sardonic, dark heroes?

'Thank you,' Sophy whispered.

He grinned. 'Miss Grantchester, your chariot awaits!' He gave a little bow and offered her his arm. 'Would you like to step up?'

'Miss Grantchester!' The loud voice carried and was unmistakable — Mrs Fisher!

Sophy froze, her hand in the middle of the air. She drew it back sharply to fall down by her side. Mrs Fisher and Mrs Johnson hastened into the inn yard. She had better explain that Lord Hart was her cousin or the supposed impropriety would be all over Wiltshire before she even made it home.

Mrs Fisher had seven children and was in an interesting condition, which her voluptuous blue cloak could not disguise. Mrs Johnson had been widowed before she came to Stickleton some years ago. Stick-thin and buttoned up to the neck in lilac, she wore a dashing felt bonnet, entirely fashioned by a hatmaker and such as Sophy could never afford, and kid gloves. Sophy tucked her own woollen mittens behind her back.

'Mrs Fisher, Mrs Johnson, I don't believe you know *my cousin*, Lord Hart.'

'Oh no, your lordship.' Mrs Fisher would have tugged her forelock had it occurred to her. Silly, fawning woman!

'Lord Hart and I are acquainted.' Mrs Johnson smiled in a way that made Sophy

17

wonder if Mrs Johnson was one of her cousin's rakish conquests. Rakes were supposed to favour widows, were they not? The thought was vexing, somehow.

'Good day, ladies.' Lord Hart appeared to have no interest in prolonging the conversation any longer than necessary, which was good because neither had she. He jumped into the curricle and patted the seat beside him. 'Sophy?'

She started at hearing her given name on his lips. Only her father ever called her Sophy.

She took a deep breath and climbed into the curricle, aware of the women's scrutiny. Why had Lord Hart addressed her thus? Yes, they were cousins, but they were not well acquainted and she had given him no leave to do so.

'Let's go,' he said, and whipped the ribbons just before she sat down, causing her to land on the seat with a thump.

The horses jolted forward and the carriage swung into action and clattered out of the inn and into the street. She raised her hand in a flimsy wave but did not look around at their audience.

The air punched her face as they picked up speed and as soon as they were round the corner, Sophy ventured to say, 'It's rather cold weather to be driving around in a curricle.'

'Are you cold? I don't think there's a rug. New, this thing. Not fully equipped yet. But we can stop?'

'Oh no, I like it. How fast does it go?'

'Through Stickleton it goes at this speed,' he said and leaned back, letting the ribbon grow slack between his fingers. He had his pair well trained. 'In the open country where I can be sure I am not about to run over a child, faster.'

Sophy regarded his profile, static, while behind it the shops and houses accelerated past. His profile would make a rather fetching silhouette.

Her bonnet was sturdy and securely fastened, though to have been able to feel the wind through her own hair as he did his would have been quite a thing.

'Oh!' she said, suddenly remembering. She didn't want to berate him. In fact, she had quite liked it now she thought about it. 'Why did you call me Sophy?'

He flickered his gaze at her before looking back at the road. 'I decided it would be wise to appear to be on a more suitably intimate footing with my cousin than the reality of the matter. Surely you can see, Miss Grantchester, that an unmarried lady, going for a drive with a gentleman alone in his curricle, is not the thing to be done at all.'

'I have heard it said that the richer a lady is, the more liberty she has. However, I am so poor as hardly to be on the scale, my lord. And also we are cousins.' She waved her hand. 'Besides I pay no heed to such things. I am not in the market for marriage.'

'Surely you aspire to marry a respectable gentleman, Miss Grantchester?'

'Oh, please call me Sophy now you've started.' She folded her hands in her lap and looked out across the dark-earthed fields on either side of them. It was too early in the year for any green shoots to have appeared yet. 'And to answer your question, no.'

'You still should be careful. A reputation is a fragile thing and once broken, near impossible to repair. And if the question is asked, we are in fact terribly distant cousins. Certainly so far removed from each other by blood that it would be possible for us to marry.'

'Despite your sudden interest in my welfare, Lord Hart, I had not researched whether or not it would possible for us to marry. I am content to take your word for it.'

'What? D'you think I'm offering you marriage? You misunderstand — '

'*Marriage?*' Sophy spluttered. He was the

rake, and one who twisted everything she said.

'Be clear on this, Cousin. If I should stoop to offer you marriage you will be in no doubt on the matter. In the meantime, I might suggest you refrain from leaping to wild conclusions.'

'*Stoop* to offer me marriage? It would be I stooping to accept such an offer. Do you think any woman aspires to marry a notorious rakehell?'

'Possibly not, I concede you that point.' His voice had returned to its amiable laziness and a smile hung from the corners of his mouth. 'But so what? I'll reform. Besides, I am probably not as rakish as women like to imagine.'

'Benedict — '

'Ben will do. Only my dear mama calls me Benedict.'

'Ben?' she whispered, forgetting what it was she'd wanted to say in the first place.

'I rather like the sound of my name on your lips.' His tone had changed again; lightened.

'What an . . . outrageous thing to say!' She crossed her arms, sat back and watched the leafless trees and empty fields gallop past. She would have imagined one would grow sick travelling at such speed but instead it was exciting.

'Are you one of those rakes who race curricles?' she said, after a few minutes had passed.

'Yes.' He flashed her a grin. 'But you haven't seen the half of what this beautiful team are capable of. Although, they are still in training.'

'Can you go faster?'

'Yes, but not with young ladies on board whose safety I have to consider.'

'Such is the burden of the female sex.' Sophy sighed. If she made a fortune she would buy her own curricle and learn to tool it. Then she could go at exactly the speed that suited her. 'Now, what was this mysterious family business you wanted to discuss with me?'

'That?' He raised an eyebrow and breathed very deeply, a tiny smile tugging at the corners of his mouth. '*That* was a ruse.'

'A ruse?'

'I realized that I had a rather pretty cousin with whom I was not that well acquainted. The company of attractive women tending to be more enjoyable than not, it appeared to be a fine idea to get to know you a little better.'

What did he mean?

The curricle swung around a corner.

Clattering towards them helter-skelter was a huge coach and four.

'The very devil!' Ben shouted. 'Hey there!' He pulled on his ribbons. Sophy gripped the side of her seat with one hand and her bonnet with the other. Their greys began to slow but not fast enough . . . the oncoming coach showed no sign of stopping!

Ben steered them violently to the left to avoid a collision. Their horses cleared the small ditch but the left wheel dropped down. The vehicle collapsed over on one side as if it was falling away from beneath them.

Sophy was thrown to one side, hit Ben and fell away from him. She tried to grab him. Too late: she saw her feet and her skirts, the sky, then the upturned side of the curricle.

2

Benedict St Michael, Lord Hart, of Hartfield Bury in Wiltshire, was a man who never took up any book. However, the consequences of this unfortunate accident were to have a profound effect on his reading habits. None of this was known to Lord Hart at the present moment, however, as he lay in the ditch beside the road. Nor was it known to the young lady who lay improperly on top of him.

Birds squawked. Sophy forced her eyes to open. Above her a barren tree. The breeze blew its branches into one another. She felt her chest rise and fall. She was still breathing. Men's shouting, the clatter of horses and carriage wheels, pushed into her ears. She wanted to close them, be still for a moment.

It was warm here. She was not lying on the hard ground but on top of a person — masculine — the scent of starch, soap and sandalwood — Lord Hart!

'Ben?' Sophy said.

No answer.

She shook. She could feel her arms, her legs. She twitched her toes in her boots and stretched out her fingers. They touched the smooth superfine of his jacket. He had completely cushioned her fall.

'Ben?'

No answer.

The voices were coming nearer. Horses whinnied. The other coach! It must have stopped. Someone, several people, must be running towards them.

'Madam? Miss? Are you hurt?'

She wasn't hurt but she wasn't sure how to move. She must. What if her weight was crushing Ben? His body felt heavy below hers, not quite right.

'Ben?' she said again. 'Lord Hart?'

No answer. A chill ran the length of her spine.

Shadows appeared over her and a man dressed in a hunting jacket reached down towards her. She grasped his arm and he pulled her to her feet.

'Can you stand?' the man said with a crisp, aristocratic accent.

She felt a little shaky but of course she could stand! The ribbons of her bonnet were askew and chafing at her neck as she gulped. She tore at them until they came undone and pulled the crumpled straw hat from her head. She threw it to the ground. She stared up at his long face and directly into his eyes. 'Was it your coach we had to swerve to avoid?'

'You are no doubt a little overset,' the man replied.

Sophy ignored him. Where was Ben? She turned around.

He lay still in the ditch on his back. His eyes were closed, his face limestone white. One arm was flayed into a pile of low winter nettles.

'Ben!' Sophy heard herself shriek. She stumbled towards him. A strong hand gripped her arm and held her back.

'Let go of me!'

'Wait a minute, madam, we'll get your husband out of there.'

'He's not . . . ' Sophy began and then pursed her lips closed. The important thing was that Ben was seen to.

A man in a greatcoat who looked like the coachman clambered into the ditch and another gentleman, younger than the one who had the effrontery to continue to hold her, followed him.

Ben wasn't dead, was he? He couldn't be. She stared at his face, long, white, drawn, his lips half-parted. No flicker; no sign of anything. He was a rake, probably did very little of worth in this world, but he didn't deserve to die! Sophy swallowed the lump in her throat.

The coachman bent down over Ben's face,

obscuring her view. 'He's breathing, sir. He's alive.'

'Well, are you going to get him out of there?' Sophy pulled her arm free of her captor. 'Or do I have to do it myself?'

'Madam.' The younger gentleman caught her glare and nodded at her. 'You take his shoulders, John, and I'll take his feet.'

'I'll see to your horses, madam,' the older gentleman said. He went over to Ben's magnificent greys, held fast in the tangle of ribbons by the damaged curricle, which lay on its side.

They lifted Ben's body up and carried him to their carriage.

Sophy followed. When they were certain they had manoeuvred him into the most comfortable position inside, she climbed into the coach and sat opposite him. Ben looked so without colour, propped up by the crimson cushions; so without vigour, not like himself at all. Dirt streaked across his clothes and his face. There was no blood; at least none that she could see.

She felt herself tremble as she leaned forward and carefully touched the top of his head with her fingers. She choked back a sob as she felt through the soft hair and to the skin of his scalp. But she had to check. Head injuries were the worst. If . . .

She could not bear to think on it. She quickly moved the pads of her fingers across and down the back and then along each side. No stickiness, no blood from what she could feel. The air tasted heavy, as if there was a thunderstorm coming. It was difficult to breathe.

'Ben?' she whispered, hardly hearing herself.

No answer came, no movement, no sign he had heard her.

How badly was he injured? How long would he be unconscious? All because he was taking her home. She should have run after Mr Camberley and caught a lift with Mr Drayman and then none of this would have happened. Sophy sat back against the squabs and rubbed her damp palms on her cloak.

'I have a flask of strong wine if he'll take it, madam,' the younger gentleman said from outside.

'Pass me the flask!' She opened it and poured a little of the wine into the silver cup.

'Ben?' she whispered, leaning forward. She took one of his hands and pressed his cold fingers. Ben's eyelashes flickered. She held her breath.

'Sophy?' he said, his voice fragile and smothered by a jangle of harnesses. His eyes did not open.

'Ben, I've got some wine for you.' Oh dear, was he very badly hurt? Bones broken? She didn't know. She reached forward and pressed the rim of the cup very gently against his bottom lip. His lips moved, fell more apart, but it was no good. He was never going to be able to drink it.

Reluctantly she let go of his hand, placing it carefully back on his lap. She pulled off her right glove, muddied anyhow, and dipped her finger into the wine. She touched the middle of his lower lip, rubbed a drop of the wine there. He managed to close his lips — taste it, she hoped.

She held the cup under his chin and brought a wine-soaked pad of her finger again and again up to his lips. It wasn't much but it was something.

'Ben, can you drink this? It's wine,' she said, and pressed the tiny cup against his lower lip. He managed to tilt his head slightly and groaned. She tipped the cup gently. His Adam's apple rose and fell as he swallowed, though a trickle of the red wine ran down from the corner of his mouth.

She hastily poured another thimbleful and repeated the exercise and fancied a spot of colour returned to his cheeks.

She bent forward and brushed a tiny kiss on his forehead. She was not sure why she did it but she couldn't help herself. It was just as well that the owners of the coach were under their own impression that they were husband and wife.

Ben opened his eyes fully and she saw he could see her and behind his uneven gaze was a dark pain — a great deal of pain he was trying to hide.

'Madam, your horses are secure.' The elder gentleman had appeared and he peered into the dimness of the coach. 'How is your husband?'

'He's . . . he's . . . he needs to go home,' Sophy said, her skirts rustling as she turned to face him. 'He needs a doctor.'

'Rather belated for introductions, isn't it, but I am Sir Horace Blunham, travelling with my son, Evelyn. We take full responsibility for the accident; shouldn't have been travelling so fast. What may we do now to assist? Are you far from home? May we take you there?'

'This is Lord Hart of Hartfield Bury, which is about eight miles from here,' Sophy said, keeping her voice clear and steady. 'And, yes, I should think that is the very least you can do.'

★ ★ ★

Hartfield Bury, a square, aristocratic house, as symmetrical as an architectural drawing, loomed into view. Sandstone, tinged with grey, its slate-tiled roof looked in perfect repair. Unlike the roof of Middleton parish church. Sophy bit her lip; glanced at the body slumped beside her. At least his chest rose and fell evenly.

'Ah, chestnuts.' Sir Horace Blunham waved his hand at the window. 'An excellent choice for a gracious avenue.' He turned his head. 'And the house! Such fine proportions! The work of Robert Adam, m'dear?'

'I'm afraid I do not know the architect, sir,' Sophy replied. The carriage was slowing. 'You must ask Lady Hart.'

'Will do. Will do.' Sir Horace nodded.

Sophy pushed down the window.

'Let me.' Mr Blunham reached forward. She sat back out of his way. There was no sense in waiting for a footman.

A final crunch of the gravel. The coach halted. Mr Blunham sprang to open the door and descended. Sophy touched his proffered arm and jumped down, then gripped her skirts and ran straight up the sweeping stone steps to the wide front door. It opened as she reached the top step.

'Lord Hart has been injured!' She gasped for breath.

The servant — the butler — looked down his nose at her.

Sophy felt herself frowning. 'Someone must be sent to fetch a doctor. Quickly!'

Surprise flashed across the servant's countenance.

'Oh, for goodness' sake! Look!' She waved towards the coach. 'Lord Hart has been in a terrible accident.'

The butler sprang into action and summoned his footmen. Sophy rushed past them and into the house. She came face to face with Lady Hart in the hallway. 'Oh, Lady Hart! Ben — Lord Hart — has been dreadfully injured. A curricle accident.'

'Benedict?' Lady Hart was a very tall lady who had kept the figure of her youth. She seemed fragile in her jonquil day dress. Her complexion better matched the eggshell paint of the hall. She blinked. 'A curricle accident? Sophy, what are you doing here?'

'There was an ac — '

'Oh heavens!' Lady Hart leaned against the stair rail. Her fan clattered to the floor.

Two footmen carried Ben into the house.

A very excited setter appeared from somewhere. The dog had only one eye and barked urgently. He pushed his way to Ben and nuzzled the side of his suspended form with his nose and whined.

'Hastings!' Lady Hart said in a raised, unsteady voice. 'Send for the doctor!'

'What the devil is going on?' came the rasping drawl of Viscount Merryford from above them. Sophy looked up as he walked down the stairs. The setter jumped back and barked furiously.

'There has been an accident.' Sophy reached forward and patted her hand on the dog's warm shoulders. The barks descended into growls.

Merryford stood at the foot of the stairs and looked about him at the scene as if watching a tedious play. Lady Hart stumbled to Ben's side and shrieked, 'He's dead!'

'He's not dead!' Sophy ran forward but she was too late to prevent Lady Hart from collapsing on the cold marble floor.

'Take Lord Hart upstairs and make sure the doctor gets to him as soon as he arrives.' Merryford waved a hand. He knelt down beside Lady Hart before Sophy could get there.

Sophy stood still, two feet away, unsure what to do. She wanted to follow upstairs, where they were carrying Ben, but Lady Hart might need her.

'Have you got any smelling salts?' the viscount asked her.

Sophy shook her head.

'Can some smelling salts be found?' Merryford bellowed, making the maid who stood beside him jump. The various female servants sprang into action. 'And someone get that dog out of the way!'

'Excuse me?' came the authoritative voice of Sir Horace Blunham. He stepped in through the front door, followed by his son.

'Blunham!' Merryford exclaimed. 'What are you doing in this neck of the woods? Very bad timing for a social call.'

Sophy inched her way towards the stairs. Lady Hart would recover easily enough. She had simply had a shock. But Ben . . . Who was to see to Ben?

She grabbed the banister, swung herself around and fled up the large, curved staircase before anyone could say otherwise.

She reached the landing, stopped and listened. Noise was coming from a room on the right and the door was ajar. She padded along the thick, oriental carpet towards it. The dog sprinted past her and headlong into the room.

Sophy pushed the door open a little further.

Ben lay outstretched on a vast canopied bed, still fully clothed. Only his boots had been removed. His eyes were closed and his pale face was half-turned into the pillow.

One servant, perhaps his valet, was putting some items away in a cupboard. The butler and two other footmen stood in front of the window discussing something in hushed tones. They stopped and stared as she walked into the room.

'The doctor has been sent for?' she queried.

'Yes, miss,' the butler replied.

'And what else are you doing?'

'We didn't want to move Lord Hart any more than necessary, in case of broken bones, miss.'

'There are visitors downstairs who need refreshments provided and Lady Hart has fainted.' All three of the male servants started. 'And see that I am brought some hot water and flannel cloths. And brandy, please, or whatever spirit you have in the house. And blankets.'

'Very good, miss.' The butler nodded and led the footmen out of the room. Only the valet remained. He shut the door of the closet and turned towards her.

'Excuse me the liberty, miss, but I am afraid I don't know your name?'

'Miss Sophia Grantchester, Lord Hart's cousin,' Sophy said in the haughtiest voice she could muster. 'I'd like some tea, please. I forgot to ask the butler.'

The valet looked somewhat taken aback but he clearly decided that while his master was thus incapacitated it could be foolish to argue with her. He bowed and left the room.

Sophy threw herself down at the bedside and took Ben's hands in her own. They were so frightfully cold. Her heart stopped for a moment. She forced herself to breathe evenly.

The dog pushed in next to her and whimpered.

'When Thomas Grainger, the blacksmith's son, was thrown from his horse,' Sophy told the animal, 'he'd only broken his arm but he grew so cold with the shock he developed a fever. We must not let this happen to Ben.'

The dog rested his chin on Ben's thigh.

'Good boy,' Sophy muttered and hoped that someone would bring some blankets quickly.

She rubbed Ben's hands in her own, pressed his fingers together and unfurled them. Such strong, noble hands; they were like a Greek statue's and equally as bloodless. She leaned forward and placed the palm of her hand on his forehead. It was cold. Too cold.

'Ben?' she said loudly. 'Lord Hart?'

His eyes flickered and opened. She saw a wave of confusion wash over them. She swallowed the lump that had formed in her throat.

'You're at home,' she said and rested her right hand over his left. 'Hartfield Bury.'

'Sophy?' She saw the beginnings of a frown. He was awake — and sentient! The dog woofed approvingly.

'Yes, it's Sophy,' she replied.

His gaze narrowed. 'What the devil are you doing in my bedchamber?'

Sophy snatched her hand away.

He tried to pull himself forward but fell back almost immediately and groaned.

'Lie still. The doctor is on his way. How badly are you hurt?'

'Not badly enough not to sit up,' he replied, and with a mighty effort heaved himself upwards, propped on his arms.

'No broken bones?' Sophy fussed with the pillows behind him. If he was going to insist on sitting up, he might as well be comfortable.

'Bruises only, I think, and the very devil of a headache.' Ben leaned back into the pillows she had arranged and breathed very deeply.

'Oh dear, I wonder if when we fell you hit your head on something?'

'What happened?'

'We had an accident in the curricle,' Sophy explained. 'A coach was coming very fast around the corner straight at us so you had to swerve to the side to avoid a collision. But we overturned in a ditch. You grabbed hold of me and stopped me from being hurt, Ben. Thank you.'

'Heavens!' He rubbed his hand across his forehead. 'Well, I appear to have lost some of my memory as I don't remember all that.'

'That can happen with concussion,' Sophy said.

'We're not married, are we?' he said, his brow creasing.

Sophy stared at his white face. She grasped one of her hands in the other and found she was trembling. 'W . . . what makes you say that?'

'You're in my bedchamber alone with me and you were holding my hand.' He sighed. 'I've done far more foolish things so I wouldn't be surprised.'

'No, we most certainly are not married.' Suddenly her head was spinning, her throat dry. How could he think they could have been married? Why in all the heavens would he want to marry her, a penniless clergyman's daughter?

'Betrothed?' he said. His eyes narrowed as he pinned her gaze.

'No.' Sophy gulped.

'Then you really are a most singular lady.'

Ben reached over to pat the dog's nose. Sophy caught the wince of pain on his countenance; he was unable to hide it. 'I'd wager you just waltzed in here as if you owned the place.'

'Yes, of course. In the circumstances — '

'Mama will be shocked,' Ben said in an indifferent manner, a flicker of pain passing across his eyes. He blinked and then looked at her again. 'I see you've made Nelson's acquaintance?'

'Nelson?'

'My one-eyed four-legged friend.'

'Oh, what a splendid name!' Sophy patted Nelson on the head.

'I rescued him from a life of crime. He was stray and in a lot of trouble when I came across him, for stealing sausages at the Eagle and Child inn.'

'You're an arrogant rake yet you adopt a stray one-eyed dog?' Sophy could not help laughing.

'You're a shrewish chit and — '

There was a loud rap on the door.

'Come in,' Ben shouted.

Sophy quickly got to her feet. Two maids, one with a basin of water and the other carrying a pile of blankets and cloths, came in and placed their wares down on the dresser.

'Do you require anything else, miss?' one of

the maids said and bobbed.

'No, thank you.'

'Quite the mistress of the house, eh?' Ben said when the maids had left. A smile pulled at the corners of his mouth that for some strange reason made Sophy feel slightly nauseous.

'Someone had to take charge with both you and Lady Hart incapacitated,' she said quickly to distract herself. 'Your mother fainted when she saw you carried in. Viscount Merryford was seeing to Lady Hart so I thought I had better come up here.' It was not the whole truth, Sophy conceded to herself. Mostly she had been anxious to see that Ben was all right but she was not about to tell him that.

'Merryford?' Ben screwed his eyes up. 'Is that bounder here?'

'Yes.' Sophy went over to the basin and wet one of the cloths in the warm water. She perched on the very edge of the bed and began to clean the dust from Ben's face.

'Hmmm,' he said, grimacing at the touch of the flannel. 'I shall just have to trust it all comes back to me. Now, I don't want some do-gooder flimflam, about why you've snuck into my bedchamber like a wanton. I want the truth!'

'The truth?' Sophy's hand and the flannel

remained suspended in mid-air. The truth was half that she was a wanton. Why, if he tried to kiss her now, she was not sure she would want to refuse. He was just as handsome as she'd remembered him and there was something about his urbane fecklessness that was potently compelling, even though it was wrong for her to be compelled.

'Ah! You're trying to trap me into having to offer you matrimony! I knew my first idea was close.'

'Nothing, I can assure you, was further from my mind.' She might be hankering after a kiss but she certainly didn't want to marry a rake.

'In that case, get out, for goodness' sake, before someone other than a servant finds you here. Unless . . . ' His eyes darkened.

'Unless?' Sophy said slowly and in a voice no louder than a whisper. She wasn't moving. She didn't see why she should have to explain herself to anyone.

He sprang up like a tiger and far too quickly for an injured man, caught her wrist with one hand, slid the other around her back, pulled her towards him and over so her head was on his pillow, his face only inches from hers.

He was going to kiss her and Sophy wanted

him to. She let the flannel drop to the ground. She had to know. Had to know what would happen when their lips met.

Her heart was beating so hard it was like having a caged bird in her chest. She had forgotten how to breathe.

He lowered his lips and as they touched hers her eyes closed. The feel was even softer than when she had touched them so intimately with her wine-wet fingers. She wasn't prepared for the shock, the jolt that leapt up like a flame on dry tinder, the multitude of butterflies cascading through her head, blinding her to her thoughts, her surroundings.

A touch so gentle, softer than the softest goosedown. A taste sweeter than marchpane. She was fixed, captured by the sensation. Paralysed when she wanted to move, to kiss him in return as he kissed her.

She grappled with her thoughts, her emotions, tried to bring them up to the surface where she could see them for what they were, name them. They remained just outside her grasp. She was losing them, losing herself in this curious fog.

He broke away, too suddenly. Left her only to breathe air that was mingled with him; the musky scent of strength, and in the far distance, the exotic promise of sandalwood.

His brown eyes caught hers and held her, tried to examine her, understand her. The smallest crease lined his brow. She wanted to reach up and smooth it away.

'Are you angling to be my mistress, or are you truly as innocent as you seem?' he said, his voice as heavy as a millstone, and as hard.

'I . . . I don't know,' she said, unhappy with her answer. He had disarmed her, somehow, with that kiss. She didn't know anything except that she wanted him to kiss her again. She needed to think.

'You don't know?' He didn't sound as if he believed her.

A sharp rap on the door and he pulled right away from her. Sophy sprang to her feet; felt heat rising up through her chest and splaying into her neck.

'You can hide in the wardrobe if you like,' he said in a low voice tinged with amusement. 'There should be enough room.'

'I've done nothing to be ashamed of!' She tried to stare at him in anger.

'Come in,' Ben said loudly, looking away towards the door. 'Ah, Merryford!'

Sophy saw the streak of pain that went across Ben's face as he pulled himself upright. She rushed forward and put the bolster and pillows behind his back. He batted her away.

The viscount walked into the middle of the room and came to stand facing the bed. 'Harty! You're looking a lot more perky than when they brought you in here. Lady Hart thought you were out for the count.' He looked Sophy up and down. 'I see your cousin has been looking after you.'

She prickled. Odious man! Sophy kept her hands held tightly behind her back and reminded herself that well-brought-up young ladies did not slap gentlemen without extreme provocation.

'How is Lady Hart?' Ben said.

'Mild shock, that's all, nothing to be overly concerned about. She's recovering in the drawing-room and taking tea with your unexpected guests.'

'Guests?'

'Blunham and his son.'

Ben raised an eyebrow but said nothing.

'It was Sir Horace Blunham's coach that caused the accident,' Sophy said.

'Ah.' Ben nodded.

'The day is getting on, you know. Being winter and all that.' The viscount raised his bony fist to his mouth and coughed. 'No doubt your cousin is anxious to get home. I'd be happy to escort her.'

'No need.' Ben looked as if he was about to swing himself off the bed.

44

'You're not going anywhere until the doctor's been,' Sophy snapped. And she certainly wasn't going anywhere with Viscount Merryford. If she ever was going to be ruined, she would arrange the matter herself, and the perpetrator was not going to be Viscount Merryford.

'Sophy, you had better stay here overnight. One of the stable lads can run a note over to your father.'

'Certainly.' Sophy walked straight out of the room, her head held high.

★   ★   ★

His head ached as if it had a pitchfork riven through it. That was no excuse, Ben told himself. How did Sophy manage to confound him so? He should not have acted with such a lack of restraint. She was his cousin, after all, not some fly-by-night opera singer or wanton widow. What if she expected an offer of matrimony? Well, she'd be waiting a long time. Getting leg-shackled was not for him.

'I take it we're not going up to town this evening?' Merryford said. He wandered over towards the window, which overlooked the back lawns, and glanced out.

'Were we to go to London today?' Ben

struggled to pull his thoughts together. But she'd tasted as sweet as hothouse peaches. Never had a kiss so easily exceeded his expectations.

'Yes, don't you remember?'

'I have to say it's all a bit hazy. I don't remember the accident.'

'We had planned to go to London today.' Merryford leaned his hand on the side of the window-frame. 'No matter. Let's see what the quack says. A day or two won't make much difference.'

'Yes, by the time the doctor's been it'll be far too late to go anywhere today.' Ben winced as another knife of pain sliced through his chest. 'Besides, I'm aching like the very devil.'

'You know your curricle's been smashed to smithereens?'

'No? Hell!' Ben slammed his fist down on the counterpane.

'A more delicate matter.' Merryford left the window, took a step forward and scratched his brow. 'You remember last night?'

'Last night? What did we do last night?' Ben tried to think but his mind kept hitting a blank wall. They must have dined, he supposed.

'We ate lamb at dinner, drank some rather fine Madeira, played cards — faro.'

Ben shook his head. 'I don't remember any of that!'

'Ah, I wondered.' Merryford's eyes did not meet his.

'What's the matter?'

'We had a wager.' Merryford scratched his nose. 'We played cards for it and you lost. I have still to collect my winnings.'

'How much?'

'Ah, now this where it gets rather delicate . . . '

'Out with it, for heaven's sake!'

Merryford's chest rose and fell as he breathed deeply. 'All in all, your debt to me came to eight hundred guineas — '

'Eight hundred guineas!'

'But this afternoon, we discussed it and I took back your vowels in exchange for your cousin. I take her off your hands and you owe me nothing.' Merryford pulled at his cravat. 'In fact, you can say you win all round.'

What? A hellish stab of pain shot through Ben's ribs and his vision blurred. He said, 'You mean Sophy? Miss Grantchester?'

'Yes. So, you see, it's a bit unsporting of you to be, er . . . spoiling the goods, as it were.'

3

In spite of the mischief of his attentions, Sophia felt a great deal of good will towards Lord Hart. She could not help thinking much of the extraordinary circumstances attending their acquaintance, and of the right which he seemed to have to interest her.

She pressed the cool back of her hand to her lips. They felt . . . she couldn't describe how they felt. It was altogether very extraordinary. She leaned against the wall; waited until the dizziness passed.

She came down the stairs. The smartly liveried footman opened the door to the drawing-room.

Papered in a feminine eggshell blue, the tall ceilings and plaster designs of the interior matched the expectation created by the outside façade of this neo-classical house. Twenty-two years she had been on this earth, yet never before had she been invited into this house. Invited or not, she was here. Sophy stepped into the room.

Three faces turned from their elegant sofas to regard her.

'How is your husband, my lady?' Sir

Horace Blunham rose to his feet, and his son likewise, nodding a fraction of a moment behind his father. There was a large fire in the marbled hearth yet Sophy found she was trembling.

Lady Hart lay reclined on a couch, looking a little pale. She folded her Chinese fan, about to speak.

'Lord Hart has woken up and certainly has no broken bones,' Sophy forced herself to say quickly. 'And I'm sorry for any misunderstanding, sir, but Lord Hart is not my husband.'

'Dear Sophy is our cousin, Sir Horace,' Lady Hart said, pushing herself upright and holding out her arms, sleeved in fine cream-coloured lace. Sophy came forward and kissed her hands. 'My, Sophy! How you have grown into a quite proper young woman. How is your dear father?'

'He is feeling better, Lady Hart, thank you.'

'Sophy's father is a clergyman,' Lady Hart explained to her guests. 'He has the living at Middleton, a village not above ten miles from here.'

She might as well have said, 'This girl is our poor relation, pay her no attention', Sophy thought.

'Now, Sophy, my dear, perhaps you want to

go and attend to your toilette?' Lady Hart looked her up and down. The attendant footman knew his duty without having to be asked and disappeared out of the room. Sophy also knew her duty and her position, and stood still awaiting her orders.

'Now you are here,' Lady Hart continued, 'we shall send a note to your father and you and I shall have a little talk in the morning.'

'Thank you, Lady Hart.' Sophy knew her clothes were drab, that she had not even paused to check her appearance in a mirror before coming in. But a little talk? What was that to be about? Sophy stopped herself frowning.

'My lady?' A stout-looking woman — a senior female servant, perhaps the house-keeper — entered the room.

'Please make Miss Grantchester comfortable in the Green Room.' Lady Hart waved her hand. Sophy knew that she as well as the servant had been dismissed.

★   ★   ★

Spoiling the goods, as it were. Merryford's words echoed in Ben's ears. He watched the dust in the bedroom air hang still. What the devil was he supposed to do? He pushed his back against the bolster cushions of the bed and struggled to get his thoughts in order. No, he couldn't recall making any such agreement.

'I am not the sort of gentleman who would wager his cousin's virtue,' he said, breaking the awkward silence. 'It doesn't even belong to me, as it were.'

'Are you accusing me of being a liar?' Merryford drew himself up and pushed his shoulders back.

'No — '

'We could duel over it, of course, but it's such a bore now duels are illegal and so unfashionable. If one wants to kill someone, one needs to go to Spain and make it a Frenchie.' Merryford laughed. It made Ben want to punch his fist into the face of this man he thought of as a friend.

'I have no recollection,' Ben said and tried to keep his tone steady, his eyes focused on Merryford's. He didn't think he would have stooped so low. What on earth could have possessed him to . . . to award Merryford with *Sophy*?

The small mantel clock on his dresser quietly struck the hour. Four o'clock.

'I'm sorry, Merryford,' Ben said, pulling himself into a more comfortable position, 'but if this is all as you say then I shall have to give serious consideration as to whether I shall honour the matter.'

'You know, Harty?' Merryford's eyes narrowed. 'Sometimes I think you are an old stick-in-the-mud. Why let a woman's virtue count for anything? It's inevitable that someone who doesn't value it will take it. Why fight nature?'

'Honour, Merryford. That's why. A gentleman's honour.'

Merryford snorted. 'You're the last person I would have expected to start lecturing about honour. Besides, I am not proposing to use the chit and then cast her aside. I'll set her up in a damn fine little house in Chelsea, a smart carriage, the lot. What other prospects has the girl got? She is far too pretty to remain immured in the country. Surely you see that?'

No. Merryford was right. Sophy's prospects were meagre indeed. But why was Sophy here at Hartfield Bury and why had she been in his curricle with him? He couldn't even remember precisely when he had last seen her. It would have been a couple of years ago.

All he could think was that he had somehow become interested in his cousin himself. That he could understand. She was remarkably pretty, if a little pert of manner. Whatever was going on, one thing was certain. Merryford was not having her.

'As I say,' Ben said slowly, 'I shall have to consider whether I shall accept that the agreement stands or whether it will come to pistols.'

'Hang on, Harty.' Merryford's expression twitched. 'You said a moment ago the girl didn't belong to you!'

'Did I? Well, why the devil did I offer her to you then? Of course, she belongs to me.' Ben raised his voice. 'Now get out. Not just of this room but this house.'

'I won her fair and square, Harty. Now if you are not going to play ball, why should I?' The eyes narrowed again and Merryford took a step closer. 'How easy it would be for all of London to know by tomorrow evening that the true identity of Ben Hyde is Benedict St Michael, Lord Hart.'

'I have no idea what you are talking about,' Ben said in as uninterested a manner as he could muster. How the devil did Merryford know he and Ben Hyde were one and the same? It had just been a game, a lark, and there was only one man in London who knew Ben Hyde's identity for sure — Jack Walden. Had Jack's tongue become loose? Would Merryford truly set him up for the hangman?

'I'm a reasonable gentleman,' Merryford said. 'I see you are a little overset by the accident and your memory loss.' He waved his hand. 'And over a female! Not something serious like a prize mount. Why don't you sleep on it? You'll feel differently in the morning.'

'You're right, of course,' Ben said and struggled to keep his tone sounding debonair. 'If it was Genii, my Arabian stallion, I'd demand satisfaction of you now, wager or no wager. But how about another wager?'

Merryford's eye seemed to brighten. 'What did you have in mind?'

Ben kept the smile off his face. Merryford was weakening. He could sense it. And if there was one thing Merryford would fall for it was the excitement of some good sport.

'I have an excellent idea for a wager,' Ben said. Actually he had no great idea except that it needed to be a wager he knew he could win.

There was a loud knock on the door and the doctor came in.

'We'll settle it tomorrow,' Merryford said and left the room.

★   ★   ★

Some hours later, near the middle of the night, Ben, bored with trying to get to sleep and failing, hauled himself out of bed. He'd taken a few drops of the laudanum the doctor had advised but it had only half-dulled the pain and fogged his mind. He limped over the window, parted the curtains and glanced across the empty moonlit lawns. All was quiet. There was nothing keeping him awake except himself. He'd have to take more of the evil stuff if he was ever going to get to sleep.

However, that wasn't the primary concern gnawing at his bones. How the devil had he agreed to sell Sophy to Merryford for 800 guineas? It was despicable and now he must, in all honour, rectify the situation.

And Merryford, whom he had considered a friend, was not to be trusted.

Hell! What if Merryford was at this very moment collecting his prize? Ben's fingers clenched the edge of the sash window-frame to steady himself as redoubled pain and nausea washed through him. He thought he might be sick. Sophy would have had the sense to lock her door, wouldn't she?

Ben breathed very deeply, steeled himself and walked out on to the corridor. His mother would have put her in either the Blue or the Yellow Room, he was sure.

He was confounded to find both were empty.

Eventually his hand tried to turn the handle of the Green Room, the very smallest of the guest rooms, and found that the door was locked. Ben breathed a sigh of relief.

'Who is it?' came a small voice from inside the room. Certainly Sophy.

'Ben,' he replied. He heard a shuffle and the soft pad of footsteps and the turning of the key in the lock.

'What do you want?' she said, her dark eyes peering out of the inch she had opened the door.

'Have you no sense?' he heard himself growl under his breath. 'What are you doing opening your door to men wandering about at night?'

She stared at the ground. 'Sorry.'

The door began to close. Ben struck it with his hand and pushed his way into the room. Yes, he most certainly did want something which he had no right to whatsoever.

She stood in a far too flimsy white night-rail and bare feet, staring at him with wide, curious eyes. Her gold hair was loose and cascaded around her shoulders. He wanted to feel it, wanted to touch her.

'Ben?' she said and a crease lined her brow. She took a step towards him. He wanted her whole body to come towards him, to be pressed against him, to belong to him. The intensity of his feelings shocked him. Her night-rail floated, moved; made him notice how it hugged her shoulders and upper chest, then from her breasts downwards, hung like the lightest of drapes. The lace at the base of its skirt skimmed the mid-point of her shapely calves. Her perfect feet were naked, her ankles smooth. Her toes — He stopped himself; stared at the ceiling.

'Keep the door locked!' He couldn't help that his tone sounded harsh.

'Yes,' she whispered.

He turned his back, swallowed and left the room. His feelings for his cousin were unacceptable.

★   ★   ★

Sophy tossed and turned. The mattress had lumps. She had never spent a night away from home before. The maids had found her a night-rail and brushed her hair for her — an attention to which she was unaccustomed. She curled herself into a ball so it was very dark, and tried to forget that Ben had just marched into her bedchamber.

She'd never credited that he — or any gentleman — would do such a thing. Not an unmarried female guest in his own house! That didn't even happen in novels.

She had endured lascivious glances and continuous attempts at flirtation from Viscount Merryford yesterday. Now she also needed to beware of Ben.

She lay flat on her back so she could watch the flickering shafts of moonlight that came in through the gaps in the draughty curtain. The memory of his dark ardent gaze when he had pushed his way into her chamber was still too vivid. His regard seemed as actual as if his fingers had touched her. His eyes had burned into her flesh so that she had felt hot in those exact places he had stared at so absolutely.

She must have got to sleep eventually because the next thing it was morning. Sophy ventured down to breakfast, embarrassed that she still should be wearing the same dress as yesterday. Her drab serge dress was ideal for going into Stickleton in cold weather but if she had thought she would be visiting her well-to-do cousins she would have worn the red linsey-woolsey dress that she had made herself with some help from Mary, their servant, and could, with a lenient eye, be regarded as somewhat fashionable.

Lady Hart sat with a plate of toast in front of her, concentrated on drinking her coffee, and didn't look up as Sophy entered the room.

'Good morning, Lady Hart,' Sophy said. His mother could not know, Sophy told herself, that Ben had kissed her and . . .

'Morning, m'dear.' Lady Hart caught her gaze and Sophy fought the urge to blush and turned sharply to the buffet just in case. She was ravenous. The household had decided to forgo dinner last night and she had received an unappetizing cold collation on a tray in her room. She helped herself to some delicious-smelling rashers of bacon, a poached kipper and three slices of toast.

'Thank you so much for your hospitality, Lady Hart,' she said, as she sat down.

'I'm sorry that I am not better company, m'dear. Yesterday was quite a shock to me, you understand?'

'Yes,' Sophy said, spreading the large linen napkin across her knees.

'I thought my son was . . . gravely ill, and then when I saw you here too, I had a double shock.'

Sophy felt herself go very still. She had been about to take some butter for her toast but she placed the small silver knife back on the table beside her plate and withdrew her hand back on to her lap.

'Then of course I realized I was leaping to unwarranted, foolish conclusions. You see, my dear . . . if I may speak to you frankly?'

'Oh. Yes,' Sophy whispered.

'Benedict is not to be trusted where women are concerned.'

Sophy found herself unable to meet Lady Hart's eye.

'Dear child, you have no mother to advise you and your father no doubt trusts in the Lord rather than attending to the practical matters of having a marriageable daughter on his hands. You shall come with me to Brighton after Christmas and under my patronage and with a modest dowry I shall provide, I am certain we shall have success.'

Sophy bit her lip. She had no intention of getting married but to say it would sound ungenerous. 'Thank you very much, Lady Hart, for your kind attentions but I am not sure I can leave my father so soon. You see — '

'Arrangements can be made.' Lady Hart waved her hand. 'Additional domestic help and so forth. And your father has a curate, does he not?'

The door opened and Viscount Merryford walked in, dressed to the nines, head to foot in Brummel-fashionable black. His lips curved into a smile which Sophy could not credit was real.

He bade them good morning and piled his plate high from the buffet. Sophy wondered how he was going to eat it all yet he tucked in with gusto.

'You are no doubt anxious to get home,'

Lady Hart said to Sophy.

'Yes, Lady Hart.'

'I can see you home directly,' Merryford drawled. He brought up his napkin and wiped the corner of his mouth.

'But — Lord Hart said — '

'He's sleeping. The doctor instructed the use of a liberal dose of laudanum. He needs to recover from the accident, m'dear,' Lady Hart said. 'Viscount Merryford will accompany you home.'

'It would be my pleasure.'

Sophy swallowed. She was being ridiculous to imagine that Viscount Merryford would foist unwanted attentions on her.

'How kind, Viscount Merryford,' she said.

★ ★ ★

Ben opened his eyes. His head felt like a brick. He wanted to close his eyes again and lie completely still. He rubbed his face. Must be the vast quantities of opiate the quack had insisted he take. It had quenched the pain and allowed him to sleep, but nothing was broken: he had no excuse to lie here.

What time was it? Light streamed into the room through the crack in the curtain. Not that early then.

He pulled himself out of bed, more slowly

than he would have liked. Eventually he was upright. Where the devil was Edwards, his valet, and what time was it?

He found his brass watch, laid carefully by Edwards on his dresser. Twelve-thirty? Hell! He went to the ewer and threw cold water over himself. In ten minutes he was downstairs.

Lady Hart was reclined on her favourite sofa in the drawing-room.

'Benedict! What are you doing out of bed?' she said, pulling herself up.

An uncanny feeling struck him that something was not quite right. 'Sophy? Where's Sophy?'

'Miss Grantchester? Viscount Merryford kindly agreed to take her home.'

'The very devil he did! When?'

'Oh, they have only just left. Benedict, you look quite queer! Benedict, about arranging a house in Brighton — '

Ben stumbled out of the room.

Something drove him, something stronger than the Devil himself. Perhaps it was Edwards and the fiendishly strong coffee he had held under Ben's nose and forced him to drink; perhaps it was his racing heart that feared the very worst that spurred him back into a proper consciousness. All he knew was what his heart told him: that Merryford was no friend of his and that Sophy was more important than any gentleman's agreement.

Ben pushed Genii straight into a gallop and as soon as they were clear of Hartfield Bury, he pulled the soft black mask out of his pocket and gripped it in the palm of his hand ready.

* * *

Sophy sat in the closed carriage and watched Viscount Merryford opposite her out of the corner of her eye. They had been travelling not more than half an hour and so far he had shown agreeable manners.

'The sun is a little strong,' he said, reaching forward. His bony fingers pulled shut the curtains on both sides.

'But it is raining,' Sophy said quietly. Outside the sky had been grey. She could hear the pattering on the roof of the coach. She tried to ignore the gooseflesh prickling at the back of her neck.

The viscount squinted at her through the dimness. *What if he had no intention of taking her to Middleton?*

Sophy lifted her hand up to part the curtain. The viscount pounced forward and slammed his hand down on the window, pinning the curtains fast where they were.

'Curious, aren't you?' he said.

The coach turned to the right, off the road on to another. Where were they going? Sophy pulled her hand back on to her lap. She lifted her chin an inch. 'I do not care much for your tone of voice, my lord.'

'You'll learn to please me soon enough.' The viscount shrugged and sat back against the puce brocade of his seat.

Learn to please me? Sophy yanked the curtain sharply and saw at once that they were not going to Middleton at all. This was the road to Devizes. What was she going to do?

Jump.

At worst she would end up with a couple of broken bones. She put her hand on the handle of the carriage door.

'Oh no you don't!' Merryford sprang forward and seized her wrist.

'Let go of me!' Sophy said and struggled to pull her wrist free. He frowned and held her all the tighter, hurting her. How dare he! 'Take your hands off me!'

She swung her other hand and made sharp, violent contact with his cheek. The slap cracked like a horsewhip.

'You b — ' Merryford ground his teeth together. His cheek reddened. He pitched forward and landed on top of her as the

64

carriage drew to a juddering, crunching halt. His weight crushed the air from her chest then went flying back into his seat.

Anger flashed across his eyes. 'Why the devil have we stopped?' he shouted and reached for his cane.

The answer came bellowing out of nowhere. 'Stand and deliver!'

The horses whinnied in distress.

The harsh scream came again. 'Stand and deliver, I say! Step out of the carriage or I'll blow your brains out!'

★ ★ ★

Sophy stumbled to her feet. The ground was wet and slippery. At least Merryford had let go of her. She shook her wrist, which hurt, and looked up. The rain stung her eyes and cheeks. She rubbed her eyes. Sat on an enormous black horse was the highway robber wearing tall black boots, buckskin breeches and a navy-blue cape. He brandished a gleaming pair of pistols. A black mask hid his face. He looked well-to-do from his clothes but they said some of these men made a very good living from the highway.

Sophy glanced at the coachman. There was fear in his eyes. One man. One mount. One shout. Enough to bring a coach to a halt.

'Ben Hyde!' Merryford said, amusement tickling his voice, not fear. He stood with his back to her, directly facing the assailant.

Sophy shifted her foot an inch to the right across the stubbly grass. Was there a chance she could run for it?

'Come on, then, sir, you'll have a tasty pocket watch for me?' The highway robber's lips were set in a straight line. 'And some coin?'

Merryford stepped back and stood beside her. He fingered his chin. 'Shall we give the dishonourable gentleman what he asks for, m'dear?'

'I . . . I don't know,' Sophy muttered. How was she going to escape now with Merryford only inches away?

'Your watch, sir.' The highwayman kept the pistols trained at the viscount and didn't flinch.

'Oh, I've had enough of this!' Merryford exclaimed, addressing the highwayman. He wiped the rain from his face with his sleeve. 'What are you playing at?'

Sophy pushed her toe slowly to the right. If she could garner a few more inches, she might be away before Merryford had a chance to grab her. They were only two or three miles from the village of Weston. She would go straight to the vicarage there and all would be well, apart from the chill she was sure to catch. She'd be soaked through by the time she got there unless the rain stopped.

Crack!

The highwayman discharged a shot into the air. The smoke and smell of powder quickly dissolved in the wet. The horses whinnied in distress.

Sophy stared up at the grey sky and pressed her hands together. Water slid down her face. She didn't care to wipe it away. There were no houses in sight, only flat countryside. No one to hear the shot and raise the alarm. Whatever happened next, she wouldn't be frightened.

'Your watch, sir.'

'Don't think I'm cowed by this ridiculous performance!' A hardened glare developed on Merryford's countenance.

The highwayman pointed his second pistol at Merryford.

The rain stopped. The horses quietened. No birdsong. The silence felt eerie. Merryford appeared to pale.

'Your watch, sir.'

'Confound it!' Merryford reached into his inner pockets and drew out a handsome-looking gold watch. His eyes flashed and he stared up at the highwayman in defiance. 'I'll get you for this. 'Twas my father's.'

There was no emotion on the highway-man's face. 'Your wife. Has she no jewellery?'

'My wife?' Confusion crossed Merryford's face. 'No, no jewellery.'

Sophy gulped. The air was cold, thick as creamed soup. The highwayman looked from Merryford to her. Pinned her gaze.

'A necklace? A ring? Come on, madam, I know the tricks. Give me one item and I'll let you keep the rest.'

'I . . . don't have any jewellery,' Sophy stammered.

A moment of chilled silence, where she could hear every beat of her heart, and then the robber broke his gaze and looked back at Merryford. 'What sort of cur denies his wife even the pleasure of a wedding ring?'

'She's not my wife.'

'Your ward, then, sir?'

'She's my mistress, if you must know. And no, I haven't given her any jewellery. She's not earned it yet.'

'I'm not your mistress!' Sophy shouted. Her voice sounded like someone else's rather than her own. She brushed her hand against her forehead. It was hot. Merryford was going to ruin her. She must escape. She glanced about at the open countryside. There was nowhere to run.

4

Pride is a very common failing. It was a failing of Viscount Merryford, who cherished feelings of complacence on many scores, real and imaginary. The viscount did not consider that pride makes us blind and comes before a fall but rather that the air was cold, that the wet was seeping into his boots and that he was an unwilling participant in this ridiculous charade.

'A damsel in distress,' the highway robber said, tucking his spent pistol away. He raised his hat. 'Madam, for a guinea, I'll take you to the nearest posting house or wherever you wish to travel.'

'I don't have any money,' Sophy said. The chit's voice sounded cracked and pitiful. Did she imagine she might appeal to the robber's gentlemanly instincts? Merryford felt like laughing.

'The gentleman can pay,' the robber said, and trained his second pistol directly at him. Merryford squinted. He'd been certain it was a trick. But this robber looked severe. His eyes were cold and black.

'Dash it! Dash it, I say!' Merryford

fumbled in his clothes and drew out a single guinea.

'Give that and the watch to the lady,' the highwayman commanded.

Merryford placed the items in Miss Grantchester's hands. Her fingers clasped the watch and the shiny coin. A drop of rain landed on Merryford's nose. He sneezed. He'd catch cold now as well . . .

'Now come to me,' the robber said to the chit. He jumped down from his mount and with his black-gloved hand took the watch and guinea from her hands and tucked them directly in a pocket without even pausing to examine them. Merryford shivered. The sooner he was home . . .

★　★　★

Sophy caught the highwayman's gaze for a moment. Those commanding brown eyes were . . . familiar?

He gave her a heave up on to his stallion and as his arms came around her she breathed in a masculine scent — Benedict St Michael, Lord Hart? A highwayman?

Fear and confusion beat in her chest.

He swung himself back into the saddle behind her, put one strong arm around her waist. Sophy drew in a gulp as her stomach fluttered in a curious fashion. The rain had begun to fall again. The water on her face obscured her vision. He said, 'Now hold tight on to the pommel.'

It was Ben! The way he spoke, more softly to her now. The feel of him, the scent of him. The warmth from his arms tucked about her waist. Sophy drew her sleeve across her eyes and saw the viscount waving his fist. 'I'll get you back for this!'

Ben kicked his mount into action. They cantered away down the road.

'Ben?' Sophy whispered, as they turned a corner, but loud enough to be heard over the wind and the hoof beats.

'Ben Hyde's the name.'

'Ben . . . Hyde? What fustian nonsense!' Of course it was Ben!

'I'm Ben Hyde all the while I've got this mask on,' came the sharp reply.

'Then take it off!'

'I've one hand holding you, and the other on the reins. You do it.'

She kept hold of the pommel with her right hand, twisted her body slightly towards him and with her left hand reached for the mask. Her fingers tapped against the black silk, against the stubble on his chin before she caught the edge of the fabric and drew the mask swiftly upwards and pulled it free of him. The wind whipped it out of her grasp. It flew into the hedgerow behind them.

'Oh no!'

'No matter,' Ben said. 'That was Ben Hyde's very last outing, I assure you.'

Wasn't it just a bit melodramatic to dress up as a highwayman to rescue her from Merryford? Sophy bit her lip. The trees, the fields and the hedgerows raced past as Ben's mount kicked up a cracking pace. She turned her face to the side, so only one cheek was battered by the wind, and luxuriated in the warmth of his strong, hard body. 'You did it to rescue me?'

'Why else?' He sounded a little indignant.

'Thank you. But, actually, I was about to escape — '

'I rescued you,' he interrupted, his voice hard as a blacksmith's hammer on iron.

'Did you not see the streak of red on Viscount Merryford's cheek?' She was grateful for being rescued but she wasn't some helpless milk-and-water miss. 'That was by my hand.'

'But you didn't escape, did you? I'm not blind and I'm not a fool. Merryford will slink away now to lick his wounded pride but he will be back. He intends to set you up as his mistress: I will not allow it.'

'I have no wish to become his . . . mistress!

I don't know where he got such an idea from.' Sophy shivered. He held her fast next to him in a way that made her feel absolutely secure and yet slightly excited.

'You can't be expected to fight off a man of six foot yourself, for heaven's sake!' The tone was arrogant, nasal.

'Don't you swear at me!' Vexation rose like bile in her chest. 'I can take care of myself. I don't need you or anyone else to do it.'

'In that case . . . ' Ben pulled up sharply and they slowed to a walk and then stopped in the middle of the road. 'Good day, Sophy. You may get down.'

She looked left and right; took in huge gulps of cold air. Not a house or other building in sight. Tears threatened to prick. 'Don't you dare . . . abandon me!'

'You admit you need my help.' Ben's voice was commanding. 'Well, thank you. I admit to occasionally being a show-off but I did not conjure up this particular charade. It would have been preferable to spend today in the comfort of my bed. I'm as bruised as a roasted potato that's been hurled down the stairs.'

Sophy stifled a sob as the image of a battered potato came to mind. Ben flicked them back up to a canter and she told herself she had simply had a fright, that was all, and buried her face into the front of his cape and hoped he was not in too much pain. She should tell him she was thankful he had rescued her but she couldn't quite muster herself to put it into words. It was easier, for now, to be quiet and concentrate on gathering her composure.

★　★　★

The wind had blown a large branch into the road. Genii snorted but didn't waver as he skipped straight over it.

'Now, breakfast.' Ben flicked his reins and tried to take his mind off what the provoking warmth of having Sophy pressed up against him was doing to him. He was a man, after all, not a saint. Genii cantered a tiny bit faster and cut the corner of the road.

'Breakfast?' she queried, as if he had suggested they go to see if the moon really was made of cheese.

'I'm ravenous. I haven't eaten anything since yesterday morning.' More importantly he needed to give Merryford plenty of time to get back to Hartfield Bury, pack his things and get out of his house by the time he got home, or he couldn't promise he'd be responsible for his actions. Having a pistol trained on a spot between that cur's eyeballs had felt dangerously good.

'Oh.'

'The Dog and Duck, makers of the best pies in Wiltshire,' Ben said, and slowed Genii down to the trot as they approached the travellers' inn.

'I've never eaten pie in an inn,' Sophy said.

Ben dismounted and helped Sophy to the ground. It felt good, holding her waist in his hands, trying to catch her blue eyes, seeing them widen and the pink blush in her cheeks when he did so. He didn't want to let go. How dare Merryford think it was his right to take her in lieu of gambling debts! Yet it was he, Benedict St Michael, who had shamefully agreed to it.

Ben considered that he could chuck her over his shoulder now and, well, the landlord would be bound to have a spare chamber . . .

'Thank you, Ben,' she said and smoothed her skirts straight.

Ben cast his gaze to the ground and looked at the uninteresting mud and pebbles, ashamed of himself. He reminded himself very sternly that while he had done his fair share of misdeeds, he was a gentleman of honour. He clicked his heels and led the way into the inn.

'In here,' he said, opening the heavy oak door for her.

He regarded Sophy as she took in the scene of the taproom, empty save for a couple of coves in the corner. Her nose wrinkled at the pungent smell — beer, tobacco and goose fat.

'Lord 'Art, what a pleasure.' Mr Hicks, the landlord, wiped his hands on his apron and stepped out to greet him.

'Hicks, you've a private room, haven't you, where we might take some victuals?'

'Certainly, your lordship. Follow me.'

He watched Sophy take in every detail of their surroundings as they followed the landlord along the dim corridor and into a small dining-room. Why on earth was she interested in an old inn like the Dog and Duck? Heavens, he didn't have time for such luxury of thought! He'd never get anything done. It was interesting nevertheless and he couldn't deny that the idea that she might notice more things than he did unnerved him slightly. What the devil did she think of him?

He reminded himself that she was a woman. A delightful woman he wanted to play with, cosset and do all sorts of forbidden things with, but a woman who had a woman's mind. Women's minds became terribly interested in pointless fripperies such as choosing exactly which shade of ribbon would be the correct match for their bonnets. Just look at the inordinate amount of time his mother spent regarding fashion plates in magazines!

Ben placed his right hand on the mantelpiece over the small fire and put on his most urbane and dashing expression. It would be a rum thing indeed if his cousin, whom he was going to all this bother over, didn't look up to him and feel like swooning.

Sophy flickered her gaze in his direction but appeared to be more taken with the flames licking the grate.

'You're interested in fashion, aren't you?' he asked her, undoing his navy cloak at the neck and whipping it off. Apart from the cloak, he was attired excellently, all in black apart from his buckskins and starched white linen cravat. Had she not noticed?

'Yes,' she replied, and looked at him with a slight frown. He liked the way she stuck her nose in the air. It extended her neck and reminded him he wanted to touch and kiss it. 'But I can't afford to be fashionable.'

Ben grunted mildly as he draped the cloak over the back of a chair, and felt a small stab of satisfaction. That would certainly not be the case once he had seen to her wardrobe.

A maid arrived with two tankards of porter, plates and cutlery, and one enormous steak pie. Ben regarded Sophy, who had not bothered to remove her own drab grey cloak before sliding into the high-backed chair and resting her hands on her lap.

'I thought you were hungry?' She looked up at him expectantly. Her eyes sparkled.

His fingers itched to take that hideous garment off her. 'Are you cold, Sophy?'

He rested his hands on the back of his chair.

'No, but I expect the pie is getting cold.'

She was right. He should not be standing staring like an ill-mannered schoolboy. Ben tore off his gloves and swooped down to pick up the pie slice. 'Let me.'

'It looks delicious,' she said, as he heaped a lady-sized portion of pie on to her plate. Her eyelashes feathered as she looked from him to the pie and back to him again. He set her plate down on the table in front of her a little abruptly.

Ben served himself and swung himself into his chair.

'Am I supposed to drink this?' she asked, looking at him directly, teasing the handle on the mug of porter with her fingers.

'You're a country lass,' Ben said. He had to touch her; he couldn't take it any longer. He slid his arm across the table, brushed her fingers with his. They recoiled, but only an inch. He touched them again; began to intertwine her fingers with his own.

She did not withdraw.

In the far distance of his early youth, when contriving incidents to shock innocent débutantes had seemed an amusing sport, Ben had ventured to hold many a lady's hand. The reactions he had received had ranged from violent disapproval to a grudging acceptance.

Not this. She was wary, he could see, and yet she explored his own fingers in equal measure. She ran her forefinger up the back of his middle finger and then across the back of his hand, and then back, and then again. It was too slow to be a match to tinder, too delicate to inspire lust. Yet he was captivated, cowed even, the intimate sensations he could not name and could not recall ever feeling before.

He looked into her eyes. Had to. Something stronger than his own will propelled him. Her gaze did not waver. It asked, questioned. What was he doing?

What was he doing? He certainly wasn't doing anything. He was a gentleman of honour, as he unfortunately had to keep reminding himself.

'I'm ravenous,' he said, hating the gruffness in his voice. He pulled his hand away. Her eyes dulled; looked confused. Couldn't she see that he would much rather continue holding her hand?

Ben stabbed his fork into a piece of steak and ate it.

'It's very nice,' she said, after she had eaten a couple of small mouthfuls.

'Splendid pie, very good. Got a prize cow weaned on good Wiltshire grass, I should think.'

'A prize cow?'

'For the butter.'

'Now I would not have credited you knew about pies and butter, Ben.' Her eyes danced. Ben felt his throat tighten.

'Wait until you taste the greasy rubbish they serve up in London,' he said quickly. 'Made of tallow, I'd warrant.'

'I have no plans to go to London,' Sophy said. Of course she would love to go to London and see everything: Piccadilly with its bookshops, Hyde Park and the General Post Office . . .

'Everybody should go to London,' he said breezily. He didn't meet her gaze.

Everybody does not have the means to go to London, Sophy felt like telling him. 'What's London like?' she said instead. 'Tell me.'

'The finest city in the world. If it's not in London it ain't worth having.'

Ben's world was not like hers. His existence was so very different, Sophy considered. He attacked life like he attacked the pie on his plate — with vigour but in a way she only half understood, with a passion that, on consideration, should make her quake.

It didn't. It sent thrills of excitement through her. He had, after all, a rather active life dashing about all over the place. She sat at home and wrote about places she'd only ever seen pictures of in books.

'Apart from the pies,' she added. 'The pies in Wiltshire are better.'

'And the eels. They eat eels from the Thames, y'know, and the Thames is the biggest sewer in the place.' Ben scraped up a final mouthful on his fork.

'I am not terribly fond of eel in any case.'

'Splendid.' Ben pushed his plate away to one side and wiped his mouth with his napkin and then cast the linen down on the table. 'Because I can't stand the creatures.'

He was so very different from her father, who ambled through the days in his kindly, abstract fashion. Ben was so real, so very corporeal, that every inch of her begged to be allowed to feel him, even though it was wrong.

Sophy pushed her knife and fork together on her plate and dabbed her lips with her napkin. He watched her and the corners of his lips quirked, and she felt a swell of something disturbing rise in her chest, as if it was his lips that dabbed hers, not the cloth.

'Shall we go?' he said and raised his eyebrows.

She was falling, and in such a terribly headlong fashion, for the charms of a rake! She got up quickly, pulled on her gloves and cloak and went straight outside, breathed the cold, refreshing air thankfully. What was she thinking! He was a rich aristocrat and she was a poor parson's daughter, and besides, she had no wish to marry. Mary Wollstonecraft had written that marriage was akin to slavery, and so it would be. For no husband would allow her to do what she wanted — be a lady novelist. And none would marry her once they found out she already had a novel published. She had set her course for her life the day she had sent her final manuscript off to her publishers in London.

Ben appeared a moment later, striding out of the Dog and Duck in his tall black boots as if he owned the place. For all she knew, perhaps he did. She envied his confidence, his assured manner. Admired it even, though logic said it was easy for Lord Hart of Hartfield Bury, a man of his position, an aristocrat by birth and upbringing, to be so.

She needed to take her mind away from the temptation to commit mortal sin and back on to things that mattered, like looking after her father and her writing, on which she'd been stuck for weeks. Now she would put some life into the hero in her story. A dashing rake would do wonders — '

'Sophy, you're staring into the sky and you look awfully perplexed.' He stood before her, only inches away.

It was at moments like this, when he spoke to her as one sentient being to another, that he struck her in her most vulnerable spot. Sophy swallowed. 'I was just . . . thinking.'

'*Thinking*? Heavens! There's no need for a woman to *think*!' He shook his head and turned to give his horse, whom the ostler had led over, a pat on the nose.

Every grain of her skin bristled and her jaw clenched. Just for a moment he'd let her believe he might care to understand her. Then he smashed the illusion irrevocably. She was sure she hated him. A rake who was prejudiced, ignorant, self-important . . . yes, he'd be in her book with all those qualities and she'd make him learn the hard way that he was wrong.

She steeled herself, trying not to let the warm, sensuous proximity of being pressed against him on horseback erode her antipathy towards him.

Tried and failed. The breeze was strong, its

cutting coldness unforgiving, and yet Ben was solid as a wall heated by the sun and more comfortable. They reached Middleton too quickly. It vexed her that she would have been content to close her eyes to the elements and lean against him for hours.

The parsonage looked the same as it always did, squat and small, a cottage really, made of local stone and thatched, with three rooms upstairs and down, and with a pretty but unruly garden where Sophy managed to grow peas, beans and onions in between the flowers.

His fingers burned into her sides as he helped her down to the ground. As her feet hit the ground a hot, violent emotion clenched her stomach and rose up from it. She didn't want to go home. She wanted to speed off with Ben and spend the days riding around the countryside and stopping at inns to eat pies. I've only been away one day, she told herself. It seemed like longer.

Sophy shook herself as he let go and tied Genii to the gatepost. Then he was through the small gate and at the front door of the parsonage before her, being polite to Mary, their servant, and inviting himself in to see her father.

He shook his cloak off in the hall and Sophy crushed her fingers into the woollen material as she hung it up for him, but it was cold compared to when she had felt this same material on him, on horseback.

'Would you like tea, Lord Hart?' she asked.

'Ben, m'name's Ben,' he replied, and ran his hand across his face and through his hair.

Yes, but it feels strange to be calling you Ben in front of Mary, Sophy thought.

Let alone Father! Her father appeared from his study and walked towards them in his slow, shuffling gait. He smiled. 'Sophy, you're home. I got the note so there was no need to worry. Lord Hart, thank you.'

'Reverend Grantchester, good afternoon.' Ben took a striding pace forward and shook her father's hand. 'How is your health, sir?'

'I'm up and about, as you see, my lord,' her father replied. And he did look better, Sophy was relieved to see. There was a certain colour in his cheeks and lustre in his eyes. 'Good to see you, m'boy. You remind me of your father in his Oxford days.'

'I didn't know you knew my father at Oxford, sir?'

'Oh yes, we were at the university at the same time.' Mr Grantchester paused and rubbed his back. 'Oxford. Best not to mention that to Lady Hart, eh? Probably still a sensitive subject.'

'Sir?' Ben looked as if he had no idea what

her father was talking about. Sophy had an imprecise idea that there had been some scandal at Oxford and this was why her father had ended up rector of Middleton and not in some greater position in life.

'You will join us for some tea, won't you, Lord Hart?' Mr Grantchester asked. 'Lady Hart always — '

'Yes, of course.'

'Now, m'boy, before you go, it is, I feel, my duty to bring up the subject of the church roof with you.'

'The church roof?' Ben struggled to find the right words. 'I am sorry. I have a manager who should have brought this to my attention.' Hell, goodness knows what other responsibilities he had and wasn't aware of. He assumed Mr Simmons, whom he paid to manage everything, managed everything.

'Mr Simmons came about a month ago,' Mr Grantchester said, his busy eyebrows bent into a frown. 'But we have heard nothing since. Would you like to inspect the state of the roof yourself?'

'There really are a great deal of holes in the roof,' Sophy added. She looked at him with her very large eyes and managed to pin his gaze while she spoke. Ben watched her face with interest.

'I'm sorry? Curtains?' He'd lost the last

thing she'd said. He'd seen a spark flicker behind her eyes and it had excited him.

'We had to take out the sarsenet curtain last year after it was ruined by the damp.' She glared at him as if to say, 'How dare you smile?'

Merryford was right. His cousin had bed-sport promise and it was useless to deny these elemental feelings that she provoked in him by her very presence. To keep a smile off his face, Ben frowned. 'I'd better see the church for myself, sir. Ascertain the exact nature of the problem so we can progress with the repairs without any further delay.'

Her expression softened. Silk. Her cheek, when he stroked it, would feel like silk.

'I am delighted to see you take such a personal interest, m'boy,' Mr Grantchester said. 'I had wondered whether to write to you about it again but providence has intervened at just the right time. Sophy, would you kindly show Lord Hart the church roof?'

'Yes, Father.' Her countenance was artificially contrived, Ben noticed.

'If it is not too much of an inconvenience, Miss Grantchester?' He raised his eyebrows and could not wait to see her reaction. He knew he looked polished and urbane. He'd had mistresses who had tried to throw his insufferable arrogance back in his face. He'd enjoyed every minute of it, and he was sure that Sophy would do the same.

'My lord.' She rose to her feet. Even the way she said those two small words smacked of defiance. Bravo! It was like a challenge rising up before him. More potent than striving to win any curricle race; more thrilling than any wager he could possibly imagine. The challenge of getting Sophy into his bed, and the reward . . .

'Miss Grantchester.' Ben rose, motioned with his hand to say, 'After you'. Hell, she was fortunate he was a man who had a great deal of honour and who was master of his baser instincts. Unfortunately.

Yet this was tempting, so very tempting. And if it really came to it, Ben wondered, which was stronger — his honour or his lust?

5

Vanity working on a weak head produces every sort of mischief, Sophy reminded herself. She allowed herself only the most ordinary of breaths and tried to ignore the overbearing presence of Ben, who followed on her heels.

The grass was wet, speckling the inferior brown leather of her boots before she had even reached the parsonage gate. She could have opened the low gate in the dark, but, as she reached out, his long black superfine-clad arm appeared from behind her and lifted the latch. The intolerable arrogance of the man!

'Let me,' he said.

Sophy snatched her hand back and hurried through the gate as quickly as she could. His fingers might have landed on the latch at the same time, have touched hers. They did not.

He was too near. Even as he stepped out of the parsonage garden and on to the road, she could hear him breathe through his long nose as if he intended taking in all the air in the village in one go.

He paused to shut the gate and Sophy moved a few steps away so that there was at

89

least a distance of four feet between them.

Hearing the click of the gate and seeing Ben standing up and turning towards her, Sophy hurried ahead up the lane. He'd have difficulty in catching up with her and offering her his arm. Not that he was certainly obliged to do such a thing, she supposed. He was a lord and she was only the parson's daughter. But then again, they were cousins. Anyhow, if it was all the same, she would rather not give him the opportunity. At least from the parsonage door to the church door was only around a hundred paces.

He was beside her while there were still a good twenty paces to go before the churchyard. Sophy quickened her step so that she was ahead of his shadow but his long strides equalled two of her steps.

'Sophy?' he said, holding his arm out towards her. He had obviously decided to address her informally now they were alone again. Really, he wasn't so impossibly tall, she decided, finding herself staring at the line of his clean-shaven chin. If she stood on tiptoes, why —

A wave of confusion hit her like cold water from the pump on a hot summer's day.

'No need.' Sophy was dismayed to hear her voice sounding breathless. She plunged ahead up the road and into the churchyard, ignoring him and the quiver in her chest.

The long iron key hung on a nail, hidden by the foliage on the trunk of a yew tree. He stood watching her as she drew the key off its hook.

It fitted in the lock of the nave door and she paused for a moment before giving it its final turn and decided to be sensible. Ben was a rake who made her breathless because of some foolish whimsy of hers to see him as a hero, but he had the money to repair the church. It was her primary duty to make him attend to the roof, not be swayed by his handsome countenance into becoming a blushing, inarticulate maid.

She waved her arm and bowed, gushing with the fluid grace of the master of ceremonies announcing the arrivals at a ball at Stickleton Assembly Rooms. 'Middleton parish church.'

He stepped inside. The building echoed with his firm footsteps on the grey stone floor.

Sophy shut the heavy oak door and came over to stand in front of him. He stood in the middle of the nave and looked around at the ordered wooden pews. Light filtered in through the coloured stained glass at the altar window — St Francis with the birds and the beasts, the gift of Ben's father. She wondered if he noticed, or even knew.

His gaze seemed to skim the uneven collection of white and grey marble memorials along the far wall before looking up. Sophy counted the holes in the roof that were visible. She assumed Ben could see what her naked eye could, and count at least to ten.

'A holey church indeed,' he said.

Sophy swallowed the beginnings of a giggle. She said instead, 'So you find it amusing, my lord? That children catch colds and elderly ladies have their rheumatics aggravated by doing their Christian duty and coming to church?'

'It's beyond repair.'

'What?' Sophy could feel her brow creasing. She straightened it. Ben had better keep his promise to repair the church roof. If he didn't . . . well, she supposed she might write a letter to one of the newspapers.

'Quite beyond repair.'

'But it must be repaired! What will happen if — '

'A new roof, that is what is needed. If it is patched up to the extent that is required, it will put additional stress on the supporting timbers. If they are half-rotten . . . collapse.'

'It's even worse here.' Sophy walked up the step and into the chancel. He followed.

She was dismayed to see a new puddle of water had appeared even since yesterday. She looked up at the dark timbers and then down again at the puddle, and heard the rhythmic splash of the drips.

'Those struts are sodden,' she heard him say. Then a creak loud enough to wake the dead.

Sophy was about to swing her gaze upwards again when she became transfixed by a mass of black and buckskin hurtling towards her. It hit her with force and pushed her back. She stumbled, lost her balance and felt herself falling. She wanted to call out but it was as much as she could do to realize that Ben's arms had enveloped her.

She didn't hit stone — he cushioned her fall to the ground and rolled his body on top of her as he pressed her against the floor. She was completely shielded by him as the groan of timber grew swiftly louder and turned into a splinter and then a frightening crash. Sophy struggled to breathe. She had cold stone behind her back and a crushing warm weight on top of her.

'A piece of beam, that's all.' His voice was so close to her ear she felt it resonate and his hot breath fanned her cheek. Gentle prickles of gooseflesh tripped down her neck. 'Umm? Your scent. Jasmine?'

His scent was indefinable yet unmistakably male. And he was making her feel confused. What was she thinking?

'Please . . . unhand me!'

He moved and her chest had room to breathe again. She swallowed the cold, damp air in large gulps as he untangled himself from her gently and she tried to ignore the heavy, racing thump of her heart. Sophy kept her gaze pinned on the starched crumple of his white linen cravat, now askew, rather than meet his eyes.

He jumped to his feet and she listened to the scrape of his boots as he found his balance in less than a moment. He reached down to offer her his hands.

It would be churlish to refuse so she slid her gloved hands into his and leaned on his firm grip as she pulled herself up. Even through gloved hands his fingers seemed to send a searing heat into her. She looked up at his countenance, his steady gaze. Something flipped over in her stomach.

His brown eyes held her a moment too long. Sophy looked away. She pulled her right hand free and placed it on the cold stone wall. Slowly, her left hand fell from his. Her cheeks were burning. She said, 'It was completely unnecessary for you to throw me on to the floor — '

'This section of the roof is unsafe. We were lucky.' He stepped over the fallen piece of beam and blinked upwards.

'Nevertheless the piece of beam which fell is small.' Sophy bit her lip and tried to keep her anger in check. Why did she feel so piqued? 'I would certainly not have been killed, probably not even injured. I could have quite easily jumped out of the way.'

His eyes narrowed. His lips remained straight. Could he see she was still shaking? Sophy pressed her hands together. The disturbing sensations of being so intimately encased by him still lingered. How could she forget he was a lord and her cousin? 'Do you have . . . designs on my person?'

He flicked some wood splinters off his jacket. 'If I was interested in you in that way, you would be in absolutely no doubt.'

'Ah . . . I have no experience of . . . rakes . . . '

'And you never will,' he said with a frown, the end of the sentence cut short by the clank of the church door being opened.

'Miss! Miss Sophy!' Billy Entwhistle, looking more ruddy-cheeked than usual, leant on the oak shelf next to the door and took in large gulps of air.

'Billy? What is it?' Sophy felt a drip on her nose. Her heart stopped. Billy lived in the cottage opposite them. Had something happened?

'Oh!' Billy said, biting his bottom lip as he looked up and took in the scene, and last of all the tall presence of Ben. 'Oh, pardon me, sir.'

'Carry on, lad,' Ben said in a tone that sounded unnecessarily stern.

'M-Mary said for Miss Sophy to come quick, sir. The reverend's taken a turn, he has.'

Sophy pushed the palm of her hand over her mouth to stop herself shrieking; hardly knew how she got home in so little time. One thing was certain, this time the doctor would be sent for. She would find the money somehow.

Her father lay propped up on the *chaise-longue* in the sitting-room. Mary had brought pillows and blankets from upstairs. Sophy felt a tiny bit dizzy and wanted to sit down. Actually she wanted to be sick but she leaned forward instead and plumped at her father's pillows.

'Not to fuss,' he muttered. His tired-looking eyes shut for a moment.

Sophy swallowed and rushed over to the window and half-pulled the curtain to keep the bright light out of his face.

'May I come in?' followed a gentle tap on

the door. Of course, Ben had followed her back to the rectory, but right now the last thing her father needed was to be disturbed further.

'No — '

'Of course, m'boy,' her father croaked.

'Father — '

'Hush, Sophy!'

Ben stepped lightly into the room and came over to stand beside her. The skin on the back of her neck prickled. She wanted to move — but what if her father needed her suddenly?

'Has this happened before, sir?'

'On occasion.' Her father managed to lift and wave his hand. 'But nothing to be concerned about.'

'And you have sent for the doctor?'

'No.'

'Yes,' Sophy said. 'I have. Billy Entwhistle has gone to Stickleton to fetch Dr Latham, so he will be due his fee for coming here in any case.'

'I don't need a doctor. Doctors are for people with more money than sense.'

Ben tugged at his cravat. 'I would recommend you engage the services of a doctor, sir.'

'Very well.' Her father sighed. The prospect of the doctor's fee would be what was worrying him. If only she had received her advance from London, such worries would be needless! Why had she not finished the novel manuscript sooner?

'I shall personally look into the matter of the church repairs with all speed, sir. You have my word on it. The chancel must be roped off and out of bounds until we are sure it is not dangerous.'

Her father nodded.

Ben smiled. 'It was a pleasure to see you again, Mr Grantchester. And I wish you a speedy recovery.'

'You are welcome any time, m'boy. Any time.'

What does Father think he's doing, inviting Ben to come and visit them again? Sophy thought, stopping her brow from creasing.

Ben nodded at her father and then turned towards her. He caught her eye and allowed the corners of his lips to curve upwards before he turned abruptly towards the door. She amused him for some reason. 'And you, Miss Grantchester.'

'Likewise, Lord Hart.' Sophy swallowed.

'Might you be so kind as to see me out?'

'Certainly.' It would be a relief to be rid of him!

In the hall, as he slipped into his cloak, he said in a low voice, 'Please have your doctor send his bill to me and I shall see it is settled.'

'That would be very kind of you.' Sophy tried to smile but it was impossible. She would rather have told him his charity was unwanted but pride was too expensive.

'I hope your father is feeling better soon.'

'Thank you.'

Sophy watched through the open door as her cousin, the rake, strode down their short path through the front garden, his navy cloak lapping around him. He untied his black horse, threw himself up on it and cantered off. She was glad to see him go — for now.

★   ★   ★

'What a splendid young man,' her father said a little later with a curious look etched across his face. 'It has been proved time and time again that if the good Lord is asked, we must trust He will provide.'

'Yes, we are fortunate that Lord Hart appears in earnest about seeing to the church roof,' Sophy replied. 'Now, Father, will you excuse me? I have a few things to do before it gets dark.'

'Of course, Sophy, dear, and I must finish the sermon for Sunday.'

'No, you must rest, at least until the doctor has been.'

Sophy went upstairs, unlocked the drawer of her bureau and pulled out the sheets she had been most recently working on. She sat down, briefly read the last page and prepared her pen. She began to write from where she had left off. No, that wasn't right. She crossed out the sentence she had just written and tried to rephrase it.

She sighed, laid her pen down and pushed her fingers into her temples. All that was coming into her mind was Ben looking mightily dashing in his buckskins. Maybe the hero of her story would have to be a handsome rakehell after all?

She forced herself to pick up her pen again. She must get this book finished. The advance she had received when the publisher had accepted her first novel had been invaluable but it had all gone. And if Ben had not offered to see to the doctor's fee, where would they be? And what if her father should need the doctor again? She could not presume to ask Dr Latham to send all his bills to Hartfield Bury.

With her first advance she had purchased the material for new curtains and clothes, and the wools to make the tapestry covers for the dining chairs. She had also paid the cobbler to repair all their shoes and seen that the outhouse was well stocked with coal and wood for winter. All things she could do without her father noticing. He would be ashamed to think they were so poor that she was forced to try to earn a living.

This was her secret alone and she must make it her future, her guarantee against becoming destitute should anything happen to her father or to the living. Without her own income, she would have to throw herself on the mercy of one of the well-to-do farmers. And marriage was another name for an employment contract in which she lost everything and had to live in trust that her husband would provide. She would rather rely on herself.

The pen dropped from her hand and clattered on to the desk, splashing ink over her sheets of paper. Her circulating library books, her letters! One of them might be from her publisher. They were still by the side of the road with the crashed curricle! Unless someone had retrieved them and taken them to Hartfield Bury. She might have lost half a five pound note. What was she going to do?

Sophy let her head rest for a moment in her hands. It was no good. She couldn't think of any other option but to write to Ben and ask him if he would be so kind as to have her books and basket sent over and trust to the Lord that no one looked at her letters too closely.

★ ★ ★

Ben threw the drawing-room door open and with no standing on ceremony marched straight in. 'Mama, I discovered today that the roof of the church at Middleton is in an advanced state of disrepair.'

Lady Hart closed and put down on the table the magazine she had been reading before speaking. 'That, Benedict, is hardly surprising when you refuse to show any interest whatsoever in your estate affairs. I keep my eye on things relating to the house and park here, and the house in London, you know that. Everything else is dealt with directly by Mr Simmons. Don't tell me it has suddenly occurred to you it is well past time to grow up and pay some attention to your responsibilities?'

'Perhaps it has.' Wouldn't he be glad when Christmas was over and he could get back to London and his usual existence! In the meantime, he had better arrange an interview with Mr Simmons and see about setting into action these repairs to Middleton church.

'And what about Miss Grantchester?' he added. The memory of her indelible form was haunting the whole front of his body. And his mind.

'Miss Grantchester?' His mother's brow creased. 'What of her?'

'Something should be done for her.'

'I quite agree.' His mother folded her hands in her lap and confounded him with a smile. He hadn't expected her to acquiesce this easily. 'In fact I have already taken the liberty of asking dear Sophy to accompany me after Christmas to Brighton. Now, about the house in Brighton — '

'Wait!' Ben had this uncanny feeling that it all sounded a little too good to be true. 'You sponsored that distant cousin of ours for a Season last year. Did it not occur to you to do the same for Miss Grantchester?'

'No! It most certainly did not.'

'Why not, in heaven's name?'

'Benedict, it was far before your time, of course, but Mr Grantchester was involved in a most terrible disgrace. He was sent down from Oxford. Otherwise he would have been a professor of theology by now, not a village clergyman. Now, I have everything in hand because, of course, we must do something for the poor gel, so there is no need for you to trouble yourself any more about it.'

Ben pursed his lips. This was news indeed but what could Mr Grantchester have done that could possibly be so terrible as to matter now? He swung his hands behind his back and moved over to stand in front of the fire. He reminded himself that his dear mama was a professional at employing diversionary tactics. He would not be sidetracked. 'Even so . . . the gel is remarkably pretty. I am sure she would have excellent marriage prospects if she was presented.'

'Certainly not! Bad blood will be out. And don't you be getting any ideas. However keen I might be to see you wed, I shall only countenance the most suitable of candidates as the next Lady Hart.'

'What? Heavens above! You think I am planning to *marry* Miss Grantchester?' Ben watched the blood drain from his mother's face. 'Yes, indeed, I am swept away in a tide of love and passion, ready to throw myself at her feet.'

Lady Hart sat absolutely still, her pallor like grey stone. A twinge of remorse hit Ben. Hell, did she think he was being serious? Anyhow, if he did desire to marry Miss Grantchester — and he most certainly did not — his dear mama's opinion of her suitability would have nothing to do with it.

'It wouldn't surprise me,' she said at last. She picked up her fan from the table; had to flick it twice so it was fully open. She proceeded to fan herself with vigour. 'You always were set on being capricious at every opportunity. Just like your father.'

'I have absolutely no intention of marrying anyone until it suits *me* to do so.'

'I find I have a sudden headache, Benedict.' She rose to her feet and swept past him out of the room.

The door banged shut. Enough to induce a headache, Ben thought, knowing he was feeling a lack of charity. He strode to the window and looked out at the sweeping driveway and the avenue of chestnut trees that led up to the front of the house. All was quiet. Hell, he had another three weeks of this at least before Christmas would be over and he could escape back to London.

He turned on his heels, drawing a long breath, and went through to his study, a large room which overlooked the back lawns, and slammed the door. This had been his father's room up until that day, six years ago, when he had been killed, thrown violently from his horse while hunting.

Most of his father's papers lay largely untouched and stacked in folios on the shelves or in drawers. The growling dog fox in his glass case, the only exhibit or trophy in the room, remained exactly where he was on a high shelf. The maids dusted around him.

Now he wished he'd burned the fox, the lot. He didn't need the reminder now he was supposed to live up to his father.

A cautious whine came from outside the study door.

Ben turned and opened it with a sigh. It wasn't Nelson's fault he had been hit for six by his confounded chit of a cousin and vexed by his dear mother. 'All right,' he said to the dog. 'You can come in.'

Nelson pushed his nose into his leg and insisted on being patted before ambling over and jumping up to the position he had made his own on the assorted fading cushions of the window seat. Nelson rested his head on his front paws and looked at him as if to say, 'So what are you going to do, then?'

'I have no idea,' Ben replied, flipping open a book from a pile on the large mahogany desk. The title on the frontispiece leapt out at him. *Caprice and Conventionality, Volume I.* Dear Mama had accused him of being capricious.

'Am I capricious? Is it simply a whim, a fancy I've taken to my cousin, sparked perhaps by jealousy because my friend so wanted her?' he asked Nelson. 'If Merryford had not happened to be there, would I have given her a second glance?'

Nelson woofed and appeared to shake his head.

'Our delusions make us fools,' Ben muttered, and glanced again at the frontispiece of the volume. He was surprised to see the name of the author was that of a man — John Chester. How curious. The name John Chester almost sounded like Grantchester.

Written by a man, and yet it promised to be one of those melodramatic novels so enjoyed by his mama. Only fit for female consumption. What the devil was it doing in his study? He glanced down the pile. Six books in all, including Volume II of *Caprice and Conventionality*, and all novels.

Sophy's books! Of course, they must have been retrieved when he'd sent Porter to sort out the wreckage of his curricle last night.

He'd have to return them to her, he realized, and in the meantime, his interest was piqued enough to turn the pages of *Caprice and Conventionality, Volume I* to the beginning of the story.

As it was written by a man, perhaps it might not be such a tome of drivel after all. And the thought of his pretty cousin that had just sprung to mind had been so vivid and compelling he would be pleased to distract himself out of it.

It is a truth universally acknowledged that a man who marries for love will be a very happy man indeed. Mr Charles Preston —

A love story! Ben nearly snapped the book shut. How disappointing to find it was drivel after all. What sort of man would stoop to write such utter rubbish? Nevertheless, he read on a little further.

Mr Charles Preston was such a man. Having been brought up all his life to believe that, because of his great fortune, he must marry for convenience by choosing a wife who would not squander it and principally serve to please his mother —

Now there was a truth to be universally acknowledged! His dear mama certainly quite saw it as her right to choose the next Lady Hart.

. . . principally serve to please his mother by being of good pedigree and meek character, Mr Preston was surprised to find a lady whom he desperately wanted to marry who was neither.

How intriguing, Ben thought. Mr Preston certainly appeared to be a man prepared to act on his own ideas and good for him! There would be no harm in reading on a little way further. He sank into the comfortable leather armchair and flattened the volume's stiff pages open on his knees.

6

However little known the feelings or views of the man may be, the truth so well fixed in the minds of his surrounding family is that he is considered as the rightful property of some one or other of their daughters.

'My dear Sir Josiah,' said his lady to him one day, 'have you heard that Lord Hart will be at Hartfield Bury for Christmas?'

Sir Josiah replied that he had not.

'But he is,' returned she, 'for Lady Hart told me all about it. What a fine thing for our girls!'

'How so? How can it affect them?'

'My dear,' replied his wife, 'how can you be so tiresome! You must know that I am thinking of his marrying one of them.'

★   ★   ★

Contents therein? Ben raked his hand through his hair and then tipped the battered basket upside down for good measure. No, there was nothing inside except the small plaid cloth. He picked up the letter again.

Dear Lord Hart

I became detached from some posses-
sions during the accident and wondered
if they have found their way into your
keeping? Would you be so kind as to
arrange their return at your earliest
convenience. There are six books, in fact
the property of the circulating library,
and my straw basket and contents
therein.

My father is still in ill health and there
has been no one yet come with regards
to the church roof.

Yours sincerely
Sophia Grantchester

It seemed that whatever had been in the
basket had been lost. Ben picked up the
books, feeling the warm leather with his
fingers and thinking how these books would
soon be being handled by Sophy's hands. He
arranged them in the basket one by one. He
should, in honesty, have returned them before
now, but he'd ended up reading *Caprice and
Conventionality* in its entirety. In fact, he'd
read both volumes, and surprised himself, for
reading involved sitting still and he would
ordinarily rather be doing something fast

— on a horse, or driving a carriage.

But *Caprice and Conventionality* had given him rather a lot to think about. Too much; he wasn't used to thinking. It reminded him of how little he'd done in his life. So what that he had been lauded for winning a few curricle races? Or that the polite ladies of the London ton regarded him as somewhat dangerous after he'd allowed the rumours of the stunts he'd pulled off as Ben Hyde circle around him? Or that two ladies of the demi-monde had once actually fought over him?

He'd done nothing really grand and noble, nothing that put him into the heroic mould of a man such as the hero of *Caprice and Conventionality*, Charles Preston. Mr Preston had risked everything for the woman he loved, and most of all, because Mr Preston had come from a rather unhappy family and was afraid to love, he had risked his heart.

Ben did not know why he had not thought of it before, but once the thought had been seeded in his mind, it seemed inevitable, right and proper. Benedict St Michael was not afraid of anything.

He had only not thought of marriage before because he had been set in his notion that marriage was not for him and that a girl like Sophy could not be expected to warm his bed without a ring on her finger. He would marry Sophy and he would love her in every way, and she would love him in return. It gave him a warm feeling in his chest, close to the feeling that had so shocked him when they had been at the inn eating pie. But it was a feeling he wanted more of, not less.

Sophy was perfect for him, and not only did he desire her, he rather thought he had begun to love her already.

'Benedict?' came the plaintive call through the open study door. Damnation, he should have shut and locked it. Was nowhere sacred?

Not when his most vexing relatives were here to stay. 'Come in,' he forced himself to say politely. At least Christmas was over, and Sir Josiah and Lady Lincoln and their two unmarried daughters would be gone after the 6 January — today. Which daughter would this be? Ariadne or . . .

'Persephone!'

Nelson barked and jumped down from the window seat.

'Nelson,' Persephone Lincoln said with a nervous strain to her voice, holding her hands demurely in front of her as Nelson growled politely at her under his breath. 'Benedict, here you are. Mother wondered. Are you ready for our little walk we had planned?'

Nelson dared a small bark, and began to circle Miss Lincoln who was arrayed in a

112

lemon-yellow fringed walking dress complete with matching parasol.

'Oh,' she squeaked. 'Perhaps I am a little too tired after all to join you for a walk.'

'That is a pity,' Ben replied, picking up the basket of books and tucking it under his arm.

He strode outside. The sharpness of the air slapped the possibilities of the day into his face. What he needed was a damn good thoroughbred between his legs that could carry him across the countryside like the devil. All the way to Middleton.

*   *   *

Ben left Genii at the inn in Middleton, the Five Bells. No reason why he should not have ridden directly to Middleton parsonage except . . . Ben coughed into his hand and pushed open the door to the taproom. A sentiment he wasn't wholly sure of was making him feel uncomfortable. It sat, like an irritant, on his chest.

Damnation. He'd never felt *shy* about pursuing a woman before.

He enjoyed a pint of strong cider in the warmth of the inn, empty at this time of day. The problem with the village of Middleton was that it wasn't on the way to anywhere.

'The modern age not got t'Middleton yet,

m'lord.' The landlord of the Five Bells illuminated this to him fully, and managed to down two pints of his own cider in the telling. If one were to travel to Middleton from London by coach, Ben learned, then one would have to change at Calne and then go from there to Devizes. Depending on which day of the week it was there might not even be a coach running. Then from Devizes it was pot-luck.

Ben found his attention wandering to watch the rounded landlady who had bustled into the taproom, leaving the door to swing in her wake. She put down the tray of clean mugs she was carrying and then dusted each one with her cloth before bending to place them neatly on a low side shelf on the wall.

'Leave off your ramblings to the gentleman, Jim,' she said in what sounded like a Dorset accent as she caught Ben's eye in the middle of a polishing. 'What brings you to Middleton, sir, if I might be so bold as to ask?'

'I had heard Reverend Grantchester was somewhat under the weather and intend to call,' Ben replied, reluctant to tell them who he actually was.

'Ah! That he is, sir. A crying shame! You should have seen him Christmas Eve, as we all did, didn't we, Jim?'

'Yes, love,' her husband agreed.

'Midnight it was,' she said, placing her duster down. 'The whole village there in church. Freezing it were, what with the damp and all, but folks had their Christmas cheer and prospect of the holiday and that warmed 'em sufficient. Not the good reverend. He were pale as a spectre, sir. Up there on the lectern. I would say all eyes was watching him, sir, not listening to the words like good Christians. Then all of a sudden, when we was all singing, he comes over all faint like, clutching his chest and stumbles backwards. It were right horrible, weren't it, Jim?'

'Yes, love.'

'Were it not for Mr Camberley — he's the curate — and his quick thinking I don't know what would have happened!'

'A nasty fall, love. That's what would have — '

'Mr Camberley rushed up the steps to the reverend and carefully took him to sit down and we got through the rest of the service right quick. Mr Camberley took it, the reverend just sat there the whole while. I thought his face looked blue. Didn't I say that to you after, Jim?'

'You did, love.'

'And then Christmas Day it were Mr

Camberley only in church. And no one saw the reverend on St Stephen's either. Nor Miss Grantchester.' The landlady shook her head. 'Mighty sick we all were with worry 'til we heard yesterday that the doctor had been and that the reverend were all right, just laid up for a while — '

'Thank you,' Ben said, pulling out some coins and pushing his way out of the inn and into the village street. His countenance was happy to hit the fresh air.

A plump pheasant, canny enough to survive the autumn, made a running take-off along the road ahead of him and careered into the branches of a leafless tree. Ben smiled. He thought how Nelson would have given the bird a run for its money.

Then he felt his smile fall away. Mr Grantchester was gravely ill.

His frosted steps sounded lonely in the empty village street. The parsonage loomed up ahead and there was no cover. She would have the liberty, he considered, of watching his every step as he approached. His throat felt rather dry. Likely as not she would be too busy — with whatever she was doing — to watch, to care.

★　★　★

116

Sophy stretched out the two off-white flannel vests of her father's on the top of the dresser side by side and regarded them. A stitch in time would indeed have saved nine. Both needed repairing but the left one was so threadbare she feared it was completely done for. Oh well, she could use the good bits of material left on it to patch the other one.

She wandered over to the window and looked out at the familiar view. A thin coil of smoke rose up from the chimney of the Entwhistles' cottage and it took a bird to disturb the barren branches of the tall oak tree opposite. At least the wind had dropped. They would be warmer this evening and she could damp the fire downstairs earlier. She'd kept it burning much later than she ought because the warm chimney went up through her father's bedroom.

The rest of the scene outside was still, the road and the lane that curved to the church empty. No one came and went in Middleton, especially in the middle of winter. She might as well do the mending now. She wanted to write but it seemed her muse had packed its bags and gone somewhere. She had only written two pages this week and they were full of crossings-out. At this rate of progress it would be six months before the book was finished. She couldn't afford for it to take six months. Not with Dr Latham's bill due to arrive soon, and more to come.

She turned away from the window as she caught the flash of a dark figure in the corner of her eye. She looked back, curious to see who was abroad.

It was Ben walking up the road!

What was it about the man? She was simply looking at him and already her heart had leapt into her throat, her wrists were tingling and her legs threatened to quake. Like a mixture of fear and excitement.

It was quite ridiculous that the mere fact of the man should affect her so. Was his rakishness somehow *catching*? Was this why women fell so easily into the arms of rakes?

Pull yourself together, Sophy told herself sternly. She was perfectly capable of handling him and putting him in his place, if necessary.

Could she ask him if he would pay for the second doctor's bill? She must certainly mention the church roof to him.

★ ★ ★

Ben looked up at the squat parsonage, bent and flicked the small gate open, and reached the front door in six steps. He raised his knuckles.

The door opened.

Ben lowered his hand. She stood there before him, with gold flecks in her eyes that made him blink, and wearing . . . some brownish material. Well, it was a dress, he supposed. And on her head, a frilly white spinster's mob-cap. It was hideous. 'Miss Grantchester. What a pleasant surprise!'

'How so? I do live here, after all.' She tucked a loose tendril of hair behind a soft-looking ear. 'I suppose you are here to see my father? He is out at present. If you wish to wait — '

'I am relieved to hear he is feeling better, but no.'

'No?'

It was a very small word but it hung in the air like a travelling show's largest puppet. Ben watched as her eyes narrowed and then widened. He wondered what she was thinking. If he had been on a doorstep somewhere in Mayfair he could have asked the girl to join him for a spin around Hyde Park on his high-perch phaeton. Now that he was on a doorstep of a parsonage in Wiltshire he suddenly had no idea. 'I'm very bad,' he said, 'at planning things, and I also suffer from a lack of imagination. However, there is something I wish to discuss with you. And I brought your books.'

Her face brightened as he handed her the

basket he'd been holding behind his back. Ben swallowed. She had not looked so happy to see simply him.

She stared down into the basket and then rifled her slim hand down past the books piled therein. 'Was there nothing else? No . . . letters?' she asked.

'Letters? No.' Ben shook his head. 'Were they important?'

'Important? No.' She turned and placed the basket down in the hallway behind her. 'You'll be wanting a cup of tea, I suppose?'

Not particularly, Ben thought, but said, 'Yes, please.'

Then, just as she had half-turned and he was in the middle of taking a step forward to follow her into the cottage, he said, 'Wait! Would you, by any chance, care for a stroll? It is cold, but not so very cold.'

'Is there a history of insanity in your family?' Her eyes had most definitely narrowed. 'Or are you courting me? If the latter, I must certainly obtain my father's permission.'

'The very devil! What would you say if I slung you over my shoulder now and to hell with all the rest of it?'

She stared at him. Quite rightly, for he wasn't entirely joking.

'Well?' Ben pressed.

'I don't know. I never considered the possibility would come about for a parson's daughter.'

'Fair enough.' Ben seized her hand and held it firmly on his arm, pulling her forward. 'Let's walk.'

'Hadn't you better at least let me put on my cloak?'

Confounded chit! Ben let her go but didn't take his eyes off her as she went into the hall and pulled her drab cloak down from its peg. In fact, when she stretched to reach it he was able to console himself in part by admiring the sculpted curve of her breast.

He seized her hand again as soon as she was ready and within reach.

'Hadn't you better shut our front door?' She blinked, pulling up her hood and offering him a small smile.

Ben kept her fingers crushed tightly in his fist and shut the door with his free arm. He replaced her fingers on his forearm. 'Now, will they stay there or do I have to hold them in place?'

'They will stay there.' Her mild expression was pretence though. He was sure she would rather argue with him.

They walked out of the garden and Ben turned the other way from where he had come to head up the road. It was very pleasant, actually, the feel of her light fingers on his arm. He breathed deeply; felt himself begin to relax.

'I suppose this is about Brighton?' she said. 'I had the letter from your mother but with my father's state of health — '

'No, it's not about Brighton.' Ben heard his voice sound rather harsh. He softened it. 'Although it would be delightful if you were able to accompany Lady Hart to the seaside.'

'Oh,' she said. He stole a look at her rounded lips and suddenly felt the smallest bit nervous. Which was ridiculous. Benedict St Michael was not afraid of anything, particularly not a female.

'I took the liberty of reading one of your novels, Sophy,' he said, clearing his throat. '*Caprice and Conventionality*. I don't suppose you have read it?'

She didn't answer. She simply stared at him, her eyes wide and her face looking a little pale.

'Of course, I am not a man for reading, usually, but this novel was quite . . . exceptional,' he continued. 'Let me explain to you the moral of the story.'

'The moral?' Sophy gulped, tightened her free hand and struggled to get her thoughts in order. The idea of him having read her book felt uncomfortably intimate. She had been happy to share her thoughts with an unknown reader anonymously but not . . .

'The moral was that a man who has to marry for duty should not marry for duty but for love, and then the duty will have been undertaken as a matter of course.'

Sophy was impressed. He had read the book without a doubt and understood it. There was a mind underneath his rakish exterior.

'Look.' He pointed towards the pond in the middle of the village green. It was dull-coloured because of the season; what caught the eye first were the two bright white swans. They floated peacefully on the water.

'The swans?' Sophy asked and kept her voice bright. She suddenly found she wanted to have this conversation with him.

'There have always been swans and there always will be swans. Does a male swan keep one female swan tied to the nest and gad about the pond with another female swan? No, they remain together . . . for life. Well, I like the notion. I have always known that I must, at some point, marry for duty, but now I see that I do not have to marry for duty at all. I can marry for love, then the duty will be done anyhow — '

'Oh no!' Sophy interrupted. Was that what her book was going to do to the young buck about town? Inspire them to marry their mistresses? The idea was horrifying. 'A dangerous sentiment, don't you think? Radical . . . and anti-establishment — '

'You say that, but had you been privy to what goes on in London, you would have seen that it is all the fashion now to be disgustingly in love with one's wife and parade her about the place, to the opera and so forth, as if she were one's . . . ' He pursed his lips shut and smoothed his long fingers across his chin. 'Now back to the question of what to do with you and what I came to talk to you about today.'

'Do with me?'

'You should marry. You cannot live with your father for ever.'

'No . . . ' Sophy agreed, hearing her voice trail away as her thoughts took over. Her father was dangerously ill. His heart, Dr Latham had said. It would never occur to a man such as Ben that a woman might earn her own way in the world. Or indeed that if her father's health got worse she would have to nurse him. They would certainly not be able to afford to employ Mary. In fact, if her father was unable to carry out his duties, would he lose the living? Where would they live and —

'I can't see how the devil you are going to

find a husband stuck here in Middleton in the middle of nowhere. Can you? And you need a husband who can appreciate your . . . unique qualities.' Ben frowned. 'Might not be so easy to find, wouldn't you say?'

Sophy fought back against the prick of tears behind her eyes. 'Much as I appreciate the sudden interest you appear to have taken in my prospects — '

'No, there is nothing for it. I can't do anything without causing an almighty scandal and there's chaperons to think of and the . . . timetables a bachelor household runs to.' He shook his head. 'No, I can't possibly take you to London and launch you into society. Besides, my own reputation is somewhat . . . shaky. It might put fellows off.'

He only knew what it was like to be a rich, young bachelor. He wouldn't be able to comprehend Sophy's household and how they lived on her father's small stipend. She could not think of anything to say for the moment and found herself staring at the curve of his dark eyebrows, as perfect as if they had been combed or carved from wax. She wanted to know what they felt like if she brushed the tip of her finger over them. Soft, she supposed.

'Have you any progress to report on the church repairs?' she said, interrupting her own thoughts. 'When is the work to be done?'

'Has no one been?'

'No.'

'They should have.'

'Please could you kindly inform whoever you have arranged to do the repairs that they are expected with all speed. Or give me their direction and I shall write to them myself and make the arrangements.'

'*That* is absolutely unnecessary. I assure you the matter is in hand. Now, where were we?'

'Your bachelor household.'

'Quite.' He stopped and turned to face her, pressing his hand more firmly on to hers so that the heat singed into her fingers and made her lungs jolt with a sudden cold breath. His brow creased into a frown. 'Sophy, you agree with everything I've said so far?'

'Yes.' She supposed so, except the necessity for her to marry. If her writing could be made to pay enough, she would not need to marry.

He brought her hand up to his lips, so slowly that with each blink it seemed only to have been raised another inch. Even through her woollen gloves she felt the tingle that ran through her arm and tickled the corner of her heart.

'Sophy,' he said, his eyes looking very dark, very sincere. 'I think I . . . love you.'

What?

What nonsense!

'Are you . . . ?' She bit her lip. 'Are you proposing to make me your mistress?'

'I am proposing nothing of the sort! A gel of your quality shouldn't even be aware of such . . . arrangements.'

'Oh, I see. Marriage, then.'

'Marriage!' Ben spluttered.

'A lady's imagination is very rapid. It jumps from courtship to matrimony in a moment.' She felt his muscles tense as he held her hand.

'A gentleman's imagination is certainly not so engineered, I assure you.' He fixed her with a stern stare. 'Has my dear mama set you up to this?'

'How could that be so? Lady Hart would never consider me a suitable wife for you.'

'You're a gentlewoman, aren't you?' Ben snapped. He kicked a small mossy stone that lay by his foot. It skittered across the road and into the ditch. 'You are clever and challenging and . . . well, I shall tell you more on that on your wedding night.'

A smirk had stolen on to his face and she wanted to slap him, despite the compliments. Was this a proposal of marriage or was he simply teasing her?

'We shall turn back.' Ben clicked his heels

and stared at the blue winter sky with a smile she could not fathom.

'Thank you,' Sophy said, adding an artificial brightness to her voice. The tips of her fingers brushed his arm and she swallowed a large lump that had grown in her throat.

Ben did not reply and led them back to the parsonage.

She was too hot and she struggled to pull her cloak off speedily. And she had completely forgotten to ask him about the doctor's bill! She must do so before her father returned. What was it about Ben that seemed to turn her into a witless idiot? If he wanted to do something for her, he could pay the doctor's bill.

She threw her cloak at the peg and watched as it hit the wall and slid to the floor.

Ben swooped down, picked it up and gave it a good shake and brushing down before reaching up with ease to hang it on a peg.

Sophy felt her hand on her forehead start pushing stray locks of hair back under her cap. She snatched it back and forced her eyes to stare at the pattern on the curtains at the window. 'Thank you,' she muttered and led the way into the sitting-room.

Think quickly, she told herself. What do rakehells drink?

'Would you like some brandy?' Sophy hoped there was some brandy in the house. Middleton parsonage was not accustomed to entertaining rakes.

'Brandy? At three o'clock in the afternoon? Good Lord, no!' He brushed a piece of fluff from his shoulder.

There was a tap on the sitting-room door and Mary came in, looked at Ben with a surprised expression and bobbed a curtsy. 'Miss Sophy, you're back. Would you like some tea?'

'Tea would be just the thing,' Ben answered before Sophy had a chance.

'Lord Hart, please do take a seat,' she said as Mary nodded and disappeared. He seemed to fill the whole room. There were only a few inches between the top of his head and the ceiling. And the way he watched her was making her feel nervous. Sophy sat down and thankfully he followed her lead. He flicked his coat tails back and sank easily into the chair opposite her.

He stretched out his long legs and looked strangely at home, which didn't seem right. Sophy stared at the fire quietly crackling in the hearth.

'I suppose you do not spend a great deal of time in the country?' she said at last.

He leaned back and crossed his legs. 'No, I

don't suppose I do. Not Wiltshire at any rate.'

The clock on the mantelpiece ticked. Sophy refolded her hands in her lap. Where was her father?

Mary brought a tray laden with the tea things and a large creamware plate piled with scones.

'Mary,' Sophy said, 'is my father home yet?'

'I think he is, miss. I'll go and see.' Mary bobbed her head and shut the door behind her.

'Well, I must say I am pleased we have got to know each other better.' Ben bent forward and regarded her closely. It was quite unnerving. She liked his eyes though. They were chocolate-coloured and made her wonder about the man. She was still curious at the incongruity of a rake who pondered on novels. He was more complex than she had previously thought.

The door creaked open. Her father, looking a little wind-swept and rosy-cheeked. Thank heavens!

'Mr Grantchester.' Ben rose and shook his hand. 'Might I have a brief word with you alone, sir?'

'Certainly, m'boy.' Her father cleared his throat. 'Come through to my study if you don't mind the disorder.'

Why on earth did Ben want to see her

father alone? It couldn't be? No, she was imagining things. A lady's mind leapt very quickly from courtship to matrimony, and besides, Ben was not courting her.

Sophy leaned back in her chair. She gazed at the blue and mostly cloudless sky through the window. It was rather cold today but without any clouds, unlikely to snow.

The door swung open. Ben! He'd not been with her father above a few minutes. His eyes shone and the corners of his lips twitched as his smile developed into a grin. Sophy could not resist smiling in return. He looked so appealing when he smiled like that; already her heart was quickening.

He shut the door very quietly and advanced forward. He fell to his knees on the floor in front of her, and seized her hands in his.

'Sophy,' he said, and planted a kiss on her wrist that sent delighted shivers all the way up her arm and to her neck. 'Your father has no objections. None. In fact he's splendidly pleased. Sophy — '

He leant forward quickly, and caught her lips. She was stung, by his words, by the fire that leapt from him to her from the first moment of his kiss. Her skin had no time to tingle — it simply stiffened, trapping the fire inside her. She could see only velvet blackness, taste only passion, breathe only the heady scent of him; horse, leather and sandalwood.

How she wanted to lose herself in it all: discover, explore and, most confusingly, share.

His hands found the back of her neck and their soft fingers teased their way up her hairline and pulled her closer towards him. His touch burned; his kiss became harder, more challenging.

His kiss was sealing their betrothal!

7

Who can be in doubt of what followed? When any two young people take it into their heads to marry, they are pretty sure by perseverance to carry their point, be they ever so poor, or ever so imprudent, or ever so little likely to be necessary to each other's ultimate comfort. However, as it was not in Miss Grantchester's head to marry, she jerked herself back and freed herself from his proximity.

Sophy breathed the air in huge gulps, forced her eyes to focus on something, anything — the brass clock on the mantelpiece — and tried to recall what he had just said. Something about her father being delighted.

'What the devil?' Ben frowned. 'You were enjoying every moment of that kiss!'

'Ben, I haven't agreed to become your wife.'

'What?'

The fire spat and crackled as a log fell downwards. Sophy saw the draught rustle the sprigged curtains in the window. From another house in Middleton village a dog barked; two geese honked.

'I haven't agreed to become your wife.' She folded her hands in her lap, sat up straight and tried to keep her voice firm and steady. 'In fact, you didn't even ask me. You just assumed — '

'Women and their poetry and posies!' Ben said and the contempt that underlined his words were clear. He rose to his feet and sat down on the sofa beside her. 'Sophy, I haven't got time for all that stuff. You'll just have to take me as I am.'

'It wouldn't suit me to marry. I have my father to think of.' She also had her writing to think of but she could hardly tell him that. She would not have a moment spare if she took on the duties of a wife.

'Ah!' A smile of satisfaction stole across Ben's face. 'I've asked your father for his permission and he said, if you agreed to it, he would be delighted.'

'Oh, Father is trying to think of me. But if I married, who would look after him?'

'If he wants to stay in Middleton I'll employ him a housekeeper,' Ben replied. The determination in Ben's gaze licked through her skin, made her throat tight and her stomach curl. A shadow passed over his eyes and his brow creased. 'Why in heaven's name won't you marry me?'

'Ben, you declared you wanted to marry for

love. After . . . after that book you read. Why should I come in the way of your aspirations?'

'Yes, I did,' he said. She could see, to his credit, that he was trying to keep his anger from his voice. 'But Sophy, don't you see how you are far more important to me than some hoity-toity idea gleaned from a novel! Dash it, I've become inordinately fond of you, Sophy.' He gripped her hands in his before she could pull them away; crushed them. She wanted to fall back into the temptation of his embrace, yet how could she? 'I think I love you,' he said. 'I'll certainly grow to love you. You'll make a magnificent Lady Hart.'

She stared into his dark, unyielding eyes and shivered as she saw in her mind the countenance of another man — Lieutenant Darleton, who had declared his love for her so equally suddenly and passionately nearly four years before.

And then disappeared from her life as quickly as he'd entered it.

The only man to promise her the earth and make her believe that a fairytale love could exist between a man and woman, before shattering her illusions completely. Desire existed, certainly; and mutual admiration built up over years of a shared life together. But not love that appeared out of nowhere, as the dashing lieutenant had claimed, that bound a woman's soul to a man's with no sense or reason behind it.

'Ben, you don't know what you are saying.' She hardly heard her own voice yet knew she must speak. He desired her as a woman and she him as a man. There was a truth, of sorts, in that. But she, an impoverished rector's daughter could never become Lady Hart of Hartfield Bury. 'Can't we . . . kiss . . . outside the bounds of wedlock?'

'You want to marry me!' His eyes narrowed. 'I'll need to think about whether you deserve any kissing whatsoever if you continue to carry on in this fashion. I'm not having you dismiss the matter out of hand, as if my honourable intentions were some kind of bon-bon tray offered to you that you can turn your nose up at.'

'Ben — '

'You do know when we marry there'll be a lot more than kissing and I promise you'll enjoy — '

'No — '

'Yes,' he interrupted, pulling himself towards her. His eyes were incredibly dark. She hardly dared to blink. His hands tightened around hers, made her want to protest. Yet she didn't; she simply stared into him.

'Every speck of you is waiting to tremble at

my touch,' he said slowly, as if he were spelling every word. Her eyes wanted to close, to imagine she could feel as he suggested.

'And you, Sophy,' he said. 'You delight me to the core. And I'll be confounded if Merryford is going to have you!'

'Oh, so it's jealousy that's brought on this sudden ardour?' Sophy snapped free from his gaze and snatched her hands away. So what if she did long to tremble at his touch? That had nothing to do with marriage. She was not about to sacrifice her life to a man who thought nothing of teasing her; a man who didn't ask her what her opinion was, didn't stop to consider that she might have wishes, let alone what those wishes were.

'Sophy, don't turn your tongue into that of a shrew.'

'I won't marry you!' she shouted, vexation rising up in her like an unstoppable tide. 'I won't. Ever.'

'I know it's the thing for young ladies to turn down the first proposal as a matter of course but can't you even be a little demure — '

'No, and you haven't even — '

'A little more sensitive to my feelings?' His brow creased so that she wanted to smooth it, his eyes seemed downcast so that she wanted to brighten them, his lips unsure so that she wanted to reassure them. Confound the man! Why did he make her feel like she was clay in a potter's hands?

'Ben, I'm sorry. I — '

'Sophy, don't you see? I like you. I really do. Dash it! You're the first woman I've ever wanted to . . . enjoy in an intimate way *and* have a conversation with.'

His flattery was eating away at her resolve. Sophy breathed very deeply and considered what she should do. She was determined not to marry. Not in the next few years, anyhow, while she wrote her novels. Perhaps if she met a man she truly respected, like her father, and if she grew tired of writing . . . no, she would never grow tired of writing. She had ten books inside her, maybe twenty.

'I'm dashed eligible,' Ben continued, rising to his feet. He drew himself up to his full height and dared to look down his nose at her. 'Eight thousand a year.'

'Your arrogance,' Sophy said, surprised at her own equilibrium, 'will never cease to amaze me. Am I supposed to be grateful that you have lowered yourself sufficiently to consider matrimony to a penniless clergyman's daughter?'

'The eight thousand and all that has nothing to do with it,' he said. 'Can't you see I'm clutching at straws? Well, I've been humiliated enough for one afternoon. Good day. I have spoken to your father about this and it's all fixed. I shall see you next Tuesday or Wednesday most likely. I shall send word. Around noon, and we proceed directly to Brighton.'

'But — '

But he was gone. A flash of coat tails and black and the door shut hard behind him.

She heard him putting his cloak on in the hallway, the crunch of his footsteps outside. She didn't turn to watch him go. She forced herself to sit still, exactly where she was, until she was sure he had gone.

★   ★   ★

The discomposure of spirits that this extraordinary visit threw Sophy into could not be easily overcome. She would have to explain to her father later why she was not betrothed to her eligible £8,000-a-year cousin. For now, she had to be alone. She pushed herself up from her chair and flew straight upstairs.

She sat down on the bed, held the hem of the counterpane in her hands and closed her eyes. Breathed the scent of home, the faint tease of lavender from the sprigs she placed in her drawers, the lingering jasmine perfume, a present from her mother's sister when she had been in England two years ago from India.

India. Even the word seemed exotic. Her aunt had married a gentleman dependent on the East India Company for his living and had travelled the world. Sophia Grantchester could never go to India but she could go to Brighton. She might see the Prince Regent in Brighton! Goodness knows what she might see or do in Brighton!

Sophy stood up, unlocked the drawer of her bureau and pulled it open. She picked up the thick pile of crisp paper, around forty sheets, written in her smallest blue-ink hand-writing on both sides. She stared at it in despair.

She had lived all her life in one place and she had put everything she knew into one book. It was no wonder this story was so underdeveloped. In Brighton she would see something different, meet new people. In Brighton she could write. And she would be housed and fed from Lady Hart's purse. It would save them money at home. She must go to Brighton.

She threw the papers in the grate and watched them flare and crumple and then turn to black ash.

Ben might act like some medieval nobleman who thought it was his right, his *droit du seigneur*, to come riding into the village and pick off any girl he fancied. This was the nineteenth century, and the girl he had chosen had her own plans afoot. She would accompany his mother to Brighton but for herself, not for him. And she would enact her revenge for his heavy-handed behaviour on paper.

It was all coming back to her, even though she tried to shut her mind to it. The day she'd pulled out a piece of paper and started to write *Caprice and Conventionality*. She didn't think she would end up writing a novel, she had just wanted to get rid of her anger. She had been nineteen and those had been different days. Lieutenant Darleton had danced with her at two balls she had attended at the Stickleton Assembly Rooms; stolen a kiss from her one dusky afternoon. He had dared to offer her marriage and then withdraw that offer when it became clear his mother objected violently. Not even an apology and he had disappeared, posted elsewhere with the militia. A month later she heard he was to marry a candidate of his mother's choosing.

Mr Charles Preston had come to her in a fit of unhappy daydreams. A man who would

141

choose his own bride, love over duty; a man whose story she wanted to tell and so she had sat down and started to write.

She pulled out her handkerchief and dabbed her eyes. The vexing thing was that Ben was so dangerously, so easily, kissable. Nothing like Lieutenant Darleton's advances which, if truth be told, she had found rather alarming.

It would be so easy to let Ben do things for her, coax her, tease her. She luxuriated in his every attention. Fie to sentimentalism! Sophy told herself and pulled out a fresh sheet of paper. Benedict St Michael was about to come to life as the hero — no the villain — of her next novel. In her story he would get his come-uppance.

What would be a good title? Sophy considered. *Impulse and Irresponsibility?* Yes, that suited Ben rather well. She wrote this on the top of the clean sheet of paper, underlined it and began to write.

★ ★ ★

The wind tore into his face, pushing at his clothes and his hair unrelentingly, and yet he pushed Genii to gallop faster, not slowing when his cheeks felt so cold they stung, not slowing until they reached the long avenue that led up to Hartfield Bury.

Ben wiped the back of his sleeve across his brow and let Genii shudder home at his own pace, nostrils still flaring.

Porter, their head groom, and a lanky lad came running out from the archway that led to the stables as he dismounted. Nelson careered across the gravel towards him and threw himself up at him, barking as Ben's feet landed on the ground.

Ben ruffled Nelson's ears. He felt his wiry-haired shoulders brush under the tips of his fingers but he could not bring himself to smile.

'Afternoon, Lord 'Art.' Porter touched the front of his dull cap and raised his gruff voice. 'Quick to, boy.'

The groom, who had paused to touch his cap likewise, darted the final few feet and Ben dropped his ribbons into his eager hands.

Ben looked up, past the slate roof tiles and sand-coloured chimneys and could only see blue. It was cold; not a cloud in the sky. 'A fine morning, Mr Porter, indeed. Weather-wise.'

He turned on his heels and walked up to the house, gathering speed and with an increasing headache and desire to hit something very hard. He stormed into his study. Collapsed into his leather chair. Cursed. How dare she turn his honourable proposal down? He had not credited she would be a tease. Her large blue eyes were too serious, too compelling and too beautiful for him to be able to ignore. As for the rest of her, he wanted to —

There was a sharp tap on the door and Ben snapped to attention. It was Greaves, one of the footmen, who handed him a letter postmarked London — which Ben thrust down on to the desk — and said that Mr Simmons was here to attend him.

'Good afternoon, Simmons.' Ben sat up straight as his manager came in. 'What news of the house in Brighton? It's all fixed, isn't it, for I want to go tomorrow.'

'Good afternoon, Lord Hart.' Simmons tugged at his collar. 'About the house in Brighton, well . . . '

'Well what?'

'I wasn't able to agree satisfactory terms of lease with the owners. The — '

'Why the devil not? That house was supposed to be available right through to the summer.'

'It was the question of the rent and payment terms, my lord.'

'Rent and payment terms? Simmons, I thought we went through this. Have they upped the rent they require? For heaven's sake, unless it's completely unreasonable, you know the bounds we agreed.'

'Yes, Lord Hart.'

'So?'

'The owner required a large proportion of the rent to be paid up front and I am afraid that the money isn't there to do so. Perhaps, Lord Hart, if you were to approach your bankers — '

'What? Why the devil are we suddenly cash-strapped?'

Simmons put his hand to his mouth and coughed. 'There have been a number of large doctor's bills in the last few weeks.'

'Doctor's bills! Are you telling me there's no money to rent a house in Brighton because of Lady Hart's extortionate doctor's bills? Come on, man, let's be reasonable about his. How much are they in a twelve-month? One hundred pounds? Two hundred?'

'Erm .. Nine hundred and sixty-seven pounds, eight shillings and thruppence-ha'penny in the last twelve-month, Lord Hart.'

'A thousand pounds on doctor's bills! No wonder my pockets are to let. Heavens above! You are quite right, Simmons. There shall be no house in Brighton.'

'Yes, Lord Hart.'

'One other matter I would like you to deal with as a matter of the highest priority,' Ben said and cleared his throat. 'The repairs to Middleton church roof. I want you to go to Middleton and make sure the work is being carried out.'

'It will be done, Lord Hart.'

'Good.' Ben pushed himself up from his chair and shook his estate manager's hand. 'Thank you, Simmons, carry on.'

He gave Simmons a moment to leave. Brighton, doctor's bills and most vexing of all — Sophy. The confounded chit was making him think what he should do next. Think! He didn't want to think, to plan. He should just whisk her up the aisle and then that would be that.

He absent-mindedly picked up the letter that Greaves had brought him and pulled at the seal to open it.

Perhaps he did need to think. Sophy was a woman. Highly strung, sensitive, perhaps, like his greys.

Just as he would plan for an important curricle race, train up his team, so he needed to lure her into matrimony, coax her, tempt her in the right fashion. She enjoyed his kisses right enough but perhaps he had unnerved her in some way, made her skittish. Just as one would lull a skittish horse by stroking its nose, scotch any rebellion with soft words and master it through a gentle hand at the ribbons, so he would have to win Sophy round.

Ben ripped the letter open and unfolded it. He could see the logic of it. It would work, he was sure. He would tempt Sophy with kisses, and more, until she was unable to refuse him.

He cast his eyes down to the stiff-papered letter in his hands and read the scrawled black-ink hand while white fury gathered at the centre of his being, licking up into a huge, fiery-hot ball. And then he threw his head back and laughed.

Hart
Vis-à-vis an outstanding matter of business I believe we had agreed, another wager would be the best means of settlement. If you should care to peruse the betting book at White's, you will see I have taken the liberty of entering our wager there.

You will marry within three months of today's date — 4 January 1812 — any lady of your choosing — or the item of property currently in dispute will revert to my ownership.

There are a number of charming

*young ladies to be presented this year, so
I hear.*

Merryford

Well, Merryford would be doubly confounded when he discovered he'd solved the
last of Ben's problems by his own actions,
and that Ben had won his wager by marrying
indeed — the item of property in dispute.

Ben rose and tossed the letter in the fire as
the sounds of a young lady at the pianoforte,
and another one breaking into song, perme-
ated through the walls to him.

The sixth of January, in the year of our
Lord, eighteen hundred and twelve, and
tomorrow his most vexing relatives would be
gone.

He marched straight into the drawing-
room and sat down, closed his ears and
thought about the time he'd been involved in
a phaeton race down Cheapside at midnight.
No ordinary phaeton race, as one had had to
have a genuine Covent Garden opera singer
alongside to qualify. And yet, even with the
most inspired of memories, he could not
completely shut out the noise that comprised
Miss Ariadne and Miss Persephone Lincoln's
repertoire on the pianoforte.

'Bravo!' Ben said. He stood up and clapped
his hands, watching the girls take a bow.

'Benedict!' His mother pulled herself up on her chaise. 'What on earth is the matter with you?'

'Nothing that a trip to the seaside won't cure.' Ben wasn't able to suppress a smile. The seaside with Sophy was going to be very pleasant indeed.

'You're not coming with us, are you?' His mother frowned.

'Yes, I jolly well am.' Ben took a couple of steps forward so he stood behind the *chaise-longue* opposite her, where Sir Josiah and Lady Lincoln sat. 'I've still got bone ache from the accident and headache from . . . from this awful day. I need some sea air.'

'Benedict, why don't you take some laudanum?'

'Devil's tincture! No, thank you.'

'Suit yourself.' His mother waved her hand. 'However, if you are coming to Brighton, Benedict, I won't require the Grantchester gel for company.'

'Oh yes, you do, and we're not going to Brighton,' Ben said, and with a mighty effort kept his voice devil-may-care. 'Can't afford it. We'll go and stay with Fordham in East Bourne. That's all right with you, Fordham, isn't it?'

'What?' Lord Fordham had been taking forty winks and he looked up from his bath chair, where he was comfortably tucked up in a rug, and grunted. 'Be my pleasure.'

'East Bourne?' Lady Hart said sharply. 'Doctor Gillyson most particularly advised Brighton.'

'Dear Mama, no doubt Doctor Gillyson can now afford to buy his own house in Brighton whereas we shall have to make do with accommodating ourselves with Lord Fordham in East Bourne.'

'Benedict — '

'We are to East Bourne. I require you to get better without delay.'

The dear mama gave him a withering look but knew she was defeated and turned to the girls, still at the pianoforte. 'Ariadne! Persephone! If only I had had a daughter who could have been so dedicated to her accomplishments!' She must have gone mad, thought Ben. Either that or the Lincolns had shattered every musical ear in the room. 'Never could I tempt Benedict to turn his hand to the pianoforte!'

'Boys will be boys, m'dear,' Lady Lincoln sympathized. A woman who had produced five daughters and not a single son would say that, Ben thought.

'Just as well! Sounded to me like your pianoforte is out of tune,' said Lord Fordham. Ben smiled at Nelson, who looked up from where he had been dozing at the old man's feet. Lord Fordham was his least vexing relative, eighty and always happy to share his opinions, suitable or not, to the present company.

His mother frowned and Lady Lincoln tapped her wrist with her fan and pretended she hadn't heard.

★ ★ ★

Sophy came back with a handful of potatoes from the sack in the storehouse outside and sat down on a chair at the kitchen table to peel them. She hadn't slept well at all last night. She had written late into the night and then when she had finally fallen into bed she had so much going through her mind it had been difficult to get to sleep. Would her father be all right? Mr Camberley was moving into the parsonage to be at hand to assist him but was she really doing the best thing by going away?

'Miss!' came Mary's voice calling from the hall.

'What is it?' Sophy called back.

'He's here. Lord 'Art.'

Heavens! It wasn't even eleven o'clock and he'd said noon. At least she was packed. Yesterday afternoon she and Mary had found a very old trunk of her father's up in the attic and dragged it downstairs and all her things were now neatly folded in that. She put her knife down, washed her hands quickly and went through to the hall.

'What fine-lookin' carriages, miss. Two of 'em. You are in for a real treat.'

'Thank you, Mary. Where is Father?'

'Shall I see if he's in his study, miss?'

'Yes, do.' Sophy hastened to open the front door. He was there on the front path. Her heart stopped. Ben looked so dashing, tall and masculine.

'Sophy! Good morning. Are you packed?' He looked so urbane, so civilized, this morning it was hard to credit. Dressed impeccably in a black superfine jacket and buff-coloured buckskins, and boots so polished he could no doubt see his reflection well enough in them to shave. A different man, it seemed, from the rake she had been writing about over the last few days. Nelson bounded dutifully at his heels.

'Good morning, Ben. I have a trunk inside.' She swallowed and stepped outside. Her eyes traced the line of his jaw, so real against the stiff white of his cravat. She wanted to touch it. She reached down to give Nelson a rub on the nose instead. Nelson wagged his tail.

'Good morning, Mary,' Ben said, and he strode past her and indoors. 'Mr Grantchester.'

Sophy turned back into the house. It was cold. She should put her cloak on. A lump had formed in her throat. She wasn't going to see her father or Mary or Middleton for perhaps weeks and weeks.

'Trust in the Lord that He will show you the right path.' Her father gave her an affectionate squeeze on the hand. He had not said he was disappointed that she had refused Ben's offer of marriage but she knew it from his eyes.

⋆　⋆　⋆

Sophy stared out of the carriage window. Fordham Manor crouched in a lee of the land and was surrounded by ancient trees so that the house did not come into sight until they turned the final bend. The manor house was hundreds of years old, medieval, crooked, with half a moat wrapped around it, and probably larger than it looked from the outside.

Two long days of travelling and she was delighted they were here. She'd been surprised when Lady Hart had said they weren't going to Brighton after all but to stay with Ben's father's uncle, Lord Fordham, near East Bourne. She had also been startled to meet Nora, the girl Lady Hart had informed her was to be her maid. Nora had thick dark hair severely pinned back and an exceptionally plain and pasty complexion. She had looked at Sophy with great curiosity at first and followed her about the inn in the same fashion that Nelson followed Ben. Sophy knew she looked nothing like a lady in her old clothes but resolved not to care for Nora's opinion on the matter.

Nora travelled with Lady Hart's maid in one coach and Lord Fordham, Lady Hart, Nelson and herself went in the other. Ben had ridden his horse, Genii, for nearly all the journey and was scrupulously polite when the occasion warranted it, but aside from that largely ignored her. Better there was a distance between them, Sophy had told herself. It would have been impossible to bear if he had hounded and fussed and ordered her about in front of his mother.

Ben had galloped ahead and came out of Fordham Manor ready to help Lord Fordham into his wheeled bath chair.

'Home at last,' Lord Fordham said with feeling. 'Roads and old bones don't mix.'

'What a delightful-looking house,' Sophy said to him.

'You're smart, gel.' Lord Fordham chuckled. 'Don't let him push you around like he pushes me.'

'You mean Lord Hart, my lord?' Sophy smiled as she watched Nelson rest his chin on Lord Fordham's lap.

'Who the devil else?' the old man growled.

Sophy felt a flush of warmth rise up and into her cheeks. She turned away, towards the breeze, hoping it would cool it.

'Come on, you old rogue,' Ben said, and fastened his hands on the bath chair. He turned Lord Fordham around and started to wheel him towards the house without a glance in her direction. Ben was capricious by nature, she had concluded. It was painful to have been a passing fancy to such a man.

8

When a young lady is to be a heroine, the perverseness of forty, surrounding families cannot prevent her. Something must and will happen to throw the hero in her way. In this case it was a small and seemingly inconsequential remark from Lord Fordham.

The drawing-room at Fordham Manor was a very long room with the sofas clustered in the middle. Sophy wasn't sure what else she should do while Nora unpacked except join Lady Hart and Lord Fordham there. She sat down opposite Lady Hart and smoothed her skirts.

'We'll send for a seamstress for you as soon as possible,' Lady Hart said and then returned her eyes to her magazine.

'Take no notice,' said Lord Fordham. His eyes swivelled from Lady Hart to Sophy. 'Don't sit here like an old codger, gel. Have a poke around the place.'

'Might I?'

Lord Fordham grunted.

Sophy found the inside of Fordham Manor was as delightfully crooked as the outside. In the very middle of the house was an enormous double-height dining hall with a small minstrels' gallery. The rest of the house seemed to have been built around this piecemeal. She found another sitting-room, a still room with floor-to-ceiling shelves stuffed full of china, a library and, from a door to the right off the hall, a square-shaped masculine room with a vast felted billiard table in the middle of it — and Ben.

His long black-clad form was bent over the table about to take a pot. Sophy found herself standing in the doorway, absolutely still, as her eyes were drawn along his body to admire his agile wrists, framed with white shirt cuffs. He looked up from his aim to her, his eyelashes sweeping her into his dark gaze. He held her there for a moment and the back of her neck prickled.

'Sophy!' He abandoned his shot and stood up straight, facing her.

'Lord Fordham said I could explore the house,' she explained. How could simply looking at Ben cause her heart to flutter and cause a curious heat to rise up to her chest from her middle?

Ben's eyes flickered and he smiled and replaced his cue on the wooden rack behind him. He said, 'Let me show you around. Unless you're tired?' He lifted an eyebrow. He sounded so reasoned. It was hard to credit this was the same man who had dressed up as a highwayman to rescue her and who had so violently proposed marriage; the Ben who had kissed her so passionately. Simply the memory of it made her tremble.

'I'm not tired.' Sophy smiled.

He strode over to her so there was only a foot distance between them and then motioned towards the open door. Sophy turned and caught a faint wisp of sandalwood as he followed her out of the room. It made her neck and shoulders tingle. It was fortunate Ben had not been in the carriage with them these last two days. These brief snatches of proximity were enough to make her question her sanity. She wanted to close her eyes somewhere cold and quiet and make his presence go away.

'What do you think of Fordham Manor?' His smooth words broke into her thoughts.

'It's full of character,' Sophy replied, addressing the air as he shut the door of the billiard room behind them. 'I've read about minstrels' galleries but never seen one. And there are four staircases — '

'Five.'

'Five? Where's the fifth?'

'Follow me.' His lips twitched and made her heart leap in anticipation. Through this tiny chink she fancied Ben the highwayman still lurked and she followed his tall figure back through the dining hall and up the main staircase.

'But this is the main staircase?' Sophy queried.

'Did you not wonder how one got up to the second floor?' he said without stopping. They proceeded along the landing, across thick carpet that muffled their footsteps, past a ticking grandmother clock and a maid balanced on a stool dusting the top of a picture frame.

'I didn't know there was a second floor,' Sophy said, catching her breath as she caught up with his quick strides.

'Not used much now,' he said. She watched his wrist again as he fastened his hand around the porcelain handle of a large door and pulled it open to reveal a small narrow staircase disappearing up into blackness. 'Are you coming up?'

'Yes,' Sophy replied, feeling a faint touch of the Gothic about the hidden staircase and chiding herself for being fanciful. 'What's up there?'

'After you,' Ben said, and held the door wide open. Sophy walked past him, wanting to hold her breath as she did so. From him seemed to come a miasma which struck at her control, much more potent than any

Gothic fancies she could concoct.

She climbed the steep spiral stairs with care and came up on to a long corridor with two doors on each side. Above her was a small dome-shaped skylight window, partially clouded by outside dirt that had fallen from trees. Ben reached the top of the stairs a moment later, made for the first door on the right and opened it.

'Oh!' Sophy peered in. 'A rocking horse! It's a nursery!'

'Not used in a long while. Fordham is a bachelor.' Ben wandered over to the windows.

Sophy walked in, smiling at the delightfully child-proportioned furniture, and touching the real horsehair mane of the old rocking horse, its paint chipped in places. Such lucky children! Her only experience of nurseries was in books.

Ben's children — the children of Lord Hart of Hartfield Bury — would have rooms to themselves and painted toys from London. Not her children, if she ever were to marry a parson or farmer one day. They would make do with spinning tops and hoops and home-made rag dolls, as she had.

This was Ben's childhood, not hers, and she wondered if as a child he had been as he was now. Had he charmed his nursemaid into thinking he was the sweetest of charges or had violent temper tantrums, unable to control his fiery, passionate nature?

He stood with his back to the window with that urbane, fixed expression he wore as a matter of course, as if it were a mask against the outside world. She could not tell what he was thinking or feeling.

'What were you like as a child?' Sophy could not help asking.

His countenance wavered; a shadow passed across his eyes.

'Alone,' he answered and something in her chest crumpled as she wondered how old he had been when his father had died. 'There are bedrooms for children and a nurse opposite and . . . come and see.'

He pushed open a door in the side of the room, and ushered her in.

It was not a very large room but unlike the disused air of the nursery, the cupboards and shelves that lined this room were polished, the scent of beeswax still lingered, and it was filled with books and papers. On the walls large, framed prints — charts, Sophy saw on closer inspection, of the heavens.

'An observatory?' Sophy stared at the huge brass telescope mounted and facing heavenwards. It was magnificent.

'Yes, this is Fordham's own creation. I believe he does still come up here sometimes to star-gaze.' Ben placed his hands on the window-sill and leaned backwards. Then he frowned and picked up his hands and brushed them together to get rid of the dust.

It tickled her nose and Sophy couldn't prevent a small sneeze. She giggled. 'Oh dear, the furniture is dusted but they forgot the window-sill!'

Ben whipped a large white handkerchief out and handed it to her. He looked so solemn that she felt foolish for laughing. She bit her lip to stop herself and Ben's eyes seemed to darken.

'Just the dust,' she said and shook her head. He folded the handkerchief away without fuss.

'Tomorrow, if the weather is not inclement, we might go to Sea Houses which is the village by the sea.'

'I've never seen the sea,' Sophy said. 'Except in pictures.'

His jaw twitched and Sophy wished she could tell what he was thinking.

'You'll like the sea.' Ben pushed himself off the window-sill and walked past her to the door. He could have brushed her as he did so — he came so close she felt the air move and tasted the smell of his scent. He could have stopped very easily and swept her into his arms.

'Shall we continue the house tour?' he said, tapping his fingers on the edge of the door. Sophy started. She wanted those fingers to curl up around her neck and tease the back of her hairline. She wanted him to kiss her.

She must stop her imagination running riot! She looked away from his face, and said, 'Oh, yes.' She added, 'Where's Nelson?'

'In the kitchens being fed and spoiled like a king!' At least that brought a smile to his lips, she saw out of the corner of her eye as he swung through the door and his footsteps sounded ahead back through the nursery. Sophy gave a tiny sigh she knew he couldn't hear and followed him back downstairs and around the rest of Fordham Manor with determinedly maidenly thoughts.

★ ★ ★

The following day at the end of breakfast Ben asked her if she wanted to take a turn about the gardens. Sophy agreed and watched Lady Hart look up and stare at her with clear disapproval. Really, Ben had been such a model of good behaviour since they had been here she would have liked to tell Lady Hart that she had absolutely nothing to worry about.

'Would you like to take my arm, Sophy?' he said, once they were outside. His voice sounded sweet, like honey, and he regarded her, his eyes half shielded with a flicker of his dark lashes.

Sophy rested her fingers on the middle of his forearm. Her glove lay easily on the woollen sleeve of his coat but she could feel his arm underneath as hard as flint. She wondered if his soft gaze hid his passions or whether they had been fleeting and had now disappeared.

'Ben, you are being most charming .. of late,' she ventured to say to him as they walked down the gravelled path through the central lawns. So charming, in fact, that when she had tried to write last night, she had found it very difficult to keep him cast as the villain in her story.

'I am always charming.' He smiled. Nelson bounded around them and stopped to investigate things. Thin shafts of winter sunshine glittered down and set the dew on the lawns, leaves and branches sparkling.

Sophy wondered if she had misjudged him. Was this his true nature and before he had just been provoked into an extraordinary passion?

'Shall we go down to the lake?' he asked.

'Yes, please.' She met his eyes and smiled in

return. He breathed, very deeply it seemed, and said nothing.

It was a small lake surrounded by willow trees. Ben stopped by the water's edge and picked up a stick. With a flick of his wrist and arm he threw it a long way across the grass for Nelson to retrieve.

'I must go up to London tomorrow,' he said. 'Only for a few days, and when I return we'll go to the seaside.'

'I shall look forward to that,' Sophy replied, and found herself speculating on what business he might have in London that was so urgent.

They walked along the path by the lakeside, which took them slightly uphill and into a small woodland spinney. The air seemed cooler. Birds chirped and their feet crunched on the fallen twigs.

'Sophy, you should know that I will offer for you again on my return from London.'

She felt her every muscle stiffen. She'd thrown every objection she could think of at him when she had refused him. Why now was he telling her he intended to offer for her again? 'Ben — '

'I should like to ask you to consider carefully what your answer will be, Sophy.' The lines of his countenance were hard, as if etched on copper, and yet he spoke her name as if he were caressing her with velvet. His gentle manner, his soft approach of these last few days, was making it harder. She couldn't marry, didn't want to marry . . .

'I — '

'I don't want to speak on it now. I don't want to spoil this moment.'

Sophy saw a flame leap in his eye — passion. His fire still leapt within him; he had just been hiding it behind a sturdy guard. She swallowed. She wanted to run.

He took her hand in his, smoothed his thumb across the tops of her gloved fingers and raised them to his lips. Sophy trembled, knew that was all it took for her to respond to him somewhere deep inside her. Her own flicker, her own flame, leapt up and wanted to meet his.

She knew he was going to kiss her. She knew from the intense darkening of his eyes, a look so close to pain it was almost frightening, yet utterly compelling. She knew from a sudden stillness and quietness, as if the birds had really stopped singing and there was nothing around them. A world had been created in a moment where there only existed one woman and one man and all this he told her in the plea and the challenge of his gaze.

She had longed for it, she wanted it, and her lips came up to meet his, tasted the salty sweetness in half a moment, the hot, indefinable flavour of determination and maleness.

It was so easy to yield, too easy. Sophy yielded. Let him pull her towards him, envelop her in his arms, press her form against his so there could be no question of cold. He wrapped her up as if in the warmest cloak, stroked the line of her back, made her curve towards him, scandalously close, too close. Sophy wanted to gasp; she could feel his hard hips against hers.

He teased his fingers around her neck and played with her curls, the lobes of her ears, and all the while his kiss deepened, taking more and more. How much more was there? Already her mind was spinning, she had no thought but to ease the tips of her fingers below the line of his cravat, touch the cool linen and his hot, soft silken neck. The backs of her hands brushed the solid, rough line of his jaw.

'Think,' he murmured, drawing away from her slightly. Her hands slipped from where she had been teasing his hair. 'Think, Sophy, what it is you really want.'

He struck too close, too close to her heart. She had to get away. Sophy pulled herself back, nearly stumbled and fell but grabbed the rough trunk of a tree and kept her balance. She caught his fleeting, half-triumphant glance as she looked up, before she ran all the way back to the house.

★　★　★

Ben had two people to catch up with in London. One was his old friend Jack Walden. They'd dined together last night and Ben was pleased to discover that the full details of the dispute between him and Merryford had not made it into grist for the rumour mill of the ton.

The other person Ben wanted to see was hurrying down Haymarket towards him.

'Merryford.' Ben said, with force.

'Harty.' Merryford stopped and drew himself up, gazed at Ben but didn't quite meet his eye full-on.

'I believe we have some unfinished business.'

'Indeed.' Merryford's eyes narrowed. 'But the pavement of Haymarket isn't the place for it.'

'It's as good a place as any,' Ben replied. Merryford had not publicly disclosed the exact nature of their wager so far as Jack Walden had heard but Merryford was no longer to be trusted. The matter had to be closed. 'I received your letter and I've consulted the betting book at White's. That second wager we agreed to? I agree to it. On one condition.'

'What's that?'

'That no mention of my cousin's name is made. This is a private wager between you and me. If I hear my cousin's name mentioned in connection with any rumour, any, then we shall have to find another way to settle our dispute.'

'Down for a thousand pounds in the book, but you and I both know the real stake,' Merryford drawled, tilting his chin upwards so that Ben had to fight an incredible urge to plant a facer.

'Yes.'

'So you'll marry then? Just to spite me?' Merryford said suddenly.

Ben ignored the bait. 'Oh, and I came by a rather interesting pocket watch I believe I can throw into my side of the bargain. I thought you might like — '

'You b — '

'Good day, Merryford!' Ben doffed his hat and walked on. A slow smile crept on to his lips. Merryford could think what he liked but the fact remained that he'd already lost his confounded wager because Ben was going to marry, and he was going to marry Sophy and all honour would be upheld. Ben felt a

stiffening of his every sinew at the remem-
brance of her. She quivered like an autumn
leaf at his touch. Gosh, that was dashed
poetic. He must try and remember and tell
her. All in all, it seemed as if the gentle
approach was working. She was more delicate
than her strong nature had led him to believe
but then there had been the curious thing
her father had told him. The Reverend
Grantchester had not been backward in
sharing his delight at the prospect of his
daughter's marriage. He had believed that she
had encouraged no suitors after being
slighted in love by a caddish-sounding militia
lieutenant who had offered for her but then
left without a word and married someone
else.

His darling Sophy, jilted! He would make it
up to her a thousandfold.

* * *

Sophy managed to write early in the
mornings as no one expected to see her until
breakfast, which was very late, and then again
in the evenings as the household tended to
dine early before retiring. Yet the book was
not coming along as fast as she might have
hoped. Ben stole into her mind and distracted
her and she found herself wondering how

much longer it would be until he returned from London.

Lady Hart spent all day immersed in her books and magazines, not particularly in need of much companionship, and so in the afternoons Sophy had largely to amuse herself.

It was by chance on the afternoon of the second day of Ben's absence that Lord Fordham had been wheeled into the drawing-room by his valet and caught her fiddling with the pieces on the chess table and asked her if she could play. Thereafter he pestered her for a game sometimes three times a day.

They were in the middle of a game of chess three days later when the drawing-room door burst open and Ben strode in.

'Did you have a good journey, Lord Hart?' Sophy enquired in a demure voice.

'How many times do I have to tell you m'name's Ben?' He flashed his eyes about the room. 'Ah! Fordham's been teaching you to play chess?'

'No,' Lord Fordham growled. 'She beats me more often than not.'

Ben threw his head back and laughed. 'I doubt that is true, Fordham. You used to always win at chess, even against my father.'

That Ben should laugh was exactly what she should expect, Sophy told herself, yet she still felt upset. This was a man who didn't think women could or should think. She took a deep breath.

'Go on,' Lord Fordham said to her. 'You're not to take that, y'hear. Challenge him to a game.'

'Challenge accepted,' Ben said, before she even had time to speak herself. He swept forward and peered at the game in progress. Sophy tried to swallow the vexation that had risen in her chest. His eyes took in every piece and its position on the board in what seemed like no time at all.

'Ah, I see Fordham has already let you begin to corner him.' Ben fingered his chin. 'I had better turn it around and preserve the family honour.'

'Go ahead, m'boy.' Lord Fordham chuckled and winked at her.

'A master at chess are you, Ben?' Sophy said.

'Nonpareil.' He pushed a chair up to the table, flicked his coat tails and sat down. 'Now if I move my bishop here, see how that changes the picture and then — '

'You might not want to share your strategy so easily, Ben. I might turn it to your disadvantage.' How could she have been worrying for days about how she was going to bring herself to turn him down when he proposed marriage to her again? His masculine arrogance grated on her every pore. It was going to be very easy, but first she must beat him at chess.

'A valiant sentiment, but how are you ever going to learn if it's not all explained to you?'

'I know how to play chess. My father taught me.'

'There's a difference between knowing the names of the pieces and the moves allowed and knowing how to play a game of strategy and tactics.'

'Let's see, shall we?' Sophy replied. The odds at the moment, the way things stood on the board, were fairly even but if she couldn't beat him she was sure she could impress him with a deft move or two. In fact, where he had moved that bishop left a possibility, if he didn't notice in time, for her to manoeuvre a checkmate and victory.

Sophy felt her heart race with excitement. She bit her lip and moved a pawn she hoped he would regard as inconsequential.

Ben drummed his fingers on the edge of the table. After a moment he reached forward and moved a knight to take one of Sophy's pawns.

He hadn't noticed her plan! Sophy debated what to do next. She had a couple of options: a diversionary move or she could move her rook across for the kill. Nothing ventured, nothing gained, she decided, and moved the rook.

'Check,' she said.

'What?' Ben saw the situation in a moment. 'Oh hell!'

'Mind your language, m'boy,' Lord Fordham grunted.

'Sorry.' Ben knocked his king over with his forefinger. 'I resign.'

Sophy smiled. She'd beaten him!

'Beginner's luck,' he added and she bristled.

'I am not a beginner. I have been playing chess since I was seven or eight years old.'

He regarded her curiously. 'I suppose it is possible for a woman to understand chess?'

'Of course it is,' Sophy snapped and stood up. He had soured her victory with his opinions. She didn't have to stay here and listen to him. Lord Fordham had said she should treat the house like home and she was going to get some fresh air. 'Excuse me, Ben. Lord Fordham.'

'Where are you going?' Ben said and leapt to his feet.

'Excuse me,' Sophy repeated and walked towards the door. He sprinted in front of her and opened it.

'May I show you something?' he said in an

excited voice that was irresistible. His eyes sparkled and she hadn't the heart to refuse him.

'Here we are!' he said as they came outside the front door.

'A new carriage!' Sophy exclaimed and followed Ben down the front steps.

'Not brand new, no, but a fine curricle, don't you think? Not time to get a new one made before the London to Brighton at the end of March. I picked it up from a chap who was selling. Gambling debts. Poor fellow.'

'It looks very fast.'

'Drove it down from London and not bad. Tomorrow we'll go to the seaside and you can see what you think.'

'I am not sure I am safe getting in the curricle with you, Ben.'

'Fustian! The accident wasn't my fault. You know that! You were there. Hang on.' He ran his fingers through his hair. 'I remember the accident. We turned around the corner and . . . I don't believe it! My memory must have returned!'

'Oh Ben, how wonderful!'

He grabbed her hands and drew her up towards him before she could protest. He said, too seriously, 'Not as wonderful as you.'

Sophy stiffened, stood still in shock. He squeezed her fingers, bent his head and brushed his lips over them.

'You'll be perfectly safe with me,' he said. She was disappointed when he let go of her hands. Sophy wanted to shake herself. She shouldn't be disappointed, she should be relieved!

'I just remembered something,' Sophy lied, ran away from him all the way back to the safety of her chamber.

9

It would be mortifying to the feelings of many ladies, could they be made to understand how little the heart of man is affected by what is costly or new in their attire; how little it is biased by the texture of their muslin, and how unsusceptible of peculiar tenderness towards the spotted, the sprigged, the mull, or the jackonet.

The next morning Sophy sported a brand new sprigged muslin dress, the first truly fashionable attire she had ever owned, and Ben looked only at her eyes.

He held her hand as she stepped up into the curricle. He had been utterly charming in his usual way at dinner last night and at breakfast earlier. She rather thought she would be safe with him. It was herself that needed controlling.

The sun was shining and the sky was clear but she tucked the rug over her knees and around her in case he chose to fuss about her and do so.

He jumped up into his seat and they were off, jolted into motion, and they trotted out of the drive of Fordham Manor and on to the road.

It was only a couple of miles to the coast — they travelled through East Bourne village and then a mile further on was Sea Houses. It was really little more than a hamlet, a small cluster of houses on the seafront, yet they were for the most part very smart-looking cottages and many had a sign in the window saying *Lodgings to let*. The royal family had, according to Lord Fordham, stayed here some years previously.

They left the curricle at an inn.

The sea was a mixture of blue and grey edged with white and golden flecks of sunshine. Sophy stared at it and walked right to the very edge of the promenade. Ben came and stood beside her, his hands relaxed in his coat pockets. The breeze ruffled his hair.

'It is like the pictures I've seen,' she said. 'Only it moves. All the time! As if it were animate!'

'Shall we go down on the beach?' Ben asked and offered her his arm. Sophy took it. The shingle felt delightfully soft beneath her half boots. The air was bracing. Ben's arm was strong. It would have been nice to have a parasol like the other ladies though the feel of the sun on her face was pleasant.

'What are those? The wooden . . . caravans on wheels?'

'Bathing machines.' Ben laughed. 'Do you fancy being dipped?'

'Won't the sea water be frightfully cold?'

'Indeed. And January is the best month for sea bathing. They say the colder the water, the more efficacious.'

'You are knowledgeable about sea bathing.'

'Lady Hart has been ill for years.'

Sophy wondered if Ben was anxious about his mother's illness. He gave no sign of it and yet she had surely learned by now that often what Ben showed and what he thought were two different things.

'Unfortunately,' Ben said, 'Lady Hart's coming to the seaside is only for the sea air. I am no doctor but I wonder if there is a real benefit from sea bathing.'

'I'll sea bathe if you do,' Sophy replied.

He looked at her and then the corners of his lips twitched. 'I don't think it would be quite the thing for us to bathe together.'

'Let us maintain a fiction that you did not make that remark,' Sophy replied. 'I would venture to experience sea bathing should the opportunity present itself, would you?'

'If there weren't all these people about I should take you into my arms now,' Ben said.

'Are we to arrange the sea bathing?'

'If that is your wish.' He nodded.

'I have a feeling the cold water may be

particularly efficacious in your case.'

He grinned. 'Sea water does nothing to temper me.'

★ ★ ★

The woman who was to be her dipper introduced herself as Mrs Mary Jackson and continued to talk nineteen to the dozen. Sophy changed in the privacy of the bathing machine into a shift and waited as the machine was drawn by a horse across the sand and into the water.

'There is no need to be fearful,' Mrs Jackson said, 'Hundreds of people bathe in East Bourne every year.'

'I'm not fearful,' Sophy said. 'I just wonder what it is going to be like.'

'Cold. When you are in the water, keep moving.'

They drew to a halt and Sophy wondered what Ben was up to, whether he had arranged his own bathing machine or gone for a swim without one, as he had threatened.

Mrs Jackson opened the door and all Sophy could see stretching out ahead of them was the sea. A ladder was fastened so she could climb down into it, and an awning to preserve her modesty until she was covered by the water.

It was worse than cold, it was freezing. Sophy gasped and then held her breath as she climbed down the ladder after Mrs Jackson and into the sea. Every inch of her skin turned to gooseflesh as the cold bit into her, yet there was a lapping motion to the water which was undeniably pleasant.

The sand beneath her bare feet was soft and she could stand easily.

'Move your feet and arms,' Mrs Jackson said. 'Do you want to be dipped? Or do it yourself?'

'I'll do it myself,' Sophy said.

'Just put your head right under the water. Close your eyes and mouth and don't breathe.'

Sophy took a deep breath and sank herself downwards. The cold water washed over the top of her head. After a moment she came up and was thankful to breathe again. She licked her lips and tasted the salt.

She turned and looked out to sea, and saw a dark-haired figure. It had to be Ben. He was swimming. She watched his arms come out of the water as he propelled himself along. Then he stopped, his head bobbing in the water and facing her, and waved.

'Is that your husband?' Mrs Jackson asked.

'No, my cousin,' Sophy said, suddenly afraid of causing any impropriety. Ben should not have stopped and be watching her! She made sure the water came up to her neck.

'Keep moving!' Mrs Jackson ordered.

Sophy walked a few steps this way and that. She could see from the corner of her eye that Ben was still watching. Heavens! Would he not just go away!

She stubbed her toe on a stone.

'Ouch!' Sophy cried and tried to keep her balance. Pain shot through her toe and foot. 'I . . . I hit my toe.'

'Can you jig it?'

'I think so. Oh, it hurts!'

'Take my hand.'

Sophy grabbed Mrs Jackson's hand yet at the same time lost her balance and plunged backwards. Sea-water flooded into her eyes, her mouth. Mrs Jackson pulled her sharply back up into the air. Sophy spluttered and coughed. She gasped for air.

'Get her out of the sea, for heaven's sake!' came a deep masculine timbre. Ben!

He must have swum up to them. Sophy tried to open her stinging eyes properly as she felt herself regain her balance and her feet stood steady on the cold shingle. She caught an imprecise, watery glimpse of his broad shoulders — naked shoulders — and strong muscular arms, and the curly dark hair on the top of his naked chest. Sophy coughed some more. She should be ashamed for imagining how he continued below the water-line.

'Go away,' Mrs Jackson said to him. 'The propriety of — '

'Propriety be damned! D'you think I'm going to go away and leave my cousin to be drowned?'

'Ben,' Sophy managed to say, 'I only stubbed my toe. It's all right.'

'My heart stopped when I saw you go under,' he said. Sophy could hear the emotion in his voice and it was threatening to choke her. She spluttered.

'Thank you, Ben,' she struggled to say. 'Go away now, will you? I want to get out.'

'Yes, shoo,' Mrs Jackson added.

'I'm going.'

Ben turned and swam away out to sea with his back to them. What if Sophy had been in real danger? What if she had drowned? The simple thought twisted his insides so damnably all he could think to do was to swim harder, faster. Fight the sea with everything he had. If he lost Sophy he would be completely lost himself. He might as well keep swimming further and further out until he could swim no more.

He hadn't lost her. She was safe yet he had been scared witless and the fact of that scared him even more. What the devil was he going to do?

Gulls squawked and circled above him, taunting him.

Ben stopped and turned. He had to know that she was getting out of the water. Yet to see her small shivering form being hustled back up the ladder into the bathing box was almost more than he could bear. They had towels in there, didn't they? Sophy looked almost blue with cold; the wet shift clung to her body like seaweed. Would that he could take her into his arms now and warm her with the passion she deserved, warm her with his love.

Love? Yes, he had fallen in love with his unsuitable cousin. He loved everything about her, even when her stubbornness drove him wild with vexation. It was strange how that new knowledge didn't shake him; quite the opposite. It confirmed that his fears were reasonable. It confirmed that he must, absolutely must, make her his wife. Mr Charles Preston had shunned marrying for duty in order to marry for love. Benedict St Michael had vowed he would do the same and then had been prepared to give up all that for her.

That was before he knew for certain he loved her. Now he knew it strengthened his resolve, his belief that all his feelings had been leading to the ultimate end. He could see the end.

He turned again and swam back to the sheltered part of the beach where he had left his clothes.

★   ★   ★

'Time for a hot cup of tea,' Ben said. He took Sophy by the elbow and steered her forward across the beach and then up the steps back into the village and towards the tea rooms.

'A cup of tea would be just the thing.' Sophy tried to stop her teeth from chattering. Mrs Jackson had rubbed her raw with the towels — necessary, she had said, to get her circulation back and prevent chills — but she still felt cold.

'You are still shivering!' Ben frowned and took his cloak off. He wrapped it around her shoulders and pulled her closer to him. Sophy didn't protest — his cloak was warm. She would have liked to have pressed even further into him, closed her eyes —

'Here we are. After you,' Ben said and Sophy stepped on ahead and into the cottage which housed the tea room. A bevy of faces turned to watch them, openly curious. She was a young girl alone with no sign of any mother or chaperon — of course they were curious.

'D'you have a table for my cousin and me?' Ben pitched his voice very loud.

Most of the faces turned back to their conversations, no doubt discussing whether or not they believed it. Sophy kept her eyes looking upwards, never to the floor, and followed Ben and the waiter over to a table by the window.

'Tea for two,' Ben said and settled himself in a chair that seemed too small for him.

'You don't look right here,' Sophy said to him in a very low voice. Most of the tea room's patrons were female and elderly. The only other young man in the room looked as if he was there under extreme sufferance.

Ben's lips quirked. He said, 'I am here for you, you silly girl.'

The tea came quickly and interrupted Sophy's vexed thoughts. How dare he call her a *silly girl!* She drank her tea as hot as she could manage. It warmed her from the inside.

Ben was watching her. She looked away and out of the window at the sea. Surely the sight of her drinking tea was not of such great interest? His eyes were almost exactly the same dark brown colour as the hair on his chest — from what she had seen. The hair on his head was a shade or two darker. It looked curlier than usual, perhaps caused by the sea-water.

Sophy put her teacup down and it rattled against the saucer. She decided she needed to break the silence. 'Very reviving.'

She watched his fingers as he picked up his own cup and drank from it.

'Tastes of salt,' Ben said.

'The air tastes of salt.'

She would taste of salt, Ben was sure — every inch of her. He wanted to confirm his theory but he wasn't going to. Today was not the day. Today he wanted to propose to her — somewhere windswept, breathtaking and dramatic. Beachy Head. He said, 'I'm going to show you the view from a magnificent cliff called Beachy Head before we go home.'

Ben started when they stepped on to the street. Coming out of the lodging house at the end of the row was Viscount Merryford. That lying, deceitful cur! Ben felt his fist ball but he had wits about him enough to steer them out of the road and out of sight and back towards the curricle. What the devil was Merryford doing here in East Bourne?

★   ★   ★

'Have you not forgiven me for beating you at chess?' she said as he drew the curricle to a halt at the inn on the earthen track which went up the hill towards the cliff top.

'What? Yes. Luck, and I wasn't paying attention. You may enjoy your victory. It won't happen again.'

'I would not be so sure about that!'

'Sophy, I don't want to talk about chess. There are . . . other things about which we should converse.' Ben leapt down from the curricle. 'Take my hand.'

'Certainly,' she replied and placed her small hand in his and stepped down from the curricle.

'It's a bit of a walk,' he confessed and led her forward, not letting go of her hand.

'I expect I shall manage. I have been invigorated and revived by the sea bathing and the tea.'

'You're not going sea bathing again. Not unless I am there.'

'Ben, what — '

'Hush! There are things I have to tell you. Your eyes, they sparkle like sapphires. Your hair . . . it's long, is it? I imagine it is very long and like spun silk. I want you in a painting with all your hair cascading down, covering . . . ' Ben coughed.

'Ben! That does not sound . . . decent.'

'It shall hang in my chamber where only I shall be allowed to look at it.'

'Ben!' she admonished, but he saw the beginnings of a smile play on her lips. He took her hand gently in his and turned it over so that the inside of her wrist faced the blue sky. He lifted it and bent his head and planted the softest kiss he was able right there. He felt her shiver as she pulled her arm away.

'Look! Look how far the sea stretches,' she said, looking away from him and out to sea. Ben turned not to look at the sea but at her profile. The wind attacked her well-arranged hair, sent strands to brush against her cheek. He traced with his eyes the outline of her flat forehead, her pert, upright nose and perfect chin and the start of the graceful curve of her neck. Dammit! His eyes wanted to go much further than her clothing allowed.

'Miles and miles,' she said as she stared out to sea. 'And even from here you can see no end to it.' This spot would do, Ben decided. They were alone on the grassy cliff apart from the gulls and the strong breeze.

'Sophy,' he said. His voice sounded thick. He coughed. She turned towards him. 'Will you do me the honour of becoming my wife?'

'No.'

A large white gull sliced past them on the

buffeting wind and screamed.

'No?' Ben nearly shouted. Wild fury licked up his very core. 'How can you refuse me again?'

She pulled at a lock of her hair, did not look at him, half-turned away. He wanted to seize her shoulders and shake her.

'Sophy . . . ' He battened down his anger as best as he could. 'Sophy, I love you. Don't you love me, even a little bit?'

'I love you,' she murmured, confounding him.

'Then why the devil won't you marry me?'

He saw something in her eyes he didn't understand. Sadness? Fear? The way she looked at him with a mixture of tenderness and fire, he knew she loved him. Yet there was something else there — a shadow. If he could have somehow grasped it and destroyed it, he —

'I will explain,' she said. He had to strain to hear her. The wind seemed to be billowing more violently now. 'Mary Wollstonecraft, in her *Vindication on the Rights of Women*, says that — '

'Don't give me some bluestocking fustian!' Ben shouted. How much nonsense was a man supposed to take from a woman? 'I won't buy it. In fact, I am not having any of it. You don't know your own mind! Typical of a woman!

You will marry me.'

'I won't — '

'Your father was happy to accept my suit. You don't have a choice in the matter. Do you think I am going to let you walk away now? The woman I love, and who loves me in return?'

Sophy pressed his fingers into her palms. They felt damp. His eyes seemed to have narrowed yet they compelled her to listen to his every word. Every inch of him seemed to be arranged into a stance that said, *Listen to me; don't defy me.*

Defy him she must. He said he loved her but what sort of love was this when he couldn't accept that she might have beaten him at chess? What would he say if he found out she had written a book he had admired? 'Ben, I can't marry you. Your love . . . it's not . . . it's not the kind of love on which a marriage should be based. It's not — '

'You don't know what you are talking about,' he snapped. 'You are overset. The episode in the sea has upset you. I will take you home and we will resume our conversation later.'

She meekly took his arm and allowed him to lead her back to the curricle. His face was hard set, his jaw clenched and his gaze determinedly forward. His arm felt taut and his shoulders looked stiff. She had upset him, she knew. If only he had let her explain then he might have understood. She was not so completely averse to marriage that she would never marry; it was that it had to be a love that encompassed mind, body and soul. He would have to want her to be a novelist, support her dreams as keenly as if they were his own. Not deride them.

★ ★ ★

Ben knew he was boiling with a furious frustration; it threatened to paralyse him, to obliterate all his sense and reason. Yet he managed to keep it reined in; stopped himself from driving the curricle like a madman.

He could not forget that she sat beside him. Far too prim and contented-looking for his liking as she looked out at the passing scenery, seemingly oblivious to the buffeting wind on her face.

Mary Wollstonecraft, indeed! Dangerous, radical, revolutionary nonsense! No wonder Sophy was so completely confused as to her own mind. Wollstonecraft had argued for the abolition of the monarchy — of all social hierarchies — and had described marriage as 'legalized prostitution', akin to slavery.

Marriage to Benedict St Michael would be

nothing like that. He would never treat a woman cruelly. Sophy would have everything she could possibly want: an entire new wardrobe for a start, her own carriage, the title of Lady Hart . . . and him! He was an eligible piece. He would make a delightful husband.

He drew them to a crunching halt outside the front door of Fordham Manor and was about to go indoors when the sound of another carriage bowling up the drive caught his attention.

Ben turned and watched the closed carriage approach. From the peeling paint-work to the surly expression of the coachman, it looked hired. It came to a halt and the door swung open. Viscount Merryford descended.

A burning gorge of anger rose in Ben's throat. Sophy had turned white. His first instinct was to offer her his arm but something stopped him. He stiffened, realized he was still angry with her, and kept absolutely still.

'Hey! Harty!' Viscount Merryford whipped off his hat and strode towards them. He pulled his jacket straight.

'Merryford.' Ben nodded and tried to hide his scowl. 'What brings you to East Bourne?'

'What brings me here?' Merryford gave Sophy a lascivious glance that made Ben's hair stand on end. 'Purely a social call.'

Ben found himself hardly listening. The whole of the night before the accident came back to him in a flash. Yes, he had had a few glasses of wine and played cards after dinner. But he certainly hadn't lost 800 guineas to Merryford. It had been the other way around. Ben felt his fingers digging into his palms and freed them. Merryford was not to have any clue how angry he was.

'A social call?' Ben said and kept his tone unruffled. As far as he was concerned, their second wager now didn't stand because the first wager had been a sham. Merryford had lied to him and tricked him.

'Yes.' Merryford's satisfied smile developed into a grin that Ben wanted to smash off his face. He drew a bouquet of pink hothouse roses from behind his back. 'Miss Grant-chester, I am delighted to renew our acquaintance.'

'Our acquaintance?' Sophy said, her chin held high and her eyebrows arched. 'You must be mistaken, sir.'

Sophy pushed a curl away from her face and continued to stare at Merryford challengingly. What a girl! Heavens, how he admired her!

Ben felt her arm slip into his. There was something in her countenance which made him listen with an apprehensive and anxious attention, while she added, 'Ben, do you wish to introduce me to this gentleman? I am not sure of the propriety of accepting flowers from a stranger, now that we are betrothed.'

'What?' Merryford threw his hands in the air. 'You expect me to believe that?'

10

Ben was surprised, but after a few moments' silent consideration of her, replied in a calmer, graver tone, and as if the candid result of conviction, 'I believe she will scrub up rather well.'

Sophy lifted up her eyes, but was too much oppressed to make any reply.

'That puts rather a different light on things.' Merryford braved a smile. 'I don't believe you played me fair with the wager if you were planning to get leg-shackled to the gel yourself, eh? Now, are you going to invite me in for some refreshment?'

Ben shook his head. 'I don't believe so.'

Merryford scowled but there was nothing for him to do but get back in his coach. As soon as he was out of sight, Sophy took a deep breath and went into the house. Wager? Had there been some kind of wager's — *over her?* She would go to her chamber, she thought, and try to make sense of it all. She turned right in the hallway and felt hard fingers grip the top of her arm.

'No, you don't,' Ben said. She couldn't read his face but his eyes were fixing her like pins. 'I have some explaining to do.'

Sophy shook her arm free. 'Don't treat me like a child.'

'Sorry.'

'There was a wager, then?'

'Yes, there was a wager and also a false wager,' Ben replied. 'It is rather complicated — '

'Oh, I think I have mind enough to understand a wager, Ben. I have already proved to you I can play chess and converse on literary — '

'You misunderstand — '

'Are you telling me there was no wager of which I was the stake?'

'No . . . ' He pulled his hand through his hair. Sophy stared at him. It was not like Ben to be evasive. 'Not exactly, but . . . '

Ben broke off as Lady Hart came bustling into the hallway, her heavy jonquil skirts making a swishing sound. 'Who was that? I thought I heard visitors.'

'Someone came up the drive by mistake, Mother.'

'By mistake? Bother.' Lady Hart tapped her fan on her wrist. 'The Lincolns are arriving today. I invited them to visit on their way up to London. Miss Grantchester, you will no doubt enjoy their company, though they are a degree younger than you. Persephone is nineteen — a delightful gel. She is to be presented this year. Ariadne is sixteen or seventeen.'

Sophy wasn't sure if she imagined it but she thought she had heard Ben groan.

In the privacy of her own chamber in front of a well-banked fire, Sophy luxuriated in the warm soapy water of a bath; a hundred miles away from the cold sea-water of earlier. That Ben should have wagered ownership of her person with Viscount Merryford she found both vexing and, somewhat to her surprise, hurtful. She had believed he lived to a code of honour that meant he should not have done such a thing.

Sophy felt her skin prickle. Then she shivered. She had developed feelings for Ben that went deeper than simple desire or even friendship; she had begun to believe that he might, in his own arrogant way, come to care for her.

The bath water had become a little cold. Sophy stood up carefully, holding on to the side of the bath, and stepped out. She pulled the calico towel Nora had left draped ready for her over the screen and rubbed herself vigorously to get dry and warm again.

The wager could explain Ben's ardour to marry her, she thought. He might have agreed to the wager after having too much to drink and then regretted it the next morning and sought to make amends. She knew enough of Ben's character to believe that could be possible and she could forgive him if he had realized he had been wrong and was trying to make good.

She would speak to him about the wager when she had an opportunity, Sophy decided. It seemed important that she knew the whole, for good or for ill.

Nora washed her hair for her, and then began to dress it into fashionable ringlets. This would be her life if she married Ben, she found herself thinking as Nora attended to her hair. It would be a life of idleness, frivolity and pampering. What else was a poor wife, with nothing apart from cotton wool between her ears, supposed to do to fill her days apart from worry about her appearance?

Sophy could see herself in the mirror opposite, completely still while Nora fussed about her head.

'Ouch!' Sophy said as Nora pushed a pin in far too close to her skin.

'Sorry, miss.'

The idea of being such a lady was horrifying! Sophy felt an involuntary tear prick. She was safer pinning her own hair.

Yet what if Ben could be brought to realize that she wanted something more? Would he allow her to spend a portion of her day writing her novels? Would he agree to their publication?

Could a leopard change his spots?

The thought that perhaps it could took the edge off the pain of having her hair so tightly and heavily bound. Sophy smiled as she regarded herself in the mirror. The arrangement was far superior-looking to anything she could have done herself. And, despite the frivolity of it, Sophy found herself feeling particularly pleased to be able to wear one of the new dresses the seamstress had hastily run up for her. It was a simple cream sarsenet and muslin evening gown trimmed with butterscotch and coquelicot striped ribbon.

Meeting new people was always such a thrill! Sophy could hear that the guests were all assembled before she even entered the drawing-room. She took a deep breath as the footman opened the door for her.

'Ah, Sophy!' Lord Fordham said. 'You look a picture!'

'Thank you, my lord,' Sophy said, coming over to where he sat in his bath chair and allowing him to kiss her hand.

Ben stood slightly apart from the company, by the fire with his back to it. It struck Sophy how he was the tallest and most engaging-looking person in the room by a hundred miles. No one else drew the eye as surely as he did.

'Sophy,' he said, a smile playing on his lips, 'come in and meet some more of my family.'

Lady Hart stepped forward. Whether Ben had intended to perform the introductions himself, Sophy did not know, but his mother blocked his path.

'Sir Josiah and Lady Lincoln,' said Lady Hart, 'this is Miss Sophia Grantchester, a *distant* cousin on my husband's side of the family.'

Ben looked on with the amused smile still on his countenance.

'How do you do.' Sir Josiah Lincoln beamed. He was a short, rotund man who wore horn-rimmed spectacles. His wife, the same height as her husband but half the volume, echoed her own greeting but looked less enthralled to meet her. Lady Lincoln's hair, a mixture of grey and gold, was fastened with an enormous tortoiseshell comb and though her pallor was somewhat grey she had high cheekbones and would have been a real diamond of the first water in her day. Both her daughters took after her, Sophy noticed at once, and appeared, from the way they held themselves, to be extremely shy.

'Miss Grantchester, we are pleased to make your acquaintance.' Persephone, the elder daughter, spoke on behalf of herself and her sister.

'I am most delighted to meet you,' Sophy said.

'Shall we adjourn into dinner?' Lady Hart said. 'Benedict, I shall give up my arm to Miss Lincoln.'

'Yes, Mother,' Ben said, stepping out from his position by the fire to offer Persephone Lincoln his arm. She was an inch or two shorter than her younger sister, positively petite with a dainty figure and delightful pale auburn curls. Against Ben's tall, stiff black frame, she looked fragile, yet Sophy could see how he didn't hurry or alarm her — the perfect gentleman. Lady Hart and Lady Lincoln's faces were a picture of interest and expectation. They have Miss Lincoln lined up as Ben's bride, Sophy thought, and felt a stab like a hot poker in her chest.

Sophy told herself to pull herself together. She walked with Miss Ariadne Lincoln to the dining-room and found herself seated at the far end of the table from Ben, who was, quite rightly, flanked by Lady Lincoln and Miss Lincoln.

Never before had a dinner seemed so long and of so little enjoyment. Sophy had been looking forward to meeting the Lincolns, to being admired in her dress. Yet no one had

202

commented on her appearance apart from Lord Fordham. In fact, she had been largely ignored by everyone, including Ben.

The conversation around the dinner table revolved around the coming season in London and was mainly between Lady Hart and Lady Lincoln. Every so often Ben interrupted and directed a question at one of the Lincoln girls, kindly trying to assist in drawing them out of their shells, Sophy thought. Yet how she wished he would direct a question at her!

When the ladies adjourned to the drawing-room after dinner, the Lincoln girls sat next to each other on a *chaise-longue* and looked like a pair of dolls. Neither spoke and Lady Hart and Lady Lincoln continued their conversation veering off into gossip about people of whom Sophy had never heard nor would ever meet. Sophy picked up one of Lady Hart's magazines and sat down on a chair beside the fire.

It was only about ten minutes before the gentlemen joined them. Sophy looked up and caught Ben's eye and the tiniest curve of his lips. He strode over to the fire, towards her, and stopped with his back to the fireplace, only a couple of feet away from her.

Sir Josiah remained standing in the doorway. He coughed and then said, 'Let us retire, my love.'

'Certainly,' Lady Lincoln replied, and rose. 'Ariadne, it is time you were in bed too.'

'Yes, Mama.'

'I have a bit of a headache myself,' Lady Hart said. 'I think I shall retire. Miss Grantchester, it is late, isn't it?'

'Not so late,' Sophy said, glancing at the ormolu clock on the mantelpiece. It was only just after nine o'clock. Why had Lady Hart developed a sudden interest in her welfare? Of course! She wanted to leave Ben alone with Miss Lincoln. Well, she wasn't going to show Lady Hart any consideration on the matter. 'I think I shall stay a little while and finish reading my magazine. Thank you, Lady Hart.'

'It is late for the country,' Lady Hart said. 'I am sure you are tired after your exertions today?'

'In fact quite the opposite,' Sophy replied, even more determined to stick to her decision. It went completely against the grain but the prospect of leaving Ben to enjoy Miss Lincoln's charms alone made her feel quite unsettled. 'The sea bathing was invigorating.'

'You went sea bathing, Miss Grantchester?' Miss Lincoln said, her voice sounding for the first time since dinner. For a moment stunned silence hung in the room. Sophy saw Ben suppress a smile.

'Yes, shall I tell you about it?' Sophy placed her magazine down and turned to face Miss Lincoln, whose eyes widened.

'Mother, I shall see Miss Lincoln and Miss Grantchester do not stay up too late,' Ben said.

'Good night, then,' Lady Hart conceded but did not look best pleased. She followed Sir Josiah and Lady Lincoln and Miss Ariadne Lincoln out of the drawing-room.

'Tell me about the sea bathing,' Miss Lincoln insisted as soon as they were left alone in the drawing-room. Sophy moved and sat beside her. She saw Ben wander off towards the window.

'It was cold,' Sophy said to Miss Lincoln, 'but quite delightful. Bathing in January is apparently the best for one's health. The colder the sea, the more invigorating. Will you sea bathe while you are here?'

'I don't expect I shall be allowed. Mama would be terrified I catch my death and with everything so carefully set for my debut . . . it really would not be the thing. Have you been presented, Miss Grantchester?'

'No, my background is far more modest than yours, Miss Lincoln.' Sophy folded her hands in her lap and fixed her expression to look modest and demure as Miss Lincoln's did.

'How I wish I did not have to be presented!' Miss Lincoln said with a remarkable lack of emotion. 'I quake at the thought of it. Yet one must go through it if one is to acquire one's town bronze, and of course a husband.'

'Surely it will not be so terrible?' Heavens, Sophy thought, if she had had the opportunity she would have been wild with excitement, not awed by it. London! And all those people to meet!

'Had I your confidence and ease of manner, Miss Grantchester, no doubt I should find it as simple as you suppose. I am terrified of all the young bucks I shall have to deal with.'

'You deal with Ben very well,' Sophy could not help saying.

'Yes,' Miss Lincoln admitted, but Sophy saw how she twisted her hands in her lap. 'But Benedict is so very kind, he would not harm a fly. I am quite at ease with him. It is the rakes and rogues of which I am afraid.'

Sophy could not quite believe what she was hearing. Miss Lincoln seemed to be quite unaware that Ben was a rake.

'Your mother will see no harm comes to you in London, Persephone,' Ben's voice came in. 'If you follow the correct form at all times, nothing, I repeat, nothing can happen to you.'

Ben appeared in front of them. His steady steps and the depth in his eyes made Sophy want, more than anything, to belong to him. She would have never thought she could feel this way about a man, yet she did. Miss Lincoln was right when she said that he was kind.

His expression when he looked at Miss Lincoln was exactly that, yet when he turned his gaze to her, the fire, the promise that leapt in his eyes was unmistakable. It was as if he was capable of sending her a kiss through the air. Her lips seemed to quiver at the memory of his. She pressed her fingers on them, hoped that any colour in them or her cheeks could be attributed to her having sat so close to the fire.

'I think I will retire to bed,' Sophy said quickly.

'Yes, I shall do the same,' Miss Lincoln agreed.

Ben nodded and strode ahead to open the door for them. Sophy felt every inch of her skin prickle as she walked past him. 'Good night, Miss Lincoln. Good night, Ben.'

She fled as quickly as she could to her part of the house and safety. She needed to think, to write. Putting her thoughts on to paper would help make things clearer.

* * *

There was only about an inch left on the candle, Sophy noticed as she looked up and waited for the ink to dry so she could turn the page over. An inch while she could keep writing and then she must get undressed and go to bed. She could hardly creep about the house in the middle of the night looking for a new candle.

An owl hooted in the distance. She thought she heard a tap. At her door? It couldn't be. She breathed on the ink. The candle flame flickered.

Another tap. There was someone at the door! Nora? Sophy got up, padded over to the door and whispered, 'Who is it?'

'It's Ben.'

Another midnight visit to check her door was locked! Would he never realize that she was perfectly able to take care of herself!

'I'm locking my door now,' Sophy said.

'No,' he replied. 'Let me in.'

She hesitated and watched as the door handle turned and Ben walked into her chamber. He shut the door behind him. His eyes flashed. 'Sophy.' His voice cracked. 'I want to explain . . . about the wager — '

'No.' She didn't want to know now. She would rather stay in ignorance and give him the benefit of the doubt, because more than her need to know, and rising up inside her, was the burning need to kiss him and to be kissed by him.

'Kiss me, Ben. Please,' she heard herself say.

'You throw my words back in my face,' he said, advancing towards her, his eyes darkening, 'yet you respond to my kisses.'

She felt as fragile as a soufflé. She was unable to move, to think, to speak. He placed his arm around her middle and drew her into his embrace.

She tasted everything she had come to expect, to desire, and with it the sweet berry flavours of port wine. She needed this kiss, this assurance that he was not angry with her.

The kiss did not last long enough.

The warmth that had been growing inside her felt cheated as he broke away to plant tiny kisses across her face. She stiffened, and shivered, as he trailed downwards, kissing her too-sensitive neck.

'I love you . . . I want you,' he said.

Her fingers had found their way to the cravat of his evening dress and sunk into the silk.

'You say you don't love me enough,' he murmured, his eyes pitch black as he regarded her. 'I'd wager I'll persuade you to love me *enough*.'

'Kiss me again,' she heard herself say.

'Sophy.' He leant in very close and nipped at her ear. 'You're going to be mine. And then you'll have no choice, you'll have to marry me.'

She was breathless and yet something inside her stiffened. His words jarred.

'No,' she said. 'No, I won't marry you.'

'You'll have to, once I have ruined you.' His lips trailed down her neck, sending shivers across her back and to her spine. She was already bending towards him in a sudden need to feel his chest against hers when the meaning of what he had said sunk in. Sophy gasped for breath, trying to grasp sense.

'How dare you try and bribe me into marriage with . . . lust!' she managed.

Ben stopped kissing her. He drew himself up some inches so she had to face his countenance. He fixed her gaze.

It was becoming clearer to Sophy now. She pushed at him; she wanted him off her, away from her. She could not bear to look at him. His eyes were too dark, too focused, too much. She needed to think.

'It seemed like a rather good plan,' he said,

his voice hard as ice. 'You seemed most receptive to *these* advances. You would try the patience of a saint. I am not a saint.'

'Ruin me, if you will. I still won't marry you!' He could do what he liked and the way it was going she was going to like it too. But he wouldn't push her into marriage like this.

'You don't deserve my favours until you have agreed to my terms,' he said.

'Ben,' she said, swallowing all her pride as she realized that she was willing, for him only, to sacrifice her immortal soul and reputation, and the risks of pregnancy. She had obviously lost her reason, she decided, as she heard herself say, 'I will become your mistress. I would like to.'

'Sophy, I shall take that in the spirit it is intended but you don't know me if you believe for one moment I would be low enough to agree to such an arrangement. Not only would your reputation be utterly ruined — '

'I don't care for that!' she insisted. 'Why should I? What am I anyway save an impoverished parson's daughter? I have no high society reputation that must be pro-tected.'

'And what would happen were you to . . . have a child?'

She had no answer for that. She hung her

head, suddenly ashamed. There were very good reasons young ladies did not do what she was proposing and she had no answer for him.

'I want all of you, Sophy, tied to me for ever. My terms are marriage, nothing less,' he said without hesitation and closed the door of her chamber firmly behind him.

11

There is one thing a man can always do, if he chooses, and that is his duty.

Ben placed the palm of his right hand flat on the wall, leaned on it, bent his head and stared into the darkness of the floor. Had she lost all leave of her senses? He brushed his forehead with the back of his left hand, felt small damp beads of perspiration and wanted to curse. She had not been brought up to be a diamond of the first water but she was the daughter of a rector and his cousin. If she was somehow determined to ruin herself it was just as well he had rescued her from Merryford.

Yet he was sure she was a complete novice at the arts of love. An experienced woman would know she was driving him mad with desire and frustration.

Ben pushed himself away from the wall and stood upright. From the dim moonlight that came from the stair window he could see his way forward, downstairs and back into the main part of the house and his own chamber.

It was absolutely clear where his duty lay. Sophy needed protecting — from herself.

Through the fog of his anger, the memory was as clear as day. He'd been about eight years old and was trotting by his father's side down to the stables one summer day.

Standing by a large barrel of water were two of the stable boys, not much older than himself.

'What the devil are you doing?' his father had bellowed.

Ben could recall the pitiful mewing that came from the small sack one of the boys held in his hand and the moment he had realized what was going on.

'No one — no one — destroys the life of an animal on my estate,' his father had shouted and, engulfed in a sudden rage, Ben had watched him cuff both trembling boys around the ears.

Later, as he watched his father directing the boys to return the litter to the distraught mother cat in the stables, he had said to him, 'Ben, it is your privilege that one day you will be man of all this and it is the duty of the strong to protect the vulnerable. With your privilege comes your duty and do not ever forget it.'

His duty was clear. The question that remained was how, when she was so unwilling to marry him.

★ ★ ★

Sophy woke to see a shaft of sunlight streaming in through the gap in the curtains. She did not feel like sunshine. Her head felt stuffy, from the tears that had scalded her cheeks until she had finally fallen asleep late into the night.

She had never felt so alone. Not since her mother died when she was five years old, and her sister, a babe of only a few weeks old. They had both been claimed by a fever within three days of each other. From then on she had only had her father and he had never shown any inclination to remarry.

She was late down to breakfast. Her heart slowed thankfully as she observed the dining-room to be free of Ben. Only Lady Hart and Lady Lincoln sat at the table.

After she helped herself to some toast, Sophy perceived from the clattering of her teacup and her expression that Lady Hart was not in good humour.

'How are you this morning, Lady Hart?' she enquired, thinking she owed her hostess at least a daily solicitation as to the state of her health.

'As well as usual,' Lady Hart replied.

It was not until later when the rain resulted in everyone gathering in the drawing-room with nothing to do that Sophy discovered the reason behind Lady Hart's ill temper and the reason she had been fortunate not to see Ben — he had gone quite unexpectedly to London.

Sophy told herself that she should, in all logic, be thankful. His absence should allow her to imagine that things were quite ordinary. But that she in some way must be the cause of his going away did not rest easy with her. When would he return? Indeed, would he return? It was hardly to be considered; her heart would certainly break. She must see him again.

'Like his father.' Lord Fordham coughed. 'Wont to go where the fancy took him.'

Lady Hart flicked her fan open and ignored him.

★ ★ ★

The tall front door to White's, a celebrated club of long-standing pedigree, was that through which Ben stepped from St James's Street. He tapped the step jauntily with his thin, ebony cane and hurried the male servant in the lobby, who'd stepped forward to assist in divesting him of his outergarments. He met Jack Walden upstairs on the first floor with a grin on his face.

'It's all bang up to the mark so far,' Ben said and rubbed his hands together with satisfaction. The cold of the outdoors still stung his cheeks. 'Had to wait for hours but I have the licence.'

'Capital!' Jack smiled and pushed the waiting glass of brandy over to Ben. 'Come and sit down by the fire and drink this. Now, if only it was so easy to find a man of the cloth ready to be greased in the fist.'

'Indeed!' Ben tossed back his brandy as he sank into the comfortable horsehair chair.

'She's a regular out and outer, I take it, this cousin of yours?' Jack himself looked a regular out and outer with his severe black town attire. He raised a dark eyebrow. 'A prime looker too? I can't wait to meet her. I'm intrigued.'

'Stunning, my good fellow. Magnificent. I can't say this havey-cavey business is ideal by any means but I must marry her before some other devil starts dangling after her. Or worse. That business with Merryford has made me devilish uneasy.'

'Ha!' Jack threw his head back. 'Harty, I do believe the day has come I thought I would never see. You're smitten! And you are to marry her. How positively splendid!'

Ben stared into the fire. The oranges and reds crackled solidly in their iron grate. 'Not so smitten as to be blind,' he replied. 'She's a shocking bluestocking and as stubborn as a mule.'

★   ★   ★

'Sophy?'

It sounded like Ben's urbane voice. Sophy snapped volume two of *The Adventures of Peregrine Pickle* shut. Not quite the kind of reading she'd have expected to find in Lord Fordham's library, but found it she had. Mr Pickle was a rogue with an indecently moderate sense of shame.

'Sophy, I'm back.'

His hair was ruffled as if he had just come in from outside. His eyes sparkled. His lips . . . she did not dare look at his smile. It had been five days since . . . since . . .

'Ben, you're back.' She hoped her voice sounded ordinary.

'Yes, but no one knows yet,' he said and put a finger to his lips. His gaze made her feel undressed. 'Come with me for a drive.'

A doubt that his proposition was slightly clandestine niggled at the back of her mind but she placed *Peregrine Pickle* down on a table and watched as he smiled.

She knew that she loved him. She didn't care that he had wagered her person. She had almost certainly made the biggest mistake of her life by refusing to marry him. He would ask her again, wouldn't he?

'Come.' Ben held out his hand. Gingerly she placed her fingers in his and rose to her feet. He raised her hand to his lips and brushed it with the lightest kiss. Sophy quivered. Her heart was beating far too fast.

His very presence was potent. He clasped her fingers in his, a little too tightly, and swept her out of the library, through the hall, without meeting anyone except Lord Fordham's butler Dawson, who handed Sophy her cloak and bonnet without emotion.

Then out to his curricle waiting directly outside and they were away. Sophy tilted her head back and, despite the fresh breeze, decided there was no place she would rather be.

'I should like,' Ben said as they came into the open countryside, 'to explain the circumstances of the wager.'

'Please do,' Sophy said. She didn't really care. His manner was charming. She warmed to him like a flower to the sun.

'It pains me to admit it but I was tricked by Viscount Merryford into believing I had lost you to him in payment for some gambling debts. It was an untruth. I had lost my immediate memory following the curricle accident and did not realize I had been tricked until it was too late. By then I had already contracted into a second wager in an attempt to win you back.'

'How noble,' Sophy remarked.

'Viscount Merryford wagered that I should marry within three months. I had to agree to it. It was a matter of honour and Merryford was not to be trusted.'

'I see Merryford for what he is, Ben. Do not fear on that score,' Sophy said quickly but she did not really want this particular subject, Ben's marriage, to go any further. 'Where are we going?'

'Nowhere in particular. I just wanted to see you alone.'

'I might have guessed!' Sophy laughed.

'You are in remarkably good humour,' he observed.

'Indeed. You have been away and I venture to say that I have missed you.'

'Sophy, will you . . . will you say you'll marry me? We do rub along quite splendidly. For heaven's sake, this is a farce!'

'No — '

'Very well.' He sighed. She thought her heart might snap in two. What was she thinking? Of course she wanted to marry him? Why had she said no? She must take it back, quickly.

'Ben. I — '

'I don't want to hear it,' he cut in savagely and gave his ribbons a sharp flick. 'Let us have no more on the subject.'

Sophy stole a glance at his stiffened features; strained to hear something other than the dreadful silence. Even the birds seemed to have gone quiet. Ben's knuckles were white. He held the ribbons grasped in his hands as if they were a carving knife and fork in a very old joint. Her heart rose into her throat. She should speak, say something. Anything would be better . . . she could not.

The trees and the fields and the hedges passed by, faster than before. Sophy pulled her cloak tighter around her. It seemed colder than earlier.

After some time and several villages Ben drew them into the yard of an inn, the Red Lion. The low, whitewashed building was several hundred years old and stood quite alone, surrounded by tall lime trees. The sort of place to be frequented by smugglers and ill-doers, Sophy thought, and wondered why they should stop here. They had passed a number of far more agreeable-looking hostelries.

'Some refreshment?' he said, but she did

not believe his smile. She leaned on his hand to step out of the curricle and decided she must say something on the subject of their marriage. Her whole future depended on it. Why was she suddenly struck with fear like a goose?

'Ben . . . ' she began.

'Lemonade? I expect they will have some,' he said and she knew at once that something was wrong. Something in his expression wasn't quite right. His brow should be creased but it was smooth; his eyes should be twinkling with vexation but they were unnaturally dull.

'Ben, what is wrong?' she heard herself squeak, and below, fluttering in her chest, was a sudden, unexpected feeling of alarm.

'Wrong? Nothing is wrong. Come inside.' Yet his voice held an undertone of impatience he could not wholly suppress. Sophy hesitated but rested her hand on his arm and allowed him to lead her into the inn.

He seemed to know the place. No sooner were they inside than Ben opened a door to the left, which took them directly into a sitting-room, a square, dark-panelled room with a heartily burning fire. Not quite empty. A man stood with his back to the window — a priest!

'Ben!' Sophy pulled her hand from his arm

and turned to leave. She had no doubt what the priest was there for. What kind of low trick was this?

Ben's fingers clasped her wrist and held her still while with his other hand he calmly turned the key in the lock and put it in his pocket.

'Let me go!' Sophy said loudly. 'What do you think you are doing? You are as bad as that low fellow, Merryford!'

'Where's the priest I was expecting?' Ben said in a voice that could only be described as dangerous.

'He could not come,' the priest mumbled.

'Ben! What is going on?' Sophy demanded and shook her arm. Ben gripped it tighter but ignored her.

'I specifically asked for a priest.'

'You have a priest,' the priest said and ventured a small, uncertain smile.

'Hell and damnation!' Ben swore and dropped his hold on her and advanced towards the priest.

She had to get out of here, keep her wits about her. Sophy flew to the door but of course it was locked. She banged her fists on it and shouted. 'Help!'

She stumbled backwards as Ben's arms came around her middle and pulled her away from the door.

'For heaven's sake, Sophy!' he said as if she was a disobedient child.

'I am not standing for this!' Sophy said, and struggled to be free of him even though the traitorous sensations of being pressed next to his body were suggesting a completely different response entirely. She stamped her feet.

'Sophy!' he shouted. His anger sounded so developed she stilled for a moment, uncertain. Not defeated, only uncertain how to proceed.

He took the advantage, swinging her around and into his arms properly, pressing her into his chest, capturing her lips in a single, well-executed movement, laying siege to her confused heart.

It beat all the more erratically. Pulses of joy as well as anger swept through her.

He pulled away as forcefully as he had begun to kiss her, let her go apart from one hand he held firmly in his.

Sophy pressed her free hand to her lips. They stung. That they had been kissing in front of a man of the cloth! Heat flooded her. Her knees were threatening to buckle. Her head began to throb. 'Ben?' she muttered so low he did not hear her.

'Shall we proceed?' Ben said to the priest.

The priest, who seemed lost under a mass

of grey hair, fumbled in his cassock and pulled out a small black leather book and leafed through it.

Ben pulled her forward. She almost lost her balance. Finding it snapped Sophy back to attention. His urbane manner grated on her, raised the goose-flesh on her back. So he thought he could kiss her into submission! Ha!

She aimed a sharp kick at his ankle; hit his boot with frustratingly little result. 'How dare you think you can make me marry you in this way!' She kicked his shin, still to no discernible effect. 'You are an ogre of the worst kind!'

'If there was another way, Sophy, I would have taken it,' Ben said. His eyes darkened. Outside it had begun to rain heavily, pattering against the small windows and casting everything in a grey gloom.

'Have you a licence?' Sophy said, breaking his quelling gaze and determined to muster her thoughts. 'We can't be married without a licence. And can we be married in an inn? Do we not have to be in a church to be married legally?'

Ben pulled a piece of folded paper from his pocket, shook it open and thrust it under her nose. It looked like a special licence for all she knew and someone had certainly signed it with a flourish in brown ink.

'We can't marry without my consent!' Sophy said, knowing her voice sounded off-key and that she was trembling now. She longed to be able to shake Ben off yet he stood firm, holding her with a grip that did not hurt her but was iron nonetheless and impervious to her twisting. If Ben could not be persuaded, she must try to deter the priest. 'Father, sir, listen to me. I have not given my consent to this marriage.'

The priest looked at her and cleared his throat. Despicable man! Her father would never agree to such a clandestine commission. Ben must have paid this corrupt fellow handsomely.

'I was given to understand your father consented to the marriage?' the priest mumbled and stroked his grey beard.

'He did, yes . . . but . . .' Sophy shook her head sadly. Tears were welling behind her eyes. In a moment she would not be able to see, let alone think. She blinked rapidly.

'Sophy!' Ben said and she thought the anguish she heard behind that one utterance of her name would choke her. She coughed and spluttered. He let go of her wrist and cupped her shoulders, gently. 'Don't cry! For heaven's sake!'

'Ben, why are you doing this?' she managed

to say, in a voice not much louder than a whisper.

He pulled out a large handkerchief and dabbed her eyes with it. He stroked her hair away from her forehead, kissed her there. It only made the tears come the more. How could he be so domineering and yet tender? 'You are going to be so delightfully happy, my darling Sophy!'

'How can I be happy when you insist on forcing me into this?' she demanded. Would it do any good if she threw herself down on the floor at the mercy of the priest?

There was a silence so loud she wanted to press her fingers in her ears and shut her eyes. She did not. She stared out of the window at the enveloping, menacing grey and tried to remain standing — lucid, aware, steady.

'Get on with it!' Ben said to the priest in a voice brimming with muted anger. He stuffed his handkerchief into her unwilling hand and seized her other hand, which he brought up and kissed with hot lips before settling it fast and enwrapped in his own.

There was no escape and even if he had let her go, unlocked the door and opened it for her she would have been in an utter confusion over what to do.

The priest began to read the marriage

service from his book. Sophy pressed the cool cloth on to her eyes, removed most of the damp and bit her lip as she tried to listen. She was about to be fastened to this man for ever, until death parted them. Wasn't this what she wanted?

Yes, but not this way. Yet something stopped her protesting too much. Ben was impetuous, headstrong and determined. She could be stubborn also, this she knew. Heavens knew how Ben had tried every trick in the book to bend her will to his and this was his last resort. Perhaps there could be a future for them? Perhaps.

She had stopped listening to the priest. She drew herself back to the present and took in the expectant silence around her.

'Repeat these words after me,' the priest said, and she did, and yet didn't hear a word of it. A buzzing as loud as a swarm of bees driven from their hive crowded her mind. More than anything else she wanted this to be over and she wanted to go home.

She would never go home, she realized, as she mouthed the last of her promises.

She tried to listen to Ben as he spoke his vows. His voice was firm, determined, everything she would expect to be yet there was an underlying unhappiness. He was not wholly satisfied it had come to this either but that knowledge gave her no comfort.

He had a ring — gold — but she hardly noticed it. The priest kept speaking but she did not hear the words. She saw Ben's unhappiness, which he tried to disguise under the feathering of his eyelashes, and she wanted instinctively to share it, to ease his self-inflicted burden, despite everything.

Yet she could not. Even when he pressed her into his arms, all she felt was limp, wrung out like an old cloth. He had gone too far.

He let her go. The shock of being away from his warmth and being able to lean on him struck her. Sophy noticed the priest began to shuffle away. Was it all over? What now? She felt curiously dizzy. The edges of her vision were clouding. She reached out towards Ben, needing to steady herself. The ground was moving. She was falling into blackness.

★   ★   ★

Sophy felt rather faint but that was not half as alarming as the fact that she was moving — and quickly — but without her feet touching the ground. She was being carried in a pair of strong, male arms. It could only be Ben. She flicked her eyes open and found herself staring at his hard, clean-shaven jaw.

'Ben?' Oh dear, her voice sounded very shaky. 'What on earth — '

'Hush!' he said. Sophy stared at the dark oak-beamed ceiling and breathed the sweet smell of beer and pie crust. Why was Ben carrying her through a public house?

'Ben, where are — '

He fixed her with a piercing but strangely gentle gaze. 'I am going to find somewhere to put you down, Sophy, so you can have a rest.'

'Rest? Why — ' It hit her forcibly as she remembered. She wanted to be sick. Her every sinew went limp; she struggled to breathe, to think, to speak. 'Ben? We are married, aren't we? Tell me!'

'Straight upstairs, my lord,' she heard some firm tones say.

'Thank you,' Ben replied and immediately she was being carried up the stairs. It got darker. There were other people with them as well. She caught a glimpse of a large ruddy-faced lady wearing an apron as Ben swung around in the upstairs landing and strode into a bedchamber.

He placed her very gently on top of a large feather bed and looked down at her with such open, sympathetic eyes she thought she would cry.

A snap and crackle. Someone had lit the fire.

'Sophy, you are indeed now my wife, I am pleased to say.' Ben sat at her side on the bed and pulled her hands into his. They were warm, comforting. If only she could stay here like this and by some miracle it would all go away!

'Mrs Best,' Ben said to the lady in the apron, 'would you by any chance have some laudanum?'

'I don't want laudanum!' Sophy pulled her hands away and pushed herself so that she was sitting upright. 'I want you to tell me exactly what has happened. Exactly.'

The tears were already brimming but she told herself she must hold them back. She could do this. She could face it. She must know.

'Sophy, you said your vows,' Ben said quietly. 'We are married.'

So it was true. She had known it in her bones. She felt frozen. She didn't need emotion. What was the use when nothing could be done to get back to how they were before?

'Is it really so terrible?' he said. 'I can protect you properly now; look after you! Mrs Best, would you please have some tea brought up here? Thank you.'

'Certainly, your lordship,' the woman said. She curtsied and left them alone.

There were so many things Sophy would have liked to say to him, but all of them were so vicious and unworthy that she did not. He had behaved abominably but the intentions behind it were good, and this situation was, at least in part, of her own making. Stupid fool, she told herself. This is what happens when you play with fire.

She had said her marriage vows in front of a man of the cloth. It wasn't as if Ben had held a pistol to her. She had married him of her own volition.

She wanted to laugh. That was hardly appropriate.

'I had better go home and tell my father,' she said, in a voice that didn't sound like her own.

'Are you sure?' Ben said. His brow creased. 'We can, of course, leave for Middleton tomorrow if that's what you want?'

She had no idea what she wanted.

Ben bent towards her. She was aware that they were alone in the room. Was he going to kiss her? Only her forehead. His lips brushed across her skin with the lightest of touches.

'Don't!' she heard herself exclaim, even though his kiss made her tremble with wanton excitement. She ignored the hurt appeal in his eyes and said, 'Please, Ben, don't. Don't kiss me. I don't think I can bear it. Not yet. Let me be for a while. I need to get used to what has happened.'

He pushed himself off the bed and walked away. By the time she'd wits about her to sit up he had gone and she was left alone in the inn chamber. A small room with one leaden window, a dresser, a chair, the bed and her unhappiness!

Oh, would that she were a romantic poet and could have channelled her sadness into a few artful, meaningful, paper-bound words!

With no one watching, it was too easy to give in to womanish tears. She hugged her knees up against her chest and rocked herself, as if she imagined she was still a child and it would somehow comfort her.

12

Benedict St Michael, handsome, clever and rich, with a comfortable home and happy disposition, seemed to unite some of the best blessings of existence, and had lived nearly thirty-one years in the world with very little to distress or vex him.

Now he slammed his fist into the cracked bark of the trunk of an oak tree. Shock jolted the bones and a searing pain shot through his arm. He stopped himself crying out, lifted his fist to see that it was grazed and pressed it into the palm of his other hand to ease the stinging.

He looked up at the sound of crunching footsteps on the gravelly ground and saw Jack Walden, ridiculous-looking in his priestly garbs, running up the lane towards him.

'Harty!' Jack called. For heavens sake, his priestly grey beard was half hanging off! Hadn't he used enough glue to fasten it to his chin properly?

'There is no point punishing yourself over it — what's done is done,' Jack said, as he came to a halt in front of him and tried not to appear out of breath. He placed his hand on the tree trunk and leaned on it. 'Come on, let's go back to the inn and see what the landlord can haul from his cellar that will be a better medicine for your temper.'

'You don't quite seem to realize exactly what it is I have done,' Ben said savagely. 'Nor did I until I saw it for myself. Hell! I've ruined everything!'

'Does she suspect the marriage was false?'

Ben gave a snort of pained laughter. 'No, it seems my faux-wife is not so well versed on marriage law.'

'Well, then — '

'That is not the point. The point is that . . . hell! It's like breaking a horse before it's ready to be broken. The look in the eyes and you know the animal will never truly be yours.'

'If she believes she is yours, though?'

'For how long? How long before someone finds out, before she finds out it's just not legal to be married clandestinely in such a fashion? Why the devil couldn't you come up with a real priest? I thought that was what we agreed?'

'Don't turn it back on me!' Jack pulled himself up straight. 'I did find a fellow but he got cold feet at the last minute. He offered to lend me his things for a small donation, however. What would you have done?'

'I would put the robes on myself,' Ben replied and sighed. 'Sorry, Jack. You did what any decent friend would do.'

'Harty, listen. Tell her it would upset your family too much to know the true circumstances and so invent a lie about your wedding for public consumption.'

'Lies, lies and more damn lies!' Ben swung himself about and stamped his feet on the ground. As if that would do any good! 'What an absolutely fine start to a marriage! A marriage that is itself a lie . . . Oh, it will never do. I'm going to have to confess to her and be done with it.'

'Ah! Guilt. Well, Harty, I'll say this. Don't do anything rash. You don't want to lose her now, do you? Surely that's the last thing you want?'

'Rash? Heavens, the whole scheme was rash and ill-thought-out from the start! But you're right. I've dug myself this hellish hole and I have to get out of it but in the meantime at least I've got her, so to speak. But what if the price is too high, Jack?'

Jack pressed at the errant beard, fingering it with some signs of uncertainty. 'That's for you — and her — to decide.'

★ ★ ★

Sophy poured some cold water from the ewer into the basin on the dresser and then splashed it on her face. She found a ragged but clean towel in one of the drawers and dried her face and hands. The tea that had been brought up by one of the inn's servants was still hot and she drank some quickly.

That felt better!

She took a moment to inspect her face in the mirror. Her eyes were still a little red but that could not be helped. She patted her cheeks vigorously to put some colour in them and tucked her stray curls back into place as best she could before putting her bonnet back on.

That would do. Sophy took one last glance in the mirror and then made purposefully for the door. Out on the empty landing she spied the stairs and hastened towards them. Now where was Ben?

She found him, following a slightly improper search of the inn's public rooms, in the yard. He was sitting on a bench next to the water trough, his back to her — he was staring out towards the road. She saw him run his hand through his hair. Her husband now, for better or worse; she would make sure it was for the better. As Mary would say, 'There ain't a purpose in grieving over spilt milk.'

'Ben?'

He turned and regarded her. An unusual expression that suggested repose had settled on his countenance. Sophy could not believe he was that tranquil underneath. He had better not be that unperturbed by the day's events!

'Let's head back to Fordham Manor,' he said and rose. He called over to the ostler. 'Hey!'

Sophy refused the offer of waiting inside while the curricle and pair were prepared and sat on the bench where Ben had been. If that was not appropriate behaviour for the new Lady Hart, he only had to say. What did she know! She had been brought up with the expectation that she might marry a curate or some such lowly gentleman. Not a lord!

She amused herself by staring at a cat who was walking along the ridge of the stable roof.

Ben said nothing to her of any consequence until they were in the curricle and away.

'Lady Hart is likely to be somewhat distressed by our news,' he said, after clearing his throat.

'Very true,' Sophy agreed.

'I suggest it is presented to her in a favourable fashion. She would not like it to know the marriage took place in an inn — '

'And behind a locked door and by the hand

238

of a corrupt priest! No, I can quite see that.'

Ben coughed. 'We had better say it was all agreed by us both beforehand.'

'Oh yes, why tarnish a good story with the truth!'

'I went to London to procure the special licence. That is true.'

'Always some fire behind a lot of smoke.'

Ben frowned.

Sophy pulled her cloak up tightly around her chin and looked away towards the fields.

'We must . . . ' Ben began. His voice was trying to be firm! 'We must explain that we were prompted into such rash behaviour because it is . . . a love match.'

'How romantic!'

'Sophy, it *is* a love match, d'you hear? Why the devil do you think . . . ? What do you think made me . . . ?' Sophy turned her head to see Ben staring straight ahead, his lips firmly pressed together.

Benedict St Michael was having some difficulties! How the mighty have fallen, Sophy thought, and then regretted her lack of charity.

'It is possible,' she said gently, 'that you and I disagree somewhat on that definition of love.'

'I didn't know what love was until I met you!' Ben snapped. 'Had I known I would have avoided you like the plague! In fact, that is the perfect metaphor. You are like a disease and yet you dangle the prospect of a cure in front of me that I absolutely must have!'

He whipped the ribbons with force and they accelerated.

'Ben, I do want our marriage to work out well, however inauspiciously it has started.'

Ben tore a glance at her and pulled the ribbons. They slowed.

'No reason why you shouldn't have a devil of a good time married to me,' Ben said. They stopped and the horses chafed at the bit. He leaned forward. The trees rustled above, echoing his heavy breath. They could not temper his closeness.

She saw him coming like a blur yet the touch of his lips on hers was a shock. Sophy started. Yet in a moment she had yielded. He insisted on gaining entrance; plundered. She tasted his purpose, responded to his force.

Honey- and sugar-laced. But behind, from some depths, were short stabs of a curious bitter taste. Frustration? Something she could not name.

She heard the chirp of a songbird; felt a cold rush of breeze against the side of her face.

She broke away.

She had to breathe! Sophy took in large,

gulping breaths. Ben raised her fingers to his lips and kissed them intimately.

'We shall enjoy ourselves splendidly, if we put our minds to it,' Ben said, and grinned in a way that invited her to join him.

Sophy could not help smiling. Perhaps a way could be found where they could rub along together?

'Let's go,' Ben said. His lips twitched and he flicked the ribbons hard. The curricle jolted into motion.

* * *

Lady Hart looked as white as a sheet. *Please don't faint*, Sophy said to herself, as if Lady Hart might somehow be able to read her thoughts and obey them.

'Mother — '

'Don't!' Lady Hart managed to snap. She turned her head away towards the drawing-room fire, which was blazing merrily. 'I can't bear it!'

'Why all the fuss? The gel is delightful, m'dear. What he needs,' Lord Fordham said grumpily and shifted in his chair. At least the Lincolns were absent, Sophy thought. Ben had requested this interview in the drawing-room with his mother alone as soon as they had arrived. They must have sensed the crackle of tension in the air as the Lincolns had left soundlessly. Lord Fordham had remained where he was. It was his house; he was entitled not to have to be inconvenienced by the goings-on of his guests.

'Mama, the expediency was *necessary* — '

'Heavens!' Colour shot into Lady Hart's cheeks. She stood up with haste and patted the seat she had vacated. 'Benedict! Of course! Sophy, m'dear, sit down.'

Sophy didn't think she'd seen Lady Hart move with such rapidity on any previous occasion. After a pause she moved towards the proffered chair.

Lady Hart seized the rug from across Lord Fordham's knees in one fell swoop and shook it in Sophy's direction. Sophy sat down very quickly.

'What the devil?' Lord Fordham grunted and woke up from his unexpected doze.

'Here,' Lady Hart said and tucked the rug around Sophy's knees and ankles.

'Mother!'

'Benedict!' Lady Hart's brows snapped into a fierce frown. 'We must look after her now that's she's breeding!'

Breeding! Sophy swallowed.

Ben shot her a hard stare.

'Oh, thank you, Lady Hart. It may well be a false alarm, you know.'

'My rug!' Lord Fordham said querulously. He slapped one hand across his knee and opened one eye very wide and accusingly in Lady Hart's direction.

She did not appear to notice but Ben did and he moved over to ring the bell for a servant.

'Now you sit there quietly, m'dear.' Lady Hart gave her a motherly look. Sophy smiled in return. There was nothing to be done for the moment but accept these unnecessary solicitations, it seemed. Unless she was to be the recipient of the second ever virgin birth in the history of mankind, there was no danger that she was increasing at all. But it put in her mind that it was a future possibility. More than that, it would be expected that she would produce an heir, would it not?

'About time there were the patter of tiny feet. I'm getting bored with the company of old people,' Lord Fordham said.

'Thank you, Mama, for your kind solicitations but Sophy and I have some things of import to discuss. You will excuse us?'

Ben flicked his gaze at her and Sophy rose. In truth she would rather go with Ben than sit here in the middle of such awkwardness.

'What shall I tell the Lincolns?' Lady Hart insisted.

'Tell them what you will.' Ben waved his hand.

'Benedict, do you not wish to break the news yourself? Miss Lincoln — '

'Miss Lincoln had never been so foolish as to expect an offer of marriage from me, despite the best efforts of her mother to encourage her to do so.' Sophy saw the white flush of impatience on Ben's countenance.

He turned on his heel and made purposefully for the door. Sophy caught up with him and he grasped her hand and took him with her, out into the hall and straight through to the billiard room opposite.

'Ben?' she gasped, almost tripping on her skirts in her haste to keep up with him.

She stood on the deep-coloured and patterned oriental carpet with her back to the billiard table as he locked the door. He rounded on her, an eyebrow raised. 'I would rather we were not disturbed.'

Something about the way he said it made her insides tingle. She shivered.

'Why on earth is there no fire in here?' Ben exclaimed, his brow creasing.

Sophy turned to regard the empty brass grate that had been polished and had a fire laid but not lit. She felt his arms wrap around her shoulders and draw her into his warmth. It was so easy to sink into him. His lips

244

brushed the top of her head and she let her eyes close for the moment, enjoying the intimate sensation. Yet she must speak.

'Ben, is it really necessary to lie to Lady Hart?' She felt him stiffen. 'I am not . . . increasing.'

'That can be sorted out,' Ben said evenly, and caught the tip of her nose in his lips. How was it possible, he wondered, that a woman could taste so delicious? He didn't need any reminders of the deception. His mother seemed reconciled enough. In truth, he thought it would be a lot worse.

Now he had to work on making sure that Sophy was entirely his so that he could be sure, when he revealed the false nature of their marriage, she would want to marry him for real, not leave him in disgust.

Just that thought sent a hot stab of fear bolting through to his core. He must, must make sure she was his, absolutely. He pushed her hair from her face, kissed every inch of her forehead, brushed with the lightest touch her eyelids. He heard her gasp and sigh before he rewarded her by meeting her lips.

He ran his hand down to the small of her back, pulled her into the curve of him so that she was moulded to him. He rested his lips on her neck, could feel the wild flurry of her heartbeat, could not stop himself groaning.

'I had thought just a kiss,' he said, moving back and putting inches of air between them while he was still in control of his actions. 'It will never be just a kiss with you.'

'No,' she agreed, in a voice no louder than a whisper, and looked at him thoughtfully.

Ben turned the key in the lock and opened the door.

'Right, upstairs!' he said and scooped her up into his arms. He caught her by surprise so by the time she protested, they were already in the hallway and headed for the stairs.

'Ben! Someone will see!'

'What if they do?'

He hastened up the stairs. The door to his chamber was ajar and he gave it a push with his foot and swept in.

'Out!' he said to Edwards, his valet, who was putting some linens away in the armoire. Sophy's cheeks burned. Ben watched her turn her face into his chest and bite her lip.

'Edwards, you can finish that later,' Ben said in a more pleasant tone of voice for Sophy's benefit, not Edwards'. Would the man just go!

'My lord.' Edwards hastily left what he was doing and withdrew.

Ben threw Sophy on to the bed and then went to lock the door and draw the curtains.

By the time he was back at the bedside, Sophy was sitting up. Her eyes sparkled in the dim light. Heavens, how he wanted to . . .

A curtain of confusion rustled over her face. She looked down. She needed kissing, she needed unwrapping and caressing, she —

Ben's fingers found their way to her chin and raised it so that her trembling blue eyes met his. She looked so fragile, as delicate as porcelain.

A ball of anguish rolled down his throat and into his stomach. He did not deserve her love, not yet, not while he had deceived her so abominably.

Ben found he could hardly hold her gaze, not knowing everything he knew and she did not. He leaned forward. Her lips parted instinctively for him to kiss her.

Her warm sweetness stung him instantly and sent flames of desire racing through him. She let him in without hesitation, wanted his kiss to increase in force, to plunder as deep as he could. He could not ignore the invitation. Never before had the taste of a woman so comprehensively and so quickly provoked him to arousal. The excitement of a new mistress, and of one keen to prove her skill at fanning his lust, was nothing compared to this.

She pushed herself into him. The feel of

her chest against his, although they were still fully clothed, made him want to catch his breath in wonder that there was yet more to be stirred.

He would have to channel every ounce of strength in his will to rein it in. He must give her every pleasure, proceed slowly and with every care. He would take his satisfaction only once he knew she had had hers.

He eased her backwards so she wriggled beneath him but it was no good. He drew her up again to be able to undo the tiny buttons of her dress that went all down her back to her middle. She breathed and shivered in his arms, dared to kiss him as if she was trying to distract him from undressing her although he knew she was not.

She eased herself out of her dress. He pulled it over her head and then stood up to drape it carefully across the chair. He came back and noticed the flush of red across her collarbones, the push of her breasts against their stays. He would free them in a moment but first himself.

Ben whipped his neckcloth away, shook his jacket and waistcoat off and cast them on the same chair, pulled uncaringly at his shirt. It dropped to the floor. He watched her as she watched him; saw the swell of her chest, the depth of her breathing, the widening of her eyes. They darkened, and it was not because the light was dim, he thought to his satisfaction.

Then he undid and pulled off his boots and finally peeled his breeches from his legs. She would have already seen the bulge the tight-fitting buckskins could not hide, but he wondered what she thought now he was completely naked. She gave no inkling that she did not like what she saw.

He pressed himself against her, covered her soft body with his hard one, felt a quickening of her breath.

Ben groaned. He had thought this would be easy, a simple matter of seduction, but now he was confused as to who was seducing whom.

'Ben?' she muttered. Her voice sounded like music, soothed his befuddled reason. Her fingers brushed his temples. Or did he imagine it? For the moment his eyes were closed while he tried to bring back some sense of orientation. The blood pounded.

He opened his eyes for a moment, just in time to register the colour in her face, before he plundered into a hot kiss.

13

Let other pens dwell on guilt and misery. Sophy, indeed, at this very time, must have been happy in spite of everything. She must have been a happy creature in spite of all that she felt.

'What happened?' she said.

Ben groaned and buried his head in her chest. She stroked his hair. It felt pleasant, having him pressed against her, keeping her warm.

'I love you,' she told him.

Ben shifted his weight to one side, raised his head and looked at her.

'Did you . . . enjoy it?' he asked. There was a slight frown across his brow. Sophy reached up and smoothed her fingers over it. His forehead felt damp.

'Yes. It was most peculiar, but certainly pleasant!' Sophy giggled. It seemed so silly to be lying here in bed like this — in the middle of the afternoon!

Ben's lips quirked.

'You have convinced me of one thing,' she added.

'What's that?'

'That there are some very good reasons for marriage.' Even as she said it she could not ignore the feeling of foreboding. What Ben would say when he found out she was a published writer was still to be determined. That she was a novelist and that she planned to continue writing were two truths that could not remain hidden for ever.

Ben rolled over to one side and Sophy suddenly felt very exposed.

'Should we get dressed again?'

'If you wish,' Ben replied. He propped himself up on his elbow and ran his hand lazily across her front. Her skin tingled where he touched it. 'Or you could stay just as you are and allow me to make love to you over and over again for the rest of the afternoon.'

'Ben!' She was shocked. It was one thing sneaking away for a few minutes with the excuse of having a private conversation but . . . 'What will your mother say?'

Ben tucked his arm around her middle and pulled her towards him and into a masterful embrace. 'The dowager Lady Hart's chief concern will be that her first grandchild is on the way.'

★   ★   ★

'We are of course extremely upset to have missed the wedding,' Lady Lincoln said and let her spoon clatter against her soup plate.

'Naturally,' Ben replied.

Sophy tried to sit still and concentrate on her oxtail soup. She felt curiously stiff. In fact many parts of her, particularly her legs, positively ached.

'Will you hold a ball at Hartfield Bury or a celebration sooner in town, do you think?' Lady Lincoln pressed.

'We have not thought,' Ben replied.

Sophy glanced at him, curious to see the expression on his face. Ben caught her eye and smiled and Sophy felt a blush begin to rise in her cheeks. She hastily picked up her wine glass and took a large sip and hoped that she managed to hide her discomfort successfully. Where the company supposed she and Ben had been all afternoon she did not know and did not like to think.

'My dear,' Lady Hart interjected, 'it was all very sudden. Circumstances, you know, made the wedding expedient but I must say I am delighted Benedict has come up to scratch at last. Such a worry having unmarried children.'

Sophy wished she could hide under the table and cover her face.

'Mama!'

'For heaven's sake, woman!' Lord Fordham growled. 'Can't you see the poor gel's blushing?'

'I expect Persephone will take immediately! She'll be the toast of the ton.' Lady Lincoln snapped.

'That's two of 'em red-cheeked now,' Lord Fordham observed.

'Shall we talk about something else?' Sir Josiah was not a man of many words, Sophy had noticed, but she was extremely pleased he had chosen to expend a few of them now.

'Tomorrow,' Ben said to her in the drawing-room after dinner, in a low voice that could not be overheard. 'Tomorrow we leave for Hartfield Bury. Alone. And be at liberty to enjoy our honeymoon.'

'Thank you,' Sophy whispered and could not deny that her heart jumped at the promise in his words.

'It is not only for your sake and sanity!'

★   ★   ★

Ben saw Sophy up to her bedchamber, kissed her soundly but then left her for the night — a calculated move. She'd be all the more receptive to him tomorrow night when he would have her at his will in their own private rooms in a very good and comfortable inn.

Tomorrow he would insist that his dear mama remained by the seaside for at least another month, leaving him and Sophy free to return to Hartfield Bury undisturbed. Besides the honeymoon he had promised Sophy, there was the question of their marriage to be solved. It had come to him at dinner. He still had the special licence — genuine and paid for. He would be the perfect husband to Sophy in every way so that she would know she could not live without him. He hated to think in this way, but it was true that if she fell with child that would be another thing to bind her to him for ever.

He was set though that as soon as they reached Hartfield Bury, he would tell her. She would be furious and upset, but without an interfering family around them, they could arrange a quiet and true wedding without delay and all would be well.

★   ★   ★

Sophy watched in surprise as Ben bade her good night and left her bedchamber. She had thought he might stay, well, a little longer. She felt suddenly alone, which was foolish because she had gone to bed every single evening of her entire life on her own. Perhaps she would do some writing before she went to sleep.

A whine that sounded like Nelson's came from outside her door. Sophy went over and opened it and sure enough it was Nelson. He wagged his tail hopefully.

'I'm not sure you're allowed up here but come in,' she said. 'How did you know I would be in need of some company?'

Nelson gave a very low woof.

'Shhh!' Sophy said and put her finger to her mouth.

Nelson padded in and she knelt down to meet him. Nelson licked her hands and face and Sophy wrapped her arms about him and rested her head against his flank.

'Thank you, Nelson, for being such a stalwart friend!' she said. Nelson panted with pleasure and she felt him wag his tail the more.

'I might have known!'

Sophy stumbled to her feet with a start. No wonder she hadn't heard the door opening — she hadn't closed it! Ben stood in the doorway wearing an amused expression.

'Oh! You gave me a fright! I thought you had retired for the night?'

'I had, but it seems that Nelson has been spending his nights with Lord Fordham and they have become firm friends. Fordham is kicking up a rumpus that the dog must be found! I had a couple of ideas where he might have got to.'

Nelson hung his head.

'Come on, dog, you can't serve two masters. Or a master and a mistress!'

Nelson obediently trotted over to Ben.

'Good night, then.' Ben said.

'Good night.'

'You don't mind, do you? Lord Fordham adopting Nelson? I suspect he needs the company more than we do though you won't get him to admit it.'

'Oh, no.' Sophy shook her head.

'It's just that you look a little sad?' He looked as if he would take a step forward towards her.

'Good night, Ben,' Sophy said as firmly as she could and forced herself to smile. Please, let him get out of here before she did dissolve into tears! She didn't want him to see her cry. He was hardly going to respect her writing if she kept giving him plenty of reasons to believe her a weak and feeble female.

*　*　*

Twelve hours and a fitful sleep later, Sophy stood on the gravel outside the front of Fordham Manor. Everyone had gathered outside to see them off. It was going to be quite a different journey back to Hartfield Bury, Sophy mused. They had come here in a cavalcade of carriages. They were returning a *deux* in Ben's new curricle. The journey would be faster, unless the weather turned against them, but there was not even room for all her luggage.

'Do accept my sincere felicitations for your marriage,' Miss Persephone Lincoln said and squeezed Sophy's hand.

'Thank you,' Sophy replied and thought it was a shame she had not had the opportunity to build up more of an acquaintance with Miss Lincoln. She had never really had any friends of a similar age. 'Good luck with your season in London.'

'I shall write to you at Hartfield Bury?'

'Oh,' Sophy said and smiled. 'Do!'

'Are we ready?' Ben seized her hand. Sophy looked at his face with a mixture of pride and wonder. Her husband, she thought. Who would have thought that only yesterday they were not even married! So much had happened in the last few hours.

Ben held her hand as she stepped into the curricle and then tucked the rug around her legs. The closeness of him made her tremble.

'Don't give him an inch, gel!' Lord Fordham called out and coughed.

Sophy smiled and found herself biting her lip. Ben jumped into his seat in a moment and whipped the ribbons. Sophy waved and watched Lady Hart, wearing the fixed expression she had all morning of neither pleasure nor displeasure, wave in return.

They were soon around the corner and out of sight. She would not have to worry about Lady Hart for a while. Did she imagine it, or did now their marriage truly begin?

'Did you sleep well?' Ben asked. There had been such a fuss about their departure this morning, they had not exchanged above a dozen words with each other and certainly none in private.

'No,' Sophy said, surprised that she had not lied. 'I missed you last night.'

Ben thought his chest had been slain in two — with a blood axe. His jaw was set on edge. He struggled to know what to say. Hell! When had he ever felt so less in command, so less self-assured than when he was with her? It was confounding.

She glanced away. Heavens, now she would think he refused to answer her! Ben flicked the ribbons urgently. Quick! They needed a mile under their belts.

'Sophy,' Ben said, with absolutely no idea what he was going to say next.

She looked at him and he was rewarded

with that smile of hers he so loved — so delicate, so delightful, so infectious. 'Yes, Ben?'

'How . . . sorry I am to hear you missed me. I hope . . . '

She put her finger to her smiling lips. He rather thought she might wink at him for good measure. An uncomfortable sensation occurred in his pantaloons. Ah, Ben thought with a spread of satisfaction, this spinney of elm trees would do!

Ben pulled the curricle into the side of the road beneath the trees. They were sheltered to some extent from prying eyes, and the road was empty. His fingers stole on to her chin.

'Ben,' she breathed, and that was all she had time to say before her lips were his.

Blood pounded through him, obliterating every thought for a moment except the sweet, pliant taste of her. A stiff breeze ruffled the hair at the back of his neck, reminding him where he was. Ben ended the kiss swiftly, and flicked the ribbons before he was tempted to change his mind.

'Thank you, Ben,' she said, her voice sounding strangely shy. 'When you kiss me like that it puts my mind at rest and I know some of my fears are unfounded.'

'It aggravates my mind beyond compare!' Ben replied. 'Hang on, what fears?'

'Fears that things will not work out between us?'

'What the devil are you talking about?'

She did not answer immediately. She seemed to swallow and then her lips parted but it was a moment before the words came. 'There is something I have not told you.'

'What's that?' Ben felt his hands tighten their grip on the ribbons. He shot her a glance to see she was staring straight ahead and her face appeared impassive rather than troubled.

'Maybe I should tell you now?'

'For heaven's sake, woman! Is it material?'

Ben hoped her confidence was a womanish trifle and certainly not something that mattered because he had no intention of sharing his guilty secret with her yet.

'I write.'

'What?' Ben felt suddenly light-headed with relief. 'Is that it?'

'Yes.' She had turned her face towards him, Ben saw out of the corner of his eye. He couldn't look at her, although he would have liked to, because the road twisted and he had to concentrate on driving.

'What do you write? Letters?'

'Everyone writes letters! No, novels.'

'Novels?' Ben fancied smiling but didn't. He had suspected for a while that his Sophy was a little out of the ordinary. Did not her ability at chess prove her mind was rather overdeveloped for a female? Women did not have the same capacity as men to absorb complex information. Their natures were directed towards the domestic rather than the scientific.

'Yes, novels.'

'As long as it doesn't affect your health,' Ben said in a serious tone.

'My health?'

'A preoccupation with the grisly and Gothic such as one finds in the female novel could well be detrimental to health.' Ben was careful to keep his expression stern in case she was watching. 'So I have heard, both to the health of the body and the health of the mind.'

'Do you mean novels like Mrs Radcliffe's?' Sophy replied. Ben was surely not going to ban her from writing on health grounds! Did it all stem from having an invalid mother?

'The ones full of sinister and implausible goings-on, haunted castles and other such nonsense,' Ben replied. 'I've not read any m'self, naturally.'

'No, I don't write those sorts of stories. Far too much melodrama! Mine are far more ordinary. My interest is in character.'

'Good. Well, I have no objection to your

writing novels if that was your concern. I am not some tyrant!'

'You don't? Oh, Ben, thank you. No, I didn't think you were a tyrant. I thought rather you might not like it.'

'Why in heaven's name would I object? Women can have their interests — reading, playing pianoforte, painting, sewing and all that. Writing novels is not wholly regular, I'll grant you, but it's not as if you are going to be having them published!'

Oh dear. Sophy felt her heart sink. She was going to have to break the bad news to him. Perhaps it could wait for a while. She didn't want to deceive Ben but what if he banned her? Although she had promised herself that nothing would stop her writing, had things changed now? She had to consider whether it was worth potentially ruining her marriage over.

A spot of water landed on her nose. She looked up to see the sky had greyed. Another spot confirmed it was rain.

'I had hoped to get some miles beneath us before lunch but we'll have to stop at the next place,' Ben remarked through gritted teeth. He whipped the ribbons feverishly.

★   ★   ★

The rain was still pouring down outside, tapping against the window-panes solidly. It looked as if they would be here for a while, Ben thought, and crossed his legs. He stretched his arms out on the armrests of his chair and drummed the fingers of his right hand in time to the rain.

Ben picked up his teacup and tossed down some of the hot liquid. It was passable, a bit ashy-tasting. You couldn't always trust the tea they served in inns. Fortunately, overall, the first inn they had come to had turned out to be rather a good one with a nice small private sitting-room that had instantly been turned over to their disposal.

'I shall miss Nelson,' Sophy said and took a sip of her tea.

Ben glanced at her. She had a wistful look about her he could not exactly fathom but it made him feel he was in some way failing her. He shifted uncomfortably in his chair.

Hell, she wasn't lonely, was she? Lord Fordham was lonely but he lived by himself. Sophy was a young woman and had her father, and . . . ?

'Do you not have any brothers or sisters?' Ben asked suddenly. He didn't know why he hadn't asked her before. He'd just assumed not, but for all he knew she could have five brothers away sailing the sea in His

Britannic Majesty's Navy.

'No.' She shook her head. 'I did. A sister but she died when she was only a few days old. And my mother. Of the same fever.'

'I am sorry to hear that.' Ben placed his teacup down quietly on the table.

'Ben, what if we have a baby . . . ?' Sophy looked at him through her thick eyelashes and he was drawn into her gaze and stared at her. He wanted to kiss her. 'And it dies — ?'

'What?' he shouted. 'Nobody is going to die! Certainly no son or daughter of mine!'

He saw the flash of shock that went across her face. It was white. Good. The last thing he wanted was her having some fit of hysterics! Women!

'Why do you not have any brothers or sisters, Ben?' she asked. He admired her for having control of her emotions and smiled benevolently.

'I am surprised my dear mother managed to endure having me, let alone more,' he said in a kindly voice. 'I should not be surprised if I am actually some by-blow.'

'Ben, don't say that!' Sophy frowned.

'I'll say what I damn well like.' Ben pushed himself up from his chair and made for the door. He'd had enough womanish conversation for the moment and he either had to leave the room or admit that he was somewhat unsettled by it. He opened the door, stepped into the hall and shut it behind him.

★ ★ ★

And still it rained! If only it would stop and they could be on their way. Sophy wanted to kick herself. Why had she said such a foolish thing! The truth was, though, that it did worry her. And now she did not know what to think. She had either upset Ben or he simply didn't care.

Sophy stood up and walked over to the window. The water was gushing in rivulets towards a drain with a broken lid in the corner of the inn yard. The rain continued to fall like a sheet of droplets.

It would be easy, Sophy considered, to dissolve into tears. Sometimes they helped, sometimes they could not be helped. Now was not the time.

Slowly the rain began to ease although the sky still looked rather dark.

Sophy turned at the sound of a click of a door handle turning. Ben stood in the doorway; filled it.

She didn't care any more. Her stupid pride could be gone. Most important, more important than anything else — anything — was that she loved him. She held her skirts and ran over to him.

'Sophy!' he exclaimed but he could not disguise the light of pleasure that sparkled in his eyes. While there was love between them, they would find a way of working things out, Sophy was sure. She fell, like a bird coming back to the nest, into his arms.

'My Sophy,' he said and kissed the top of her head before manoeuvring her inside the room so he could close the door and kiss her properly.

She felt like she was ice melting into him and she could hardly feel her own body any more she was so close to him. His kiss was gentle, coaxing, comforting. Just enough before he broke off.

'Look,' he said.

She followed his gaze to the window where rays of sun were coming through the clouds. Lo and behold there was a rainbow! It must still be raining close by but no longer over the inn. There was a strange quietness. Sophy felt herself smiling.

'Let's go. I'd like to do some more miles before we stop for the night.'

★　★　★

'What do you mean you only have one room available?' Ben's fist crunched against the wall and he held it there, leaning very slightly on it.

Sophy put her hand to her mouth to stifle a yawn.

'Sorry, sir.' The landlord looked unrepentant.

'I am Lord Hart.'

'Sorry, your lordship.'

'Can't you see my wife is tired?' Ben's brow puckered into a frown. 'It's dark outside. The hour is very advanced.'

The landlord shrugged. 'I've only the one bed and the one bedchamber.'

'Who, may I ask, occupies your other chambers?'

'The Marquis of Rotherham and his family, your lordship.'

Sophy thought she saw Ben mouth a curse. He stood up straight and said, 'Well, then, nothing to be done. We'll take the room.'

'Who is the Marquis of Rotherham?' Sophy asked Ben later when they reached the privacy of their bedchamber.

'An extraordinarily dull fellow but he outranks me. Had it been an ordinary gentleman or mere baronet I certainly would have kicked up some dust.'

'I don't object to sleeping in the same

room with you. It might' — Sophy bit her lip — 'be fun?'

'There's the rub for it's going to be devilish difficult to get any sleep at all!' Ben pounced forward and swung Sophy up into his arms.

'Put me down!'

'Shush! You might as well start learning about society now you're going to have to deal with 'em. Lesson one. Lord Rotherham is a bore but Lady Rotherham is a hostess of the first water. They have a fine house just off Piccadilly and Rotherham's seat is in Dorset. You will meet 'em in due course, but not, I think, tonight.'

14

The novelty of travelling, and the happiness of being with Ben, soon produced their natural effect on Sophy's spirits. She skipped across the dull puddles in the inn yard, making her way towards the curricle.

'Lord Hart!' came in a thunderous boom. Sophy stopped and turned to see a tall and well-built gentleman of middle years coming over towards them.

'Rotherham!' Ben stopped and tipped his hat.

'What you doing here, eh?' Crimson-cheeked Lord Rotherham looked at her with his one eye that was permanently more open than the other. Sophy stared back at him.

'May I present my wife? Lord Rotherham, Lady Hart.'

Sophy stepped forward dutifully.

'Lady Hart, good morning to you.' Lord Rotherham gave a fraction of a bow. It was clear he did not quite believe it. 'Never thought I'd see you leg-shackled, m'boy.' He patted his waistcoat and drew out a monocle glass. He pressed it into his eye and then

269

regarded Sophy from head to foot. How dare he!

'My compliments, Lady Hart,' he said and sniffed. 'Well, m'boy, they'll be wanting to know where you found her.'

'I would be pleased if you would take your ill-mannered insinuations elsewhere, Rotherham. My bride is my distant cousin on my father's side.'

'Eh? Well, they'll be wanting to know. You know what women are like!' Lord Rotherham chuckled.

If she had felt at liberty to slap the awful man, she would have done. Sophy's fingers itched.

'We shall no doubt have the pleasure of your company soon, but for now, please excuse us. We must be on our way.' Ben stepped to Sophy's side and she felt his fingers curl in her own, determinedly, protectively.

'Good day!' Rotherham drawled and turned back to his own affairs with the ostler.

Ben handed Sophy into the curricle and within moments they were off. As soon as the inn was out of sight Sophy could contain herself no longer. 'If that is *society*, then I shall want nothing to do with them!'

'A valiant sentiment but not, unfortunately, entirely practical.'

'Why is that? I did not think you intended to go to London for the season?'

'Not this season, but there will be others, and there will be house parties and balls we must give at Hartfield Bury, and attend throughout the year elsewhere.'

'Of course.'

'There is a duty that comes with being Lady Hart,' Ben said evenly.

'I know that.'

★   ★   ★

Sophy watched the tall façade of Hartfield Bury coming nearer and nearer to them with a strange sense of foreboding. Despite the weather, which had caused them innumerable short delays and invariably sent Ben into a temper, she had enjoyed the last three days' travelling. She had learned that Ben snapped out of his tempers almost as quickly as he snapped into them and that all it usually took was a smile from her, a little gentle teasing at most. Never before had she ever felt so close to, so intimate with, another person. Even her father felt a stranger to her compared to Ben.

Now the respite was over and Hartfield Bury loomed and told her as surely as the meanest schoolmaster that it was time to buckle down. And she must tell Ben about her published novel and the ones she intended to publish. It stuck like a thorn in her side, the thought that she was withholding such a secret from him.

They crunched to a halt and Ben leapt down and offered her his hand. Sophy took it and was no sooner with both feet on the gravel than a groom had come running from the stables and the front door been flung open.

'Afternoon, Porter,' Ben said to the groom and handed him the ribbons.

Sophy could see it now, the gossip running like ripples through the servants' quarters, for they were bound to have been spotted arriving by an upstairs housemaid. Why had Lord Hart and his cousin returned alone, they would want to know. Where was Lady Hart?

She looked up at the house, braced herself with a single breath and advanced forward. Ben swept in front of her. The senior servants who had appeared at the door jumped out of his way. Sophy trotted up the steps, hardly daring to look in case she caught someone's eye, and into the house.

This was her house now but the servants did not know it yet. The butler took her cloak and handed it to the footman beside him. Would she ever get used to having all these people about her? Sophy wondered.

'Hastings,' Ben said to the butler. 'Have the house servants assemble in the drawing-room forthwith.'

'Very good, my lord.' Hastings nodded and took Ben's coat.

'Come with me,' Ben said and beckoned to her.

Sophy followed him down the hallway. He pushed open a door, which took them into a study. He shut the door.

'You will have ascertained that I shall be announcing our marriage to the servants shortly?' He looked at her, his gaze as hard as steel.

Oh why oh why had she not told him before they arrived? Now their marriage, their disagreements, were going to be acted out in front of the entire staff of the house, from whom she would never escape. Sophy stared at Ben but she did not feel she could begin to explain to him how she felt. He had grown up with this; it was all perfectly ordinary.

She would have to take her lead from him.

'Come here,' Ben said. He held out his arms and she fell into them gratefully. Some sort of communication passed between them that involved no words. Sophy was not sure if either understood the other, but it was something. She would have to pray it would be enough for when she hit Ben with the bad news.

⋆　⋆　⋆

She had sat at this table for dinner before with Lady Hart and Viscount Merryford. Dining with Ben was entirely different. He dismissed the footman at once and bade him only attend them for specific waiting duties rather than standing at the side of the room for the duration.

'Vastly fashionable now that one might wish to converse with one's wife in private at the dinner table,' Ben remarked.

'Fashionable?' Sophy asked, curious.

'Love matches are all the crack.' Ben rose and helped himself to some more wine from the bottle which had been left on the buffet. 'I predict the nineteenth century will be the century of domesticity.'

'How interesting.'

'Would you like some more wine?'

'Yes, please.' He bent over and topped up her glass. Sophy's neck prickled at his nearness. She breathed him in for a moment and savoured it.

'If the last century was all about the pursuit of pleasure outside the home, it's about time the balance was redressed.' Ben stood up straight and went to top his own glass up before returning the wine bottle to the sideboard. 'Of course, one must have a suitable house and a suitable wife in order to become domestic.'

'Ah.'

'I seem to have overachieved on both scores.' Ben flicked his tails, sat down again and smiled. Sophy's heart flipped over. She watched him pull his chair in and take a sip from his wine glass. 'Except there is one small detail about our marriage which needs to be addressed and which I would speak with you about.'

★   ★   ★

Ben held on to her gaze for far too long and then flickered his eyes downwards to watch her hand twirl the stem of her glass. He knew exactly what her soft fingers felt like when they pressed against his skin; like nothing else on this earth.

He shifted uncomfortably in his seat with the predictable tightness of his breeches. The satin of her green gown seemed to shimmer, reminding him of the smoothness of her skin. The prospect of bedding her in the very near future or the prospect of shouting and tears after he had informed her he'd deceived her

— which was it to be?

He was a coward. How, by heavens, did she render him somehow weak? How was she able to send this stab of fear right into his chest, constricting it as at the squeal of an untuned violin? Ben cleared his throat. 'We could do without pudding?'

'Will your cook not be upset?'

Ben was ready to curse the cook but reminded himself he was a civilized gentleman, not some rude half-wit like Lord Rotherham. 'Doubtless they will be pleased of it in the servants' hall.'

She smiled and dabbed her napkin at her lips. He wanted to kiss them, naturally. In fact — now.

Ben placed his own napkin down on the table and pushed his chair back. He rose and so did she; they met somewhere in the middle, about halfway down the long mahogany table. He pressed her against him, took her lips without delay and wondered fleetingly whether it would be possible or advisable to take her and now.

It would not be, but there was a very thick pile carpet in the morning-room next door and a door that could be locked.

★   ★   ★

He was tired, Ben decided the following morning, and the restlessness was because he had still not told Sophy. He'd left her sleeping upstairs for now.

Ben settled himself down in his chair in the study and gazed at the March sunshine spilling across the lawns, promising that today would be a fine day. They might go for a ride, he thought. He knew just the spot where they might stop to take in the view across Salisbury Plain. You could see for miles and all that open space might be just the place to tell her they were not actually man and wife — yet. Then, if she wanted to rip his eyes out, she could do so without the servants watching. Better that than an enforced stiff-lipped silence where he would be in danger of having no idea what she felt or thought.

His eyes flickered lazily about the room. He really must go through the piles of papers — his father's — and sort out some of this mess. Ben spotted some mud-splattered letters on top of a pile of papers on the desk and felt himself frown. Really, the postal service might at least be expected to keep one's letters clean.

He went over to investigate. He scooped the letters up. There were three of them. Ben glanced at the address on the top one and read it twice it so confounded him: the letter was not addressed to him.

The letter was addressed to Mr John Chester care of Stickleton Post Office. Still sealed, it had not been opened. He tucked that letter to the bottom of the pile in his hand and checked the second letter. It was addressed just the same, although written by a different hand, and in black ink whereas the first had been brown. And both letters had been through the post as they were postmarked London. He hastily put the second letter to the base of the pile to regard the third.

Ben felt his brow stiffen into an even deeper frown. What the devil? Another letter to Mr John Chester. Why did the name seem familiar to him? Then he remembered. John Chester was the author of *Caprice and Conventionality*. Fancy that that book's author should be having his post sent to Stickleton.

But that didn't answer the question as to what they were doing in his study.

There was a quiet knock, and the door opened.

'Ben?' It was Sophy in a bright jonquil day dress. Her eyes moved from his face to his hands, and the letters he held, and the colour fell from her cheeks.

'Good morning, my love,' Ben said with a smile and waved the letters.

'Oh dear,' she muttered and gripped the door with her right hand.

'I found these letters. For a Mr John Chester.' She knew something about these letters — he could tell from her countenance and the way her shoulders drooped. Ben took care to level a pained expression at her. 'Sophy, you might have told me!'

He was shocked to see further colour drain from her face.

'Oh.' Sophy forced herself to breathe slowly and tried to keep her mind in order. 'Yes, the letters are mine. I thought I had lost them from my basket in the curricle accident.'

'Yours?' Ben stood up and moved around the desk towards her. 'Don't you mean your father's? He's the author of *Caprice and Conventionality*, is he not? Clever to use a nom de plume. There are many who would not approve of a clergyman as a novelist.' Ben's hand clasped over hers. She thought she could feel the faintest tingle of his breath on her cheek. 'I won't tell anybody.'

'You won't?' She felt a little confused as to what exactly he was saying. She saw his eyebrows arch and felt the warmth of his nearness.

Ben straightened up. 'We had better go to

Middleton today in case any of the correspondence is urgent.'

'Oh?' Now she really didn't understand what he was about.

'There could be one in there from your father's publisher.'

'My father's publisher?'

'Yes, Sophy.' A small frown appeared but he dispelled it quickly and blinked. His voice remained light. 'A letter from your father's publishers that could be an urgent matter of business.'

'Ben.' She did not quite know how to say this. She had best say it quickly and get it over with. 'You are mistaken in thinking it is my father who is Mr John Chester. It is I.'

'You?' Ben smiled and then tilted his head back as his smile broke into a laugh. 'Oh, Sophy!'

He leaned forward and kissed her forehead, curling a finger under her chin that sent a trembling dart down her neck and to her heart. She flickered her eyes shut for a moment. It was a wrench to open them again.

'It is very sweet of you to continue to wish to protect your father,' Ben said, 'but really there is no need.'

'My father did not write the book. I did.'

'Sophy, look at me.' His tone had changed; there was an edge to it now. She did as he asked and it was devastating. His dark eyes spoke volumes, confirmed to her that he was in charge here and it was only by magnanimity that he humoured her. 'I certainly have no intention of telling anyone. I'll do everything I can to protect his identity. I read his book, remember, and it was a damned fine story.'

Sophy swallowed. His masculine assurance both overawed and grated on her. She wanted to slap him for not listening.

Something in his look made her breath catch.

He must have been able to read her mind. He pulled her into the room and shut the door with a quiet click behind her. He leaned towards her, pushed her back against the wood, and stole a hungry, before-breakfast kiss. Sophy luxuriated in it, although she knew he was doing it again. Setting her on fire when there were important things they needed to talk about.

'Ben,' Sophy said in the gap as he broke away from her lips to glide tiny kisses down her throat. 'Listen to me. I am John Chester.'

'John Chester does not have these.' Ben brushed his fingers across her nipples through the thin material of her gown. 'Will you make love to me, Sophy?'

He trapped her gaze. She blinked.

'Me . . . make love to you?' she whispered. He pushed away the small curl that had fallen forward across her forehead with the pad of his thumb.

'What happens when I make love to you?' Recalling the answer to that question sent shards of anticipation through her. Sophy trembled. Ben moved inches closer and his hot breath fanned her cheek. 'Pretend you are me. Do everything I do to you, to me.'

'Not now, Ben,' Sophy said, closing her eyes for a moment. It took every effort of will to push him away. It was not that she didn't want to make love to him, it was that she was upset and slightly cross with him. She would rather clear the air between them first, before she lost her reason to her other senses in a confusion of passion.

'I see,' Ben said and stood up. He brushed his hands down the front of his coat and then straightened his cravat. His tone was curt. 'I have a few matters to attend to this morning so I shall leave you with your preferred company of the newspaper and see you later — at breakfast.'

★　★　★

The stables were empty of people. Ben was thankful. He really was not feeling quite the

282

thing. He was angry, he knew. Not at the fact that Sophy continued to insist she had written that book — he understood why she wanted to protect her father from the public gaze — but because she had pushed him away. He had frozen at first, unsure what to do. When had any woman ever done such a thing to him before? He could not recall. Her rejection had hit him like a blow to the stomach.

Ben walked purposefully past the stalls until he came to Genii's. Black and magnificent, Genii flared his nose and snorted with pleasure at Ben's arrival.

At least his horse was pleased to see him.

Sophy had hitherto responded to his every tactile advance, fluttered beneath his every touch. Desire had leapt in her breast in equal passion to meet and mingle with his. So why not now? Ben punched his knuckles into the wooden doorpost. Genii whinnied in concern.

Ben ran his hand down the stallion's smooth flank. It was not supposed to be like this. He was supposed to have won Sophy, be so assured of her absolute love for him that he could confess his deceit, sure that she would forgive him and arrange their true marriage without delay.

And so he would. Ben drew in a deep

breath and pulled himself upwards. Sulking in a stable achieved nothing. Action did.

'Let's get you saddled up,' he muttered to Genii and gave him a sound pat on the neck.

He would go to Middleton directly. He had already asked her father's permission to approach her and now he would formally ask Mr Grantchester for her hand and if he would conduct their marriage service. He would then confess his trickery to Sophy and at the same time be able to present her with the proper wedding arrangements he had made.

★   ★   ★

Ben did not appear at breakfast.

Sophy had poured her heart out on the page, sketched the essence, she felt, of how it felt to love a man who looked at you and yet only saw the parts of you he chose to see. It had helped her decide. She must show Ben what she was about. She would prove to him who she was in her every action and then he would not be able to deny it.

He had said to her once, when he had first proposed, that she would make a magnificent Lady Hart. And this was exactly what she would do.

'Hastings,' Sophy asked the butler after she

had decided not to wait in the dining-room any longer, 'do you know where Lord Hart might be found?'

'I believe he went out, your ladyship.'

'Thank you, Hastings.' Sophy wondered where he had gone. She walked into the drawing-room and went to stand before the first wide sash window that looked out on to the drive and front of the house. All was quiet. No sign of Ben or anyone approaching. He might have at least taken the trouble to inform her where he was going and when she should expect him to return.

If she just took off without so much as a by-your-leave, he would fly up into the boughs, she was sure. He was lucky that she was of a more placid nature than he.

At least the later it got, the less likely they were to visit her father until tomorrow and she was glad of this because she had to convince Ben that she was John Chester. What would her father — who knew nothing of her writing — say if Ben confronted him with his supposed secret?

If only Ben would listen.

Sophy turned away and decided to go to the library to choose a book to read. She passed two maids in the hallway. They had been talking to each other but their voices dropped to a hush as she approached and then stopped altogether. Their gaze stayed fixed towards the floor.

Sophy swept past them without comment, unsure what she ought to do. Some things had certainly changed now that she was Lady Hart. As a house guest the servants had been polite but this was different. Apart from the very senior servants, no one presumed to look her in the eye. Should she have greeted the maids, whom she did not know by name, with a 'Good morning', or was it better to ignore them as she had done and leave them to get on with their duties unhindered?

Sophy went into the empty library and closed the door carefully behind her. So many things she did not know! She would have to consult the dowager Lady Hart on such matters, and perhaps in the meantime, Ben.

Ben. Sophy's heart sank.

She directed her eyes to the shelves and began to look along them. She needed to find a good book — with a riveting story so she could distract herself from dwelling on the unhappy subject of Ben.

The dowager Lady Hart was a voracious reader of novels and there were two entire lower shelves of them: everything from the Gothic to the comic. *The Mysteries of Udolpho, Camilla, Marchmont, Castle Rackrent* — how she had loved those stories!

An adventurous set of volumes by Jane and Anne Marie Porter caught her eye from their titles — such as *Thaddeus of Warsaw* and *The Hungarian Brothers*. She picked up *Thaddeus of Warsaw*. Was this not the book that Napoleon had banned? Intrigued, she began to read.

Sophy got to the end of the first page and turned it over and then realized she was still standing up. She went and sat down in a large leather chair by the fire.

Two hours later, after reading about a hero who defends women, children, even his horse, she could no longer stop the tears from coming. Ben would have done all those things had he been in the same situation! He had a tender heart, a character driven by honour and yet he could, on occasion, be so utterly selfish, so absolutely blind through his own prejudice.

She could read no more of the book. She cast it aside and dabbed her eyes with her handkerchief. She suddenly felt rather thirsty and realized she had become rather hot, sitting as she was beside the fire. It was nearly two o'clock according to the small porcelain clock on the mantelpiece. She would take some tea in the drawing-room, by herself if necessary.

It was cooler in the hall, and empty. Sophy

took a moment to breathe the fresher air and glance in the wall mirror to check she did not appear disordered or red-eyed.

She could not resist checking the drawing-room windows to see if there was any sign of Ben returning home.

There was not, but there was a small gig that had arrived, and a lady, all alone, was descending from it! As the lady turned, Sophy caught a flash of her face — Mrs Johnson. It would be the first of many good-wish calls, she supposed.

Sophy hurried to sit down. She did not want to be caught staring out of the window, and certainly not by Mrs Johnson. She knew very little of that lady but had never had the slightest inclination to warm towards her on the brief occasions their paths had crossed.

However, for all she knew Mrs Johnson could be one of Ben's mother's greatest friends. Sophy felt herself frowning. No, perhaps that was not very likely.

There was a tap on the door. It opened and Hastings, the butler, announced that a Mrs Johnson had called.

Sophy arranged her skirts and told Hastings she was at home.

Mrs Johnson came into the drawing-room with her chin held high. Sophy felt the back of her neck prickle, though she could not

fathom exactly why. Then she remembered how Mrs Johnson had passed them in Stickleton High Street and smiled knowingly at Ben.

A stab — jealousy or something akin to it — pierced Sophy's breast. She wanted to put her hand on her fluttering heart as if to steady it. She gripped her hands together in her lap and willed them not to move while she looked up in as urbane a manner as she could muster.

'Good afternoon, Lady Hart,' said Ben's mistress. She wore her raven-black hair dressed very high and a necklace that looked like real diamonds around her neck. She was dressed very finely indeed, for a person of her station, for an afternoon house visit.

15

'I am very much obliged to you, my dear Mrs Johnson, for your kind congratulations.' Sophy took care to arrange her lips into a friendly smile and stare directly into Mrs Johnson's coal-dark eyes. 'Please, take a seat. Would you like tea?'

'Yes, thank you. Though this is the briefest of calls. I intended to see Lord Hart — '

Oh, she did, did she?

'Lord Hart is not here,' Sophy interrupted with satisfaction, but a doubt began to bite at the back of her mind. She watched Mrs Johnson sit down on the chair opposite her.

'A rather delicate matter.' Mrs Johnson's lips thinned. She played with arranging her hands in her lap and Sophy watched her grip her wedding ring. She could not recall who Mrs Johnson's late husband had been. She had been widowed before she came to Stickleton, unless she was a widow of convenience — a lady who claimed to be a widow in order to allow herself greater latitude in behaviour than a spinster.

'How may I help you, *Mrs* Johnson?' Sophy shifted in her seat so that she faced the lady

squarely. Mrs Johnson appeared to draw a breath but was not to be cowed by the new Lady Hart, so it seemed. The fire crackled quietly. Was she still Ben's mistress? Something gripped Sophy's gut and twisted it.

'It appears that I have found myself in an interesting condition,' Mrs Johnson said, at last, as if she was conversing about the weather. 'For a widow.'

Her insides were being strangled; she could not breathe. Yes, I can, Sophy told herself. I can still think and I can still breathe.

'You have come here to inform Lord Hart that you are expecting a child?' Sophy congratulated herself on the cold, even tone of her own voice and lifted her chin a little higher. She must not let any of her pain or discomfort show in her expression. 'You are not so far advanced so far as I can discern?'

'No.' Mrs Johnson's eyes shifted and Sophy felt a small bolt of satisfaction. Really, she should not feel pleasure at another person's misfortune but she knew there was a tumult of emotions inside her.

'And you have come to lay the blame at Lord Hart's feet?' Sophy raised an eyebrow pointedly, in the same way she had seen Ben do so many times. It was a direct imitation of his style but it gave her something to grasp on to, something to keep her steady — for now.

'Indeed.' A slow smile crept on to Mrs Johnson's countenance that spiked at Sophy's control. She felt her fingers curl, stiffen, and straightened them.

'And what proof would you like to present to support your claim?' Sophy shot back. Ben was not here. He would ask for proof, would he not? Unless he knew he was guilty?

A stab of pain sliced Sophy in two, nearly made her splutter. She swallowed and kept her eyes fixed on Mrs Johnson's countenance.

'Proof?' Mrs Johnson's eyes swept wildly about the room but did not fix on anything. Somehow, it gave Sophy strength. She forced her manner to remain calm.

'Mrs Johnson, if the . . . responsibility is indeed Lord Hart's then you may be assured that I shall press for some compensation on your behalf. However, Lord Hart would need to be satisfied, do you not agree, that the child was his?'

Mrs Johnson clutched both her hands together in her lap and her face appeared to pale.

Despite the possible reality that she was sitting face to face with a woman who could be carrying Ben's child, Sophy felt a wince of pity. What could she do or say?

'What the devil!' The door slammed open. Sophy looked and there stood Ben, dressed in his tight-fitting beige-coloured buckskins and a black riding jacket. He strode forward into the room. She caught her breath; there were beads of sweat on his forehead and she could tell from his expression that he was burning with anger.

'What is she doing here?' His eyes darted from Sophy to Mrs Johnson and then to the door, to which he flung his arm out and pointed. 'Out! Get out!'

A log collapsed in the grate with a crackling crash and sent sparks out on to the hearth. Mrs Johnson looked towards the fire, her face icy-white. Sophy leapt to her feet, surprised to find herself afraid more for Mrs Johnson's sensibilities than her own. She started towards him but Ben's eyes, alight with white fury, pinned her to stand where she was.

'Lord Hart, contain yourself,' Sophy said, and heard the first sounds of a trembling uncertainty in her voice. She must quell them. 'Mrs Johnson . . . '

Ben's gaze narrowed, challenging her to continue.

'Mrs Johnson . . . ' Sophy repeated, but the rest of her words were lost in the muddle and uncertainty that was encroaching on her mind. Her lips, her tongue, felt dry.

'I am well aware who Mrs Johnson is,' Ben said slowly as if he was speaking to a precocious child. 'And I know why she is here — '

'You do?' Sophy muttered, forgetting her immediate pique at his manner. She stared determinedly at the pattern on the large china vase by the pianoforte but the tears were pricking behind her eyes.

She needed to leave the room. Now. Go somewhere where she could buckle into a ball and deal with . . . it felt like grief.

Sophy stumbled backwards, felt for and grasped the arm of the chair and lowered herself into it in as graceful a way as she could muster. The tears were not on her face yet. She tried to push her lips into a smile. They would not move.

'Go, madam, before I have you thrown out!'

Ben's voice sounded like a knife being sharpened. Sophy stared into the flames of the fire; tried to lose her vision in their orange blur.

'My lord . . . ' came the plaintive sound of Mrs Johnson's voice and Sophy too found herself wishing, uncharitably, that the woman would leave.

'Who was it?' Ben's voice cracked like a horsewhip.

'I can't . . . '

'If you wish for my assistance, Mrs

Johnson, you will do exactly as I say. Write me the full circumstances of the matter and I shall see what I can do to encourage the true perpetrator to take responsibility for his actions. Whatever the outcome, I never want to see you in this house. You had no business coming here and worrying my wife with your lies. Your behaviour is shameful. Do I make myself clear?'

'You make yourself perfectly clear, my lord.' Sophy wished she could shut her ears to the choking sound of Mrs Johnson's words. 'Please excuse me.'

Hearing the rustle of Mrs Johnson's skirts made Sophy look up. She watched her leave the room but did not dare to look too closely at Ben. She did not want to see his expression. Dimly, she heard the door slam.

'It's all lies,' she heard Ben snap with impatience.

She didn't know whether she could believe him, whether she wanted to believe him. It was all too much. Something was pounding against her hot temples. She needed to think.

'Sophy?' His tone was gentler.

She could not contain herself any longer. She thrust her head in her hands. Somehow the darkness was soothing. She must prevent the tears from coming because she knew once they started they would be even harder to stop.

'Sophy?' She heard him move.

She forced herself to look up. Ben stood in the middle of the carpet and watched her. His fists were curled and he was absolutely straight as if he had a rod of iron for a backbone. The dark anger was still there in his eyes but also a softness as he looked at her.

She wanted to melt into his arms, to feel his warm lips on hers. Yet she stood frozen.

'Ben,' she said and took care to breathe evenly, 'that you should have . . . known other women is something I should have expected.'

'The child, if there is one, is not mine,' he said. He took a step towards her. She watched the ripple of muscle in his legs — legs that his buckskins showed off to splendid advantage — and it struck her how everything about this man was right to make him the perfect father. The father, she hoped, of the child — children — she would carry.

He was a strong man but he, as though through instinct, championed the weak.

He had already fathered a child.

Sophy thought her knees would buckle beneath her. She reached out, found the arm of the chair with her fingers, tried to lean on it to steady herself, tried to think what the most sensible thing was to say.

'Ben, if you have . . . fathered a child, that is something that happened before . . . '

A strong, warm arm slipped around her waist and held her steady, made her heart leap. His face, his chocolate eyes, were only inches from hers. Her neck tingled as she tilted her head towards him. She smelled sandalwood and horse and a scent that only belonged to him.

Sophy breathed him in, pressed on. 'It . . . was before you even knew me. I cannot claim to have any objection to — '

'What?' Ben started. She saw him lose his control only for a moment. His eyes narrowed. White flickered across his face. Then his cheeks began to burn crimson. 'How can you possibly not mind?'

'I don't mind.' It was at least in part a lie and it cost her all her pride to say it but her love for Ben was worth more than her pique or hurt over his past misdemeanours. She would nurse those herself — later, and in private.

'How dare you say you don't mind!'

The tail of his low growl was lost as his lips captured hers. The kiss was hot and angry and unexpected. She thought his hands a little rough as he pulled her into the curve of him; gave her no quarter, allowed her no leeway.

She would not be mastered in this way — ever. She pulled her lips free and when he took them again without leave, without care, she pushed her fists into the rock of his chest and herself free, of his kiss if not his grasp.

His eyes burned. 'You . . . you said you loved me. Kiss me.'

'I do love you. I will not kiss you *to order*.'

'Kiss me.' His gaze was immutable.

How dare he speak to her so! 'Let go of me!'

His grip around her tightened.

'Please?'

No answer.

'Ben, if you think I am a bundle of quivering femininity ready to be used as you see fit to salve your conscience, think again.'

He pressed his lips together and appeared not to blink. Then said, in a voice as chilling as ice, 'Has it been a sham all this time?'

'Ben, you are not listening. Of course I love you. What I said was that I expect . . . well, I expect such things to happen.' She deliberately crossed her arms in front of her and took some satisfaction that his grip around her seemed to loosen. 'If the child is yours I should expect you to own up to it and take responsibility. This is an innocent child — '

'Are you saying you don't believe me?' His eyes widened for a moment and then he swung away, setting her free. Sophy stumbled back a pace but she could stand on her own two feet. She would make him do right by Mrs Johnson, provide for the child. It was a revenge of her own, of sorts, she realized.

'Ben — '

'Sophy, that woman from Hades is lying!' He swung back towards her, seized her hands in his, pulled them up to his lips before she could stop him. 'My affair with her was mercifully brief and ended six months ago. I love you, Sophy. Kiss me. Show me that you love me.'

In his hands, her own body could not be trusted to withstand him. Sophy took two paces back, putting a distance between them. They would finish their conversation and then she would kiss him. She looked at him and she hoped that her eyes showed her defiance.

'How can you be so cold?' He stared at her, brows knotted, as if she was not truly stood before him, and ran his hand through his hair. 'Hell! I thought you were a woman beyond compare. Now I see I was grossly deceived.'

That wounded her, like nothing he had hitherto said. Sophy felt herself start to shake.

She gulped and forced herself not to flinch from his merciless gaze.

'Why did you marry me, eh? Was it to get your hands on all this?'

'No, I — '

'Damn what you think!' Ben swung away and punched a fist at the air. 'Thank heavens our marriage was a sham!'

Ben's eyes swept lazily across the room and did not rest on her. His upper lip curled and then he settled his mouth in an uneasy grin that made Sophy forget to breathe.

'What do you mean our marriage was a sham?' Sophy heard her own voice as if it was coming at her from a distance. She watched Ben's fingers clench into a fist and then unclench again. He looked up at her. His gaze narrowed.

'I mean I am wholeheartedly relieved that our marriage turned out to be a sham because it will save me the expense and embarrassment of having to get a divorce.'

Divorce. Sophy thought her knees might give way.

'Hell, and I've been suffering agonies of conscience that I tricked you into believing we were married!' Ben tilted his head to one side. She did not like his smile. 'Fate, I see, was on my side all along!'

'Divorce? Fate?' Sophy heard herself

mutter. She stumbled backwards and the backs of her legs hit the chair. She tumbled down into it and grasped the cushion, pulled it on to her lap and hugged it.

'No need for a divorce.' His voice was quiet. Too quiet. 'There is no marriage.'

'Ben, we were married. I was there. What are you saying? Was the licence false?' She willed herself to look up. All she could do was try to understand what he was saying. Perhaps if she could decipher it, somewhere in the riddle might be a glimmer of hope?

'No, and it cost me a pretty penny and a lot of inconvenience! I now wish I hadn't bothered!' Ben walked towards her and came to stand directly in front of her, looking down his long, arrogant nose at her. Sophy pushed the cushion away, determined to maintain something of a stand in the face of . . . in the face of this heartbreak. She stifled a sob, hated that her hand had flown to her mouth.

'The priest was no real priest. He is a gentleman called Jack Walden — a friend of mine from schooldays and certainly could not be considered clerical by any stretch of the imagination! Ha!' He turned away.

'Ben . . . ' Sophy blinked but she could hardly see through her tears. Ben had, for some unfathomable reason, tricked her into believing they were married. Why? And why did she have the misfortune of caring — and so much?

'Save your tears and your false womanish wiles for deceiving some other idiot!'

Sophy could not prevent her anger from taking over, though she battled to control it. These were not womanish wiles. He was breaking her heart, and it hurt as surely as physical pain.

'Excuse me,' Sophy said and drew herself up and on to her feet and kept her chin pointed upwards. She put one foot in front of the other. Blinked furiously at her tears so that she could see the way ahead and out of the drawing-room. She had no idea where she was going but if she could just get out of the room . . .

She managed to walk past his stiff form; gulped back the sob that threatened to make her weaken and want to throw herself into his arms. His arms did not want her.

'You have no idea of what I am capable,' she shot blindly into the air as she reached the door. The truth of her own words stung her more than she wanted to admit. She gripped the door handle and pulled it towards her.

'Oh, no, you don't!'

Too late, Ben. Sophy flung herself out into the hall, breathed the cooler air and found her gaze looked towards the sweeping stairs.

No, she would find her balance in the gardens.

'My lady?' Hastings seemed to have appeared from nowhere. Sophy kept her gaze down towards the floor but she knew he must have seen her tears.

'My cloak, please, Hastings,' she managed to say.

'Where do you think you are going?' Ben's voice slammed through the air like a clapper to scare crows.

Sophy heard Hastings cough. She was hardly a delicate flower likely to contract a chill from stepping outside from lack of a cloak but . . . 'My cloak, please,' she said.

Hastings may have coughed but he had gone into the cloak-room and held the garment up for her to slip her arms into.

'Where the devil do you think you are going?'

She did not know, nor did she care. The moment she was able, Sophy pulled away and, as Hastings opened the front door, she raced down the steps. The cold air hit her face, refreshed it. She would go to the Italian garden, walk the gravel paths and think, compose herself.

'Sophy!'

Would Ben not just leave her alone for a moment!

Sophy pulled open the wrought-iron gate at the side of the house and let the latch fall behind her. She could hear footsteps behind her, knew it was a futile attempt at putting some distance between them, but still she sped as fast as she could down through the rose garden and towards the walled Italian sunken garden.

'Sophy!' Ben's voice and crunch was getting nearer.

She turned the corner nevertheless. The Italian garden was empty. The stone bench at one side was tempting.

No, she would not sit. She pulled her cloak more tightly around her. She wanted to walk, to run . . .

She heard Ben's footsteps behind her and turned and realized her foolishness. She was trapped. There was no way to leave the walled garden except from the entrance in which she had come — the pink brick archway.

Ben's frame filled the archway. He even leaned against one side. She watched his chest rise and fall, the sweep of his eyelashes as his gaze appraised her. There was nothing gentle in it. His eyes were black. 'I wanted to put the world at your feet,' he said slowly. She tasted the drawn-out pain of his every word.

'And I would have done because I thought, I deluded myself, that you cared for me in return — '

'Yes, you deluded yourself,' Sophy found herself throwing back at him. Her anger was rising. It burned her throat. 'Not even when I told you I wrote a book which was published did you believe me. You believed so little of me that you would rather think me a liar than an author.'

Something flickered across his vision. Dared she hope her words had some impact? There seemed so little hope — especially when her own fury threatened so strongly to blind her reason. Sophy pressed her fingers into her palms.

The breeze ruffled his hair and then the shutters came down. Sophy felt her heart sink. Where was the hope now if he would not listen?

She started as hands gripped her shoulders — firm, warm hands. She tried to pull away, could not. Ben held her fast. His dark gaze bore into her; his presence bore over her.

'Tell me you are insane with jealousy.' Only his lips moved. The rest of him was deathly still. She thought he might shake her but he did not. He only took a breath. 'Tell me that you could not bear the thought of — '

'No, Ben,' Sophy said, as quietly as the

hush around a grave, 'because it is not true. I won't be tortured by what you've done in the past. Why should I?'

'Because . . . ' His brow creased. His voice stilled. Confusion crossed his face as if he was about to change tack completely. Sophy watched him appraise every inch of her countenance from her chin to her forehead and thought for a moment he might kiss her. He spoke very slowly. 'If it was you come to tell me you were carrying another man's child I could not bear it.'

He did not continue. She could not answer. It did not matter that birds chirped or that the wind rustled the spring leaves, her ears demanded to be liberated from the awful silence.

'So, we are not married?' Sophy forced herself to say. She took a long, deep breath.

'No! I shall never marry now,' he said through gritted teeth, his voice laced with a bitterness that made Sophy's insides want to shrivel. 'I don't know what came over me to think it was such a good idea.'

'Wasn't it a book called *Caprice and Conventionality*?' She let her voice drop to a whisper though she despised her own weakness. 'A book that I wrote.'

He did not reply. His gaze was fastened towards the fountain in the middle of the garden and every bone in his face looked as if it had been set by a surgeon, never to move again.

'If it is not too much expense and embarrassment for you,' Sophy said, feigning a light tone and wishing he would let her shoulders go, 'I should like to go home to my father.'

He batted his eyelids once only before sweeping away, with a sudden vigour. He stood not two feet in front of her and looked like a sculpture forged from iron, so haughty, so superior, she thought she could teach herself to hate him.

'Be my guest,' he said. 'You may take one of the carriages.'

He turned and strode away, through the brick archway, before she had time to blink.

★   ★   ★

Ben slammed the door of his study, pacing up and down in the unnerving quietness until the clock on the mantelpiece chimed the half-hour and he could stand it no longer.

Her insistence that she had written the book was admirable — in a way. Of her seeming forgiveness of his supposed sins he knew a better man than he would be glad. Of her defiance in the face of his accusations, he should be proud that his Lady Hart could carry herself off so well — a lesser woman would have run away weeping.

And yet fear gripped every bit of his being, a terrible fear that her coldness stemmed from the fact that she did not care, not from the strength of character he had presumed of her.

'You have no idea of what I am capable', she had said, and the truth in that statement had shocked him. It was precisely because he did not know, because he had omitted to find out the finer details of his love, to understand her, that he was now in this foolish predicament. He had thought her many things but had he ever stopped to test his theories? No, he had forged ahead, blind, overconfident of her ability to match the character he had attributed to her.

If only his anger — anger directed at himself as much as her — could be sated so he could face her again and demand they established the truth. He had to know her true feelings for him. She was worth too much for him to risk throwing her away on a whim of pique or pride.

He would go to her as soon as he could be sure his temper was in check. She would not go to her father's, would she?

Ben flew out into the hallway and to the

drawing-room. It was empty.

'Where's Lady Hart?' he demanded of Hastings.

'She asked for the carriage, my lord.'

Ben pulled the front door open himself to see the black barouche gathering speed up the drive and leaving the house behind. He ran down the steps, nearly tripped but kept his balance. He wanted to shout out but the words were stuck in his throat.

Even if he got the curricle he'd be hard pressed to catch her. He wasn't sure he wanted to catch her like this. Not yet. Later, he would go to Middleton. Later, once he had figured out how he should put things right.

16

She was very feverish and had a sore throat. Mary was full of care and affection, but Sophy herself could not speak without many tears.

If her father thought it peculiar that she should appear home with no luggage but a single basket he did not say anything. Mr Camberley removed himself back to his old lodgings and Sophy sat in her bedchamber trying to write and imagine everything was ordinary — as if she had not really spent two weeks living as she had, believing that she had been married.

'Did you have a pleasant time in East Bourne?' her father asked at supper when she at last ventured downstairs.

'Yes.' The bit of lamb in her mouth suddenly turned dry and tough. Sophy could not think how to continue. She kept her eyes on her plate.

'My dear Sophy, I do not wish to pry but fatherly concern bids me to enquire whether there is something the matter? Is it some quarrel you have had with Lord Hart?'

'L-Lord Hart?' Sophy dropped her fork,

winced as it clattered on the plate and hurried to pick it up again.

'Yes. Lord Hart came to see me yesterday to enquire most particularly about arranging your wedding.'

He had? Yesterday? Did that mean that Ben had wanted to marry her properly? Oh, it was all ruined now. He hated her.

'I'm sorry, Father, but there will be no wedding.' Sophy swallowed. It sounded worse now she had said it out loud. 'Will you . . . will you excuse me? I'm not terribly hungry. Perhaps Mary might take the lamb home to her family?'

'Of course.'

Sophy did not look at him as she pushed her chair back. She dropped her napkin on the table and left the room, keeping her body straight. She climbed the stairs and her feet felt like lead.

Her dear father did not press her. Ben had not followed her or done anything to stop her leaving. She had no one to share her unhappiness with but her pen and paper. The ritual of preparing to write was a small comfort. She placed her taper down on the corner of her desk and sat down on the wooden chair. She straightened her back and opened her wooden writing box. She took out her pen and the glass inkwell. She put it on the table before her, opened its copper lid and began to unscrew her pen.

A tear splashed into the inkwell. Sophy saw that her hand was shaking and she put her pen down for a moment. She told herself to stop being foolish and unlocked the desk drawer and drew out her old papers, which she flicked through, and then bent over to take out the papers she had brought with her in her basket. Added together, it was a goodly bundle. The book was almost finished. If she could just write another twenty or so pages she would be at the end.

She drew out a fresh sheet of paper to start a new chapter and began to write. She reached halfway down the paper when tears fell on the page and the words she had just written began to run. For a few moments she did nothing except stare as her sentences were rendered illegible. Then she mustered herself to pick up the paper and scrunch it into a ball.

She must find a handkerchief to dab her eyes, and pull out a new piece of paper and start again.

⋆ ⋆ ⋆

Sophy thought perhaps Ben might come the next day, and the next. However she thought to distract herself with household tasks, she could not help coming back to the window and looking out on to the road in case she caught the first glimpse of him.

After three days her heart leapt at the sight of a carriage she recognized — the smart black barouche. But it was only Porter with her luggage. He appeared somewhat stiff of manner and said nothing beyond his own pleasantries, and gave her no note or letter.

After that, she watched the road and saw only the usual comings and goings. The sun rose high in the sky every day and bathed Middleton in warmth. A brown speckled mother duck led her troop of ducklings towards the village pond. Then came Mary, with her basket, whistling a jaunty tune, brimming with the news that her sister was soon to make her an aunt again.

Billy Entwhistle brought a fresh pitcher of milk, swinging it carelessly in his hand, and then cantered off towards the fields.

Around mid-morning Mr Camberley usually arrived. He confided in Sophy that he hoped to take a certain lady, a grown-up daughter of a lawyer newly moved to Stickleton, to be his wife. He was kind and courteous as always, made sure her father didn't overexert himself, and could not keep his happiness from his face. Even her father had spring in his step.

Ben did not come. Sophy began to realize that she had nothing but her old life — her father and her household and parish duties. She slowly began to reconcile herself. Nothing apart from memories. And yet she could not sleep, she stayed up late night after night, burning candles wantonly, working towards the ending of her novel. She changed the name — to *Perfidy and Perfection* — because the ending had proved to be different from what she had thought, although she could not end on the note she knew to be true. She could not leave things in the swell of despair she felt. She had to end it on a note of hope. In her story on paper she was determined to have a happy ending.

★   ★   ★

'A rather smoky and unusual flavour, this tea, but not unpleasant.' Mrs Johnson finished pouring into Sophy's cup and placed the creamware teapot down on its stand on the small walnut table.

Sophy helped herself to milk and a piece of sugar using a dainty pair of silver tongs. She had no desire to dwell on her own feelings, especially not now. It had been on her mind for weeks that Mrs Johnson might not be able to provide for the baby and that Ben might have done nothing, but Sophy saw that her house in Stickleton, although modest in size, was ample and well furnished.

'I apologize for the intrusion, Mrs Johnson — '

'Not at all.'

'But I must ask . . . your circumstances? I came to see — '

'That has been sorted out to my satisfaction.' Mrs Johnson jangled her teaspoon as she stirred and then laid it down on the saucer. 'It is kind of you to concern yourself, especially after my appalling behaviour, but thankfully I have no need of assistance. I was then, though, desperate . . . '

'I understand. I would have been also.' Did that mean that Ben had owned up to his responsibility and promised Mrs Johnson that he would provide for the baby? Sophy somehow wanted to know, yet did not dare ask. She picked up her cup and took a sip of her tea.

'Miss Grantchester,' Mrs Johnson began in a kindly voice. Her eyes were wide and Sophy felt her heart flutter. She paused, her cup poised, but did not go to take another sip until she had heard what was to be said. 'If you are still labouring under any misapprehension that Lord Hart is . . . responsible for my condition, let me assure you he is not nor ever was. The er . . . culprit is another.'

Sophy felt her mind spin. It felt light, as if she had just drunk a glass of wine very quickly. Ben was not the father. She put her cup down, not quite evenly. It clattered against the saucer. Fortunately nothing spilled.

'I am to move, shortly, to another part of the country where I am not known and begin my widowhood again.' Mrs Johnson wrapped one hand around the other in her lap. 'My poor husband will have had to die more recently what with the baby. It means rather a lot of black.'

'Oh, Mrs Johnson. I am so pleased to hear that you are to be . . . provided for.'

'Thank you for your sincere good wishes. I am sorry that I intruded my predicament, which I had no right to do, and caused you such distress.'

'No, things would have come to a head sooner or later, I believe, and it was for the best that things happened when they did.'

'Forgive my impertinence, but is there no remedy for your misunderstanding with Lord Hart? Did you not wish to marry him?'

'Oh, I did. But he tricked me.'

'He did *what?*' Mrs Johnson's countenance crumpled.

'He tricked me into believing that we were married. We . . . we went through a wedding but as it transpired the service was false because the priest . . . he was no priest, only a friend of Lord Hart's.' Sophy pressed her handkerchief into her eyes. It seemed such a long time ago now although it had only been a few short weeks.

'And . . . ?' Mrs Johnson frowned and Sophy tried her best to smile. She had come here to discover if Mrs Johnson was in need of any assistance and now it seemed that it was Mrs Johnson who was assisting her. 'Did you . . . take up the duties of a wife?'

'Y-yes.'

'You don't have a mother, do you, Miss Grantchester? Forgive me if I sound so very forward, but perhaps with all that has passed between us, I can say this. Have you considered that you yourself might also be with child?'

'I had thought it might be a possibility. How would I know?'

'Ah.' Mrs Johnson smiled. 'Have you had your monthly visitor since . . . since . . . '

'Yes.'

'Then you are not with child.'

Sophy felt a strange sense of relief yet it was also tinged with a sensation that was similar to feeling cross.

'It is natural, if you feel somewhat disappointed, that is.'

Yes, that was what she felt. Disappointed. It was completely irrational, however. What did she want with a baby? She wanted a tangible reminder of Ben, a small voice inside her said. Sophy gulped but it was so easy conversing with Mrs Johnson. 'I thought he might come to Middleton to try to patch things up but he has not. What can I do but continue on as before?'

'I am sorry.'

Sophy fingered the handle of her teacup and picked it up. She took another sip. At least her publisher had accepted her book — she had picked up a parcel containing a copy from the post office on her way here.

'Mrs Johnson,' she said and looked up. 'It will soon be known by everyone but can I share something with you?'

'Of course, Miss Grantchester.'

Sophy put her teacup down. She leaned over and drew the volume from her basket and handed it to Mrs Johnson. 'I wrote this and it has been published.'

Mrs Johnson stared at the book and inspected it. She opened it.

'I shall write another and another.' Sophy bit her lip.

'You have a talent, Miss Grantchester. I

hope it brings you every happiness.'

Sophy smiled but it was difficult to do so. She was not so sure that the happiness she wanted could be found through writing stories.

★   ★   ★

The wind pushed at his face, but not hard enough. Ben whipped the ribbons and upped the pace. His pair were magnificent and rose to the challenge. The countryside, the fields and woodland, raced by, but all Ben saw was the immediate wet grey of the road ahead and the red mist of his still unquenched anger.

He'd done the London to Brighton, raced like a hare and far too recklessly, and he'd won and become hero of the moment, a crown of the Four-at-Hand club. The carousing in Brighton had been top notch. He'd drunk so much he'd forgotten what day it was. Still he didn't care because the victory felt hollow and the liquor had not been strong enough.

Nothing blotted out the memory of Sophy.

Seven weeks she had been gone. Seven weeks and it was not getting better. It was getting worse. Something inside him that the finest brandy could not dull; that the speed of the fastest curricle run in England could not dissipate.

The compulsion growing inside him that he had to see her was becoming stronger and stronger, and so was his fear. It was a different kind of fear now, that he would do anything to keep her, and another fear even more paralysing, that he had no idea what he should do.

He swung hard to bring his pair into the home straight and took only the smallest satisfaction from the crunching sounds the hoofs of his horses made as they kicked up the gravel.

Hartfield Bury stood defiantly against the overcast sky. In front of the house a familiar figure was stepping down from his own curricle and stood with his hands resting lazily on his hips as Ben came to a halt.

'Jack Walden!' Ben said and felt himself smile for the first time in seven weeks. It hurt his face.

'A flying visit, no less, but no one's heard from you, Harty. We thought we might have seen you in town long before now. Marital bliss that good, eh? Then someone said you'd won the London to Brighton and I thought — '

'As you well know,' Ben said, hearing and hating the grim truth of his own words, 'there was no marriage. And there is no marital bliss.'

'Oh.' Jack fingered his chin.

Ben jumped down and extended his hand. 'No hard feelings, eh?' He breathed in the heavy, damp air. It seemed about to rain. 'Come in at least for a drink. Toast the success of my team.'

'Certainly.' Jack looked as if he was about to step forward but then stopped himself. 'Actually, Harty. I brought this. You might like to see it, if you have not done so already.'

Jack turned back to his carriage and leaned over. He pulled out a package wrapped in brown paper and strings, which had already been untied and hung loosely. He pulled away the wrapping and handed Ben a brown, calf-leather book.

Ben saw Jack's eyes were waiting for his reaction. He looked at the gold embossed title on the spine — *Perfidy and Perfection*. It sounded like a novel. He flipped it open to the frontispiece and read:

Perfidy and Perfection
~ A novel ~
by Sophia Grantchester
author of Caprice and Conventionality

Someone was pressing an uncracked block of ice against his chest. A spot of water fell from the sky on to the page, and then another, and yet all Ben could concentrate on was the fact that Sophy had written and published a novel, two novels . . .

'Harty? Are you feeling quite the thing? You look a little pale.'

'Thank you, Jack.' Ben looked up and caught his friend's eye. 'Thank you for the book. It is . . . a bit of a surprise.'

'You didn't know?' Jack raised an eyebrow and ran his hand through his hair.

'No.' Ben snapped the book shut and felt light specks of drizzle against his face. 'Let's go inside.'

Jack nodded towards the drive.

Ben looked over to see his mother's carriage bowling towards them.

'Mother, did you have a good journey?' Ben held out his hand and helped her down from the carriage. His cravat was now nearly soaked but he didn't care. 'May I introduce Mr Jack Walden?'

'George Walden's boy?'

Jack nodded and, blinking water from his lashes, looked as if he was about to speak.

'Where is Sophy?' she said, looking about her.

Ben pecked his mother on the cheek and

tasted the familiar, chalky powder.

'Benedict! Where is she? And it's raining! What are you doing outside?'

'Waiting to greet you, Mother. Sophy is at her father's in Middleton.' Ben drew himself up straight.

'Why is she at her father's?'

'Mother, would you like some tea?' Ben waved his arm in the direction of the house.

'Are you intending to tell me what is going on?'

Ben put his hand to his mouth and coughed. 'Yes. But, Mother, we have a visitor and — '

'Fiddlesticks to all that!' Lady Hart grabbed her skirts and, head bowed, hurried towards the steps. The front door was already open, footmen waiting. Ben hurried a step behind her. 'The gel is a treasure; Fordham and I are quite agreed on that score. I came home expecting to find her . . . increasing, not . . . gone!'

'Mother — '

'What on earth have you done to her, Benedict?'

★   ★   ★

'I assume you will be making every effort to get her back', his mother had said, and it was still ringing in his ears. As if he needed reminding. Ben threw himself into his favourite chair in the library while Jack took on the task of pouring them a drink from the decanter in the tantalus on the side-table.

'The thing is,' Ben said, the prospect of wallowing in his own misery suddenly seeming appealing, 'how the devil am I going to get her back? What my dear mother does not seem to take on board is that I cast her off, y'see, like a heartless brute, and now I simply don't know what to do.'

'Have you told her you love her?' Jack asked. He placed a glass of some spirit or other down on the small table beside Ben.

'Would that that would do it!' Ben said and tossed the glass back, his throat catching the thankful sting of brandy. 'Yes, I did, and I told her a great deal more besides. Too much. I doubted her at every turn and now I do not know the truth of it, of what her feelings are, or were.'

'Why don't you read the book?' Jack had brought the volume with him and he opened it and placed it in Ben's hands. Ben read from the page.

This book is dedicated to a perfidious gentleman and yet there is a lady to whom he is perfect. It is the author's dearest wish that they are granted their happy ending.

Ben pressed the book against his chest, felt the warm, soft leather beneath his fingers. Her book. His lady to whom he was perfect. He felt a prick at the back of his eyes and blinked hard until it went away. Nothing, nothing was going to be right until he got Sophy back, and he should have done it long before now.

'Excuse me for five minutes,' he said and rose. 'And then shall we go for a gallop? I'm in need of some fresh air.'

He walked straight into Mr Simmons's office in the coach house. Mr Simmons looked up and, startled, hastily got to his feet. 'Lord Hart, good morning!'

'Sit, sit.' Ben placed the book down on the desk, ignoring the strewn piles of papers right under Mr Simmons's nose. 'Read this. Today. Now. And I want a list of everything the hero does. Everything, you understand? Oh, and a summary of the entire story.'

'M-my lord, I don't quite follow. I'm not some kind of librarian, or scholar — '

'You can read, can't you?'

Mr Simmons nodded.

'This matter intimately concerns the

Hartfield estate, my good man. Come to me as soon as you are done.'

★ ★ ★

Ben felt a smile tugging at the corners of his lips.

'And the hero of the story, my lord, Lord Michael, was a subscriber to a number of charitable foundations. For example, the Benevolent Society For The Relief Of — '

'Simply arrange it, immediately.'

'W — '

'All of them.'

'Are the charities fictional? Well, find the real equivalents, Simmons. What else? How does he win her in the end?'

'Ah. In a boat.'

'A boat? Why the devil in a boat? How very peculiar.'

'The heroine is the daughter of a lighthouse keeper, and Lord Bart sails a small boat over to the rocky promontory, a boat laden with flowers. Irises, my lord.'

There was a silence in the room that Ben noted Jack did not even presume to break.

'Well, I shall need a boat. And irises.'

'But, my lord, we are in Wiltshire, hundreds of miles from the sea. There isn't much call for seacraft.'

'And no navigable rivers or canals hereabouts to speak of,' added Jack, leaning against the wall. 'Finding a boat quickly might be difficult.'

'And once you have the boat, my lord, how — '

'It must have wheels fixed on it, and be rigged up like a carriage so it can be pulled by horses.' Ben shook his head at the gawping faces. 'It's in the book, it must be done!' He slammed his fist down on the table. 'Can a boat not be built? There are carpenters employed on the Hartfield estate, are there not?'

'Yes, my lord.'

'In the meantime I am going to see a lady whose pride is her botanic garden. She will have the irises, and if not, know where they might be found. Jack?'

Jack started and stood up straight. 'Oh yes, I'll come with you.'

★ ★ ★

Sophy heaved the counterpane and heavy bedclothes back, and pulled herself out of bed. It was too warm for so many blankets, she thought. Her feet hit the cool, thin rug beside her bed and she padded across the hard, colder floorboards to her dresser and began to brush her tangled hair. It was always like this in the mornings if she had not tied it in rags to curl the night before.

She had not bothered to curl her hair for weeks.

The birds twittered their musical nonsense as she washed and dressed. After she had finished lacing up her boots, which she noticed needed a polish, she pulled the curtains back. The sun bathed the bedroom in bright warmth and she lifted the latch and opened the window to let in the cool morning air.

All was quiet. Mary had not come yet. The road was empty.

She sat down on the narrow high-backed chair for a few moments while she finished pinning her hair under her white cotton cap. The oval mirror showed her a sombre face. She pushed her cheeks into a smile but there was nothing she could do about the dullness of her eyes.

What did it matter?

The sound of horses' hoofs, the clatter of wheels and the ring of a harness came through the window. A carriage was coming past. Unusual for so early in the morning, she could not help but be drawn to her feet to look out.

A carriage it was, and shaped like a fishing

boat, trotting past the church at no great pace. In it were bunches and bunches of flowers, so that it looked as if it was a vehicle rigged up for a wedding, and yet in it sat a single gentleman dressed from head to toe in black — Ben!

The two grey horses that pulled the contraption, they too were familiar. *What on earth . . . ?* And as he got nearer and she could discern the expression on his face, her heart contracted. Fixed, focused, he stared straight ahead. She did not think she had ever seen him look so sad. And the flowers — they were all irises.

Her hand rested on the window, the tips of her fingers pushing into the cold glass. She wished her forehead, her chest, the whole of her could feel so cool. Water . . . there was the pitcher on her dresser — she could pour herself a drink but she could not tear herself away from the window.

The scene at the end of *Perfidy and Perfection*, she thought, where Lord Michael has to go to see Flora to make amends. He borrows a boat and rows it himself over to the lighthouse where she is waiting. He fills it with irises to show Flora, who is well read in the classics and will understand the allusion, how he is bringing her a message of love.

And he asks her to leave the lighthouse and

share his life, a very different life from all she has known.

Sophy felt her hand on her throat. There had always been that faint idea that Ben might find her book, might read it and understand her wish for reconciliation. That he might act on her olive branch, but this . . .

Her heart was beating wildly as he drew the vehicle to a halt outside their gate and looked up.

17

No one who had ever seen Benedict St Michael in his infancy would have supposed him born to be a hero. His situation in life, the character of his father and mother, his own person and disposition, were all equally against him. Yet somehow enough had been there both within and without him, and he'd grown from being a boy into a man.

Our hero's dark eyelashes flickered and the slightest hint of a smile played at the corners of his mouth.

Sophy stumbled back from the window. Her hands were sticky, damp, as she gripped the iron bedstead and then the round doorknob and pushed her way out of her chamber, across the landing and hastened down the stairs.

'Sophy?' Her father's unsteady voice came from above.

Sophy pulled at the bolts and by the time she had unlocked the front door, he had creaked down the stairs to the half-landing, his flannel dressing robe wrapped hastily about him.

'It's Ben, Lord Hart,' Sophy said, willing

her hand to still, to wait a moment longer to open the door. 'Don't worry, Father. Go and get dressed.'

She heaved at the door and there Ben was, still in the unorthodox-looking carriage. For a moment she couldn't move, and then her legs obeyed and the garden path disappeared foot by foot beneath her.

'Ben!' She rested her hand on the latch of the low gate.

'Sophy, I'm here.' His voice was more gentle than she'd ever remembered. She saw his eyes move from regarding her ungloved fingers, asking why she stopped where she was, to meet hers.

'What are you doing?' She saw exactly what he was doing. The irises, the curious vehicle that looked so like a fishing boat on wheels. He'd read the book! But the hero in her book wasn't Ben, he was only a figment of her imagination. Ben was Ben. 'You should have . . . you should have come in a dashing curricle or on horseback, on Genii,' she said.

'But in the book — '

'Flora lived in a lighthouse, Ben, on an outcrop of rock! How else was Lord Michael supposed to get to her but by boat?'

'I didn't read the book.' Ben waved his hand and then held it out towards her. 'Come here. Come with me, Sophy.'

'Then how . . . ?'

'Mr Simmons read it.'

'You didn't — '

'I read the dedication. That was the important bit, the real bit, wasn't it?' He raised one dear, arrogant eyebrow. 'The rest is simply the bows and ribbons.'

'Y-yes.'

'Now, might I take you away with me like the presumptuous, perfidious Lord Michael did to his dear, sweet, learned Flora?'

'Mr Simmons briefed you well.' Sophy folded her arms across her chest and watched as her action caused Ben to frown. He held the ribbons in one hand and with the other reached up and tugged at his cravat.

'Sophy, will you marry me?'

'Cor!' Billy Entwhistle dropped his pitcher and fresh milk splashed across his mother's front doorstep and on to the carefully tended flowerbeds.

Sophy felt the heat rising through her chest and up her neck. She swallowed and squeaked, 'How I am supposed to get up there?'

'How the devil should I know? You are the one who wrote in a confounded boat to the story. D'you think this was my idea? Had I know it was neither here nor there to you how I arrived, I assure you I would not have gone to so much trouble.'

Sophy couldn't find a handkerchief and so brushed a tear from her eye with her sleeve.

'Young man, do you have a stool or small chair to hand? If you would be so kind?' Ben fumbled in his pocket and tossed a shiny coin into Billy's hands. Billy caught it adroitly and raced off.

'Ben, I — '

'Hush, save it for later,' Ben advised. 'This is a public street.'

'When?' she whispered.

'We have the rest of our lives,' Ben said breezily. 'Plenty enough time for you to tell me you love me, and I shall want to hear it over and over again.'

'Sophy?' The query came from behind and Sophy turned to see her father, dressed and with combed hair, in the doorway.

'Father, look, it's Ben — '

'I'm not blind!' Mr Grantchester stepped out and came up towards them. 'Nor am I a fool. Lord Hart, I take it your intentions are now honourable, to do things right, after the shambles and your trickery, as we discussed when you came here last?'

'Father — '

'Yes, sir. I intend to take Sophy as my wife, with your blessing and by your hand if you will do it, sir.'

'But, Father, how did you know — '

'Lord Hart came here after you had returned from East Bourne and confessed his subterfuge and swore he would put things right. We have been waiting some weeks, and I did wonder . . . '

'Ben . . . ' But she couldn't think what to say except that she absolutely forgave him, which he knew already, and that she loved him even more, if that was possible. Ben sat in the boat, the ribbons slack in his hands, as if he would wait for her for ever. She looked at his dark eyes and saw them as coals, full of heat and waiting to burn, but not yet daring. He held her gaze for a moment and smiled, a real smile. He knew what she wanted to say to him, she was sure.

'Here we are, m'lord!' Billy appeared from around the side of the cottage carrying a three-legged stool.

'Down there, please, thank you,' Ben said, pointing.

Billy placed the stool on the road by the side of the boat.

'Oh, I see,' Sophy muttered doubtfully.

'I'm calling the first set of banns today,' her father said. 'And I shall expect the return of my daughter before nightfall.'

'Yes, sir.'

It was fortunate she was a girl to whom

absolute modesty was not paramount, Sophy thought, and unlatched the gate. She stepped on to the stool gingerly but the side of the boat still came above her middle. Ben reached down towards her and she blushed furiously — they had an audience including her father! Nothing prepared her for the coursing sense of completeness that ran through her from the top of her head to her toes as Ben's strong arms lifted her upwards. She pitched herself forward, trying to help, and landed on his lap, and squashed a couple of dozen of the irises.

'Here, Billy, give these to your mother,' Sophy said quickly, sitting herself beside Ben on the makeshift plank, rather than on top of him, and arranging her skirts. She took a handful of the iris bunches and handed them down. 'Oh, and some for Mary.'

Mary hurried down the road towards them, her basket swinging, her eyes wide.

'Let's go.' Ben flicked the ribbons. 'Lady Hart is most anxious to see Sophy, sir.'

'Very good.' A curious smile came to her father's face.

'We shall return anon, sir.'

The vehicle moved at the pace of a cart. Sophy waved and wished it would go faster, and that she could bury herself under the piles of flowers. How many people were going to see her, in this curious fashion?

'Ben,' she said, as they drew out of the village and into the thankful emptiness of the countryside, 'are we to drive through Stickleton? There is the other road, which would be quieter — '

'You said to me once that a lady who is rich may do exactly as she pleases.'

'But I — '

'Are assured in your heart, if not yet by the law, that you have everything you will ever want. Tell me, is that not true?'

'Ben, I love you,' she said, and ventured to clasp her hand around his.

'And besides, once all of Wiltshire has seen you in this, there is nothing, *nothing* you will be able to do to live down the shame except marry me!'

'Ben!' Sophy laughed and pressed her head into his shoulder. The vehicle slowed, and then stopped, and his fingers teased at her chin, drawing it upwards. She could not protest at his hungry, wonderful kiss.

'To Hartfield Bury, by way of Stickleton!' he instructed the imaginary coachman when the breeze hit her face again. He snapped the horses into a trot.

★　★　★

Lady Hart moved from where she was standing by the *chaise-longue* to the windows that overlooked the front drive. The chime of the half-hour from the French clock on the mantelpiece told her it was too early. They would not be here yet. She walked through the long room until she reached the windows that overlooked the back lawns. The cascading terraces had been designed at the same time as the house had been built. Ben's grandfather had been inspired by his travels on the Continent; had wanted to bring some of the majesty of the French court to Wiltshire.

She pressed her fingers together and watched the only sign of life, a blackbird, hopping in the middle of the oval lawn, pecking at the grass for worms. It would have a nest somewhere, she thought. She remembered when she had first met Ben's grandfather. Already a widower of some years, he was only in London to see his second daughter marry but when he found out about the flicker of interest his wayward only son had shown in Caroline Auld, as she was then, he had made it his business to find out all about the widow, still young enough to be mistaken for a debutante in the ballrooms of London.

A tall man, he would have even overshadowed Ben had he lived to see his grandson,

Lady Hart considered, as the memories came flooding back. He had deemed her a suitable match and her family were keen that she should have her second chance at happiness after the tragic death of her first husband in a riding accident. Pushed from every side she had agreed, and, after all, Ben's father had been a pleasant fellow. Handsome, dashing, courteous to all, she had even fancied herself a little in love with him, for a while.

How very different things would have been if they had been married there and then, and the wedding had not been delayed while Ben's father returned to Oxford for one final term to complete his studies.

'My lady?'

She turned to see Thompson, the footman, standing in the doorway. He would have knocked on the door. She must have been so lost in her own thoughts, she had not heard.

'Yes, Thompson?'

'Lord Hart, and . . . a visitor — '

'Yes, yes.' Through the window she saw the contraption had arrived. 'Show them in here, straight away.

She reached down on to the table for her Chinese fan and fiddled with it to open it. It kept her hands busy, gave her something to do while the interminable seconds ticked by. She had been Caroline Auld there again, with her heart fluttering with uncertainty. Was it any wonder when she knew what she had to do? She could not allow Ben, her dear Ben, to go to the altar, into a new life, *not knowing*.

'Mother!' Ben strode in looking like the cat that got the cream, and so he had.

'Lady Hart,' Sophy, at his side, said in her modest manner.

Their countenances were so genuinely wreathed in smiles, for a moment she thought she couldn't do it. 'So, there is to be a marriage?'

'Yes,' Sophy said. Ben wove his fingers in his bride's smaller hand and Lady Hart felt her chest constrict as if a new maid had suddenly pulled her stays far too tight.

'Mama, what's wrong?' A line appeared on Ben's forehead. He dropped Sophy's hand and stepped forward.

'Shall we all sit down?' Lady Hart held her fan closed in both hands, not yet ready to let go of it completely. 'There is something I would tell Ben . . . both of you.'

The anxious exchange of glances, the awkward movements, she could hardly bear to look. A creak. It was only the loose window sash now the breeze had risen. It was easier to stare at the pattern the sunshine cast on the carpet, to try to forget even though she now must speak of it, what had been on her conscience for thirty years.

'Both your fathers were at the university in Oxford. Distant cousins but close in age, it was perhaps natural that they would look out for one another. And your father, Sophy, did what he thought was his Christian duty, and at the time I blamed him for nearly all of it, wrongly. It was easier, you see, to blame him, and not my husband.'

'Mother — '

'Quiet, Benedict! You must hear the whole of it. Unless . . . unless Mr Grantchester has told you what I am about to say?'

'No, Mother, Mr Grantchester has said nothing of what happened at Oxford to me.'

'I'm glad of that because he promised he would not.'

Ben looked at the way his dear mama still held her fan clasped in her hands, the taut look of her fingers, her shallow breathing and her uncharacteristic hesitation as she spoke. Something was terribly wrong and until she told them, it seemed he could do nothing but sit here and try to be patient.

'Your father and I became engaged to be married. I fancied myself in love and was still grieving over the loss of my first husband. Your father was under some pressure as the only son to marry, Ben, from your grandfather, and I think he liked me well enough.

But he went back to Oxford to complete his studies and there met a girl. Anne Chamberlayne. She was the daughter of one of the masters. I don't know the whole of it but he fell in love with her and . . . well, in character you are like your father, Ben, in many ways. They ran away and were married. It was Mr Grantchester who came to me with the news, and in my irrational mind I blamed him. Then later it was he who came after Anne Chamberlayne died in childbed, and asked me, pleaded with me, that I would take the child — and the man — and be the adhesive to mend it all. And I refused, until he went back out to his carriage and brought in the nurse in whose arms the baby lay. And I knew I could do no other thing than bring that baby up as my own.'

His dear mother was not his mother? Some other woman? Ben felt his breath catch in his chest, wanted to speak, to ask; did not know what to say.

'There was another thing I feared in my heart, although I had told no one or even admitted it to myself: I had been married for three years and in all that time I had not fallen with child. I feared I might be barren. And time has proved I was right. I would never have a child.'

'Oh, Lady Hart!' Ben watched as Sophy

rose to her feet and ran over and flung her arms around his shaking mother. Dammit! She was his mother. What other had he known? And yet he could not move from where he sat.

'Ben, I'm sorry.' Lady Hart took in huge gulps of air and Ben saw the glisten of a tear appear on her white cheek. 'I'm sorry I pretended. You see it got harder, once I knew I would never have children of my own, and then when your father died there was no one else. I'm sorry you have no mother.'

'Nonsense!' Suddenly it was in him to leap to his feet. 'Of course I have a mother. She is sitting here right in front of me. I know no other.'

A smile cracked on to her dear face and Ben hastened over to plant a kiss on her cheek.

'I don't know how you came by such an idea! Heavens above! Females! And my wife nearly as bad,' Ben added, pecking her cheek for good measure. 'My nearly a wife as soon as the date is set, which I suspect my wife's father has done already. What more could a fellow want?'

Author's Note

Jane Austen was unlucky in love, and the idea of writing a story about a Regency lady novelist who fared better was very appealing. The story of rector's daughter Sophia Grantchester and her rakish cousin Lord Hart is wholly original and not based on Jane Austen's own life or that of any of her fictional characters, but being able to pepper the tale with some of Jane Austen's words and phrases has been a delight, and is intended as a tribute to Jane Austen and her works.

We do hope that you have enjoyed reading this large print book.

Did you know that all of our titles are available for purchase?

We publish a wide range of high quality large print books including:
Romances, Mysteries, Classics
General Fiction
Non Fiction and Westerns

Special interest titles available in large print are:
The Little Oxford Dictionary
Music Book
Song Book
Hymn Book
Service Book

Also available from us courtesy of Oxford University Press:
Young Readers' Dictionary
(large print edition)
Young Readers' Thesaurus
(large print edition)

For further information or a free brochure, please contact us at:
Ulverscroft Large Print Books Ltd.,
The Green, Bradgate Road, Anstey,
Leicester, LE7 7FU, England.
Tel: (00 44) **0116 236 4325**
Fax: (00 44) **0116 234 0205**